MW01125213

# The Last Football Player

John Blossom

Published by John Blossom, 2023.

THE LAST FOOTBALL PLAYER

**First edition. July 14, 2023.**

Written by John Blossom.

# Chapter One

In the family breakfast nook with a stunning view of Silicon Valley, Dude was trying to explain to his dad how much fun he had playing football despite the risk of getting injured.

"I know you love the game, son," Dudley Sr. said, "but don't you think real football's time has passed?"

Dude stopped chewing his buttered toast to punch the code into the kitchen printer for more strawberry jam. "Why? Just because most people are plugged into virtual reality all the time? Madden's not the same, Dad. Don't you remember the fun you used to have playing football on a real field when you were my age?"

"You mean in the dark ages? 8th grade? Those days were barbaric! When I played football they made me a lineman just because I was big. Absolutely it wasn't fun, and all that pushing people around ruined my knees." His dad gestured at him with his coffee mug. "Did you know that football players now have a lifespan that is twenty years less than average? And they get dementia ten times more often due to concussions? It's sad, and what for? Just so fans can see grown men destroy each other like gladiators in ancient Rome? The game is outdated. We should be beyond getting our kicks out of watching people get creamed. It's ridiculous!"

Dude could tell that despite the strong words, his dad was only partially engaged in their argument. Like every morning, Dudley only wanted to finish breakfast and fly him to school as quickly as possible so that he could scurry off to work. Dude watched him chewing like a madman and already blinking nervously into his company phoneglasses.

He wished his dad could relax. Even though he liked to spout off about most subjects, Dudley never said much to him about his job at the biggest corporation in the country, but Dude sensed that things had been especially intense for him lately at Circle Headquarters. More than once, Dude had overheard his usually super-confident father whisper a little too loudly to his mom about lagging sales and the possibility of getting demoted.

"But you used to like throwing the football around with me, didn't you?" insisted Dude, bringing his dad's eyes back to him.

"Sure, son, it was a blast when you were little, and I wish I still had the body to do it. But casually tossing a ball around is different than having to play actual football and getting beat up on the field like a hunk of dying meat."

"Dad, it's not really like that. You just don't remember. Actual football's way more fun than just tossing the ball around. Dying meat! That's not going to happen to me," Dude laughed. "I'm too fast and coordinated."

"You can't really say that. I told you, statistics don't lie. I found out that football accidents are almost guaranteed to happen to every player eventually. Your mom knows it makes me very nervous to have you out there risking your life. Your health is too important. She tells me about how hard you get tackled sometimes in your games. "

"Relax, Dad. You're so dramatic. It's really no different than us playing catch. It's fun, and nothing is going to happen to me. Besides, the season's over, and there's only the championship game left. It's against Zinkerberg, and they're evil. Please come, okay? I can't wait for you to see me play!"

"Well, we'll see. Go zap your teeth and get in the helicar. We're a few minutes behind schedule."

# Chapter Two

Dude lined up on the far left side of the scrimmage line for the last play of the championship game. The fans are going wild because the score is tied, and Zinkerberg just turned it over on a fumbled hand-off. Honeycrisp has one last chance with the ball deep in Zinkerberg territory.

*Catch this pass and we win the game,* thought Dude. *I can do this; I'm the best receiver on the football team, and Dad is finally here to watch. I've caught a dozen passes already this afternoon. I'm a* machine! *All I have to do is concentrate and just be me. I've got this!*

"Hut, hut," said Zagan, his quarterback. Zagan glanced at the cheering fans and dropped back to pass.

Dude made a quick move and once again got the jump on the larger Zinkerberg defender. Pumping his legs hard along the sideline, he cranked his head and saw the ball arcing toward him over his opponent's helmet. *Zagan threw it too high, but I got this. I'm Dude McPherson, I can catch anything!*

Just outside the endzone, he exploded into the air, snagging the pass with the fingertips of his right hand and guiding the ball securely to his chest. But just before his feet hit the ground, a Zinkerberg safety came out of nowhere and plowed hard into his exposed ribs, collapsing his body like a doggy squeeze toy.

Wondering what the heck hit him, Dude lunged painfully across the goal line, clutching the football.

A moment later, still holding the ball tightly but lying flat on the ground and struggling to breathe, he knew the game was over and that Honeycrisp had won, but he couldn't decide whether to cry out in triumph or in pain. He did both.

His cheering teammates piled on, oblivious to his injury. They rolled on top of him, slapping each other in celebration. He smiled underneath the pile of his friends. He had caught the clutch pass no one else could have caught! He was their hero! Then he gasped for breath and tried to ignore the horrifying pain in his side that worsened with each movement.

Through the clacking of shoulder pads and shouts of joy, he heard his dad screaming for his teammates to get off him. When they did, and he could finally expand his lungs, his first full breath was an explosion of unbelievable pain. Had one of those dirty Zinkerberg players stuck a knife into him? He snapped off his helmet and looked at his jersey. No blood, thank goodness. He groaned from the effort, held his ribs, and tried to breathe. The coaches came running and hovered. His dad yelled frantic orders. It was chaos, but eventually, his teammates helped his dad and the coaches carry him off the field on a stretcher and lift him into the passenger seat of their family helicar.

The pain was growing by the minute, and as he looked out the passenger side window at the worried faces of his coaches and fellow champions, he couldn't help thinking that maybe his dad had just won the argument about the dangers of football. Still, despite the agony, he had to smile about what he had accomplished. His beautiful catch had won the game! They had beaten Zinkerberg, a nasty team from a much larger school. He was a hero to his friends at Honeycrisp School! How good was that?! What a triumph! He gave a big thumbs up to his teammates and fans as his mom climbed into the back seat.

"Hang in there, son," shouted his dad, bringing him back to reality. "We'll get you there in a flash. My buddy Mike will take care of you." His Dad waved a hand over the navigating screen, and said, "Calling Circle Emergency Code 2. Send Dr. France to meet me at the Circle heliport in five minutes. Tell him it's my son, a football accident. Eve, why haven't you activated the envelosupport on Dudley's seat yet? Are you just going to let him slump like that?"

"Oh, no, dear. Yes, dear. I was just going to do that. My poor baby!" She touched a pad on the side of her son's chair, and pillows of air surrounded Dude to hold him steady in his seat. The helicar lurched into the air.

Dude loved his mom, but it always annoyed him that her idea of "helping" when his dad got ridiculously wound up like this was to just agree with him and do everything he said. To her credit, she always excused herself for that later by saying that Dudley was hung up on the "only child thing." Would a younger sibling have siphoned off some of his dad's fear and anxiety? He didn't know, but right now he was in too much pain to think about those things.

The extra pressure from the envelosupport on his tender ribs only made the agony worse, but he didn't say anything for his mom's sake. Instead, he just groaned and let her hold his hand as the helicar rose to its assigned altitude and engaged its jets. The helicar was as fast as his dad promised, but each jerk of Dudley's impatient flying felt like getting hit in the side all over again.

Dude watched his dad's hands dance over the controls. The helicar would be zipping over their house soon on their way to the medical center at Circle Headquarters, a sprawling complex that dominated the west side. Circle Corporation had bought out all the other tech companies and was now the only one in the valley except Zetta across town, the sponsor of Zinkerberg Academy. Until recently, Dudley's only admitted complaint about his job had been that Circle hadn't managed to swallow up Zetta Corporation too. As his dad liked to put it, "I'd rather be a worm in Circle's apple than a face in Zetta's book." There were about as many warm and fuzzy feelings between the two tech giants as between their schools' football teams, although, as neighbors, the corporations had been forced to work together begrudgingly a few times in the past.

Dude thought about how he lived with the divide between Circle and Zetta during the school day, too. Honeycrisp School and Zinkerberg Academy had always hated each other. He personally might have liked going to Zinkerberg Academy, despite its reputation, because of the larger football program, but his dad insisted he stay at Honeycrisp because of its academics and, more importantly because it was expected that Circle execs would *always* send their kids there if they were smart enough to get in.

His dad landed the helicar with a bump at the Circle heliport and jumped out barking orders. In a flash, Dude was taken out of the helicar and put on a gurney wheeling his way with Dr. France into the glittering building.

Minutes later Dr. France finished running Dude through the center's state-of-the-art Medical Diagnostics Tunnel and taped him up. Dude was relieved to find out that his bruised and cracked ribs, while parent-worryingly painful, were not serious. His mom stayed silent, and all his dad could do was shake his head. He'd get better soon enough, but Dr. France pronounced him retired from all sports and other activities for six weeks.

Those six weeks were a nightmare, as it turned out.

Dude had to rest at home and watch in horror as his dad channeled his righteous outrage over Dude's injury into organizing the Honeycrisp Parent Action Committee On Rethinking Sports. Dudley convinced the trustees of the school, most of whom were his colleagues at Circle, to sign a petition to ban football, and all other contact sports in one swoop. "They're *all* too dangerous," said his Dad.

Dude had to spend that horrible time icing his ribs on the couch and listening to Dudley spout off every morning at the breakfast nook about the progress of his terrible "school improvement project."

"Dad!" he said, arguing with him about it for the hundredth time. "You can't ban all these sports, especially football! I'll be on the JV team next year. My teammates will kill me!"

"I know you love it, son, and you're great at it. That championship game was a thriller all the way to the end, and I wish it would be okay for you and your buddies to still play football, but it's not. Not anymore. You dodged a bullet there. You're going to be okay, but contact sports are very risky and frankly unneeded in the modern world."

"But there's no other sport in the world like it! It's the best! Not everybody can play football. It takes talent, and you have to be smart and tough!"

"You're sitting there with very painful cracked ribs, and you want *more* violence and mayhem?" He gestured at the living room console. "Why don't you and your smart friends just play Fortnite? It might rot your mind, but at least you'll be able to walk and think straight when you're fifty."

"Fortnite? Dad, are you *serious*? No one plays Fortnite anymore unless it's Retro Week on Immersion Vision." He rolled his eyes.

"Whatever. It doesn't matter. You can play anything you want here or in the VR Booth downstairs. You can even play on your phoneglasses now, for crying out loud! Circle Marketing says Orchard Core Sports Suite is 97% realistic. That's close enough to the real thing, don't you think?"

Dude tried not to shake his head in frustration but failed.

"What, that's not good enough for you?" his dad said, getting more and more wound up. "Do you want the Sports Suite to program in broken bones and concussions so it can be 100%?"

"No, Dad, that's ridiculous." Dude sighed, then said, "What happened to me was an *accident*. Accidents are part of it. They're the risk you take to play the game. Video games are not the same as being out there on the field. Don't you remember the sound of the ball landing in your hands, the smell of the grass, and how hard you had to run and breathe? You don't get those feelings playing it safe on the bench or in a VR booth."

"That rib-crushing you endured was a very close call. It could have punctured your lungs! I'm sorry, but until there is a way to play real football safely—*which there never will be*—you and your friends are never going to play again. I suggest you try to get over it. Your mom and I are not paying an arm and a leg for that school so you can end up in a wheel-chair or depressed forever from a concussion, and that's that!"

"I could transfer out of Honeycrisp, you know. I don't particularly like STEM, and football is still offered at San Jose High."

"That's *not* getting over it. *San Jose High!* You've *got* to learn that most schools just aren't as advanced as Honeycrisp yet, and not just in STEM. Public schools will catch up slowly, eventually, maybe, if our country's lucky. Zinkerberg Academy is getting there, except it's all stupid PC-based. If other schools are smart, they'll do the same thing we did about these barbaric, dangerous, life-threatening sports: ban them! The data is clear. Play football, and injury and even sometimes death is a certainty."

This was the way it always went when he argued with his dad, but this time was by far the worst. For the first time in Dude's life, he dreaded going back to school. He was doomed. Even if he *could* accept Dudley's thinking about this, Zagan never would. Neither would his friend Gary, or the other members of the team.

*Well then, maybe I'll just have to drop out*, he thought, but he knew better than to say that out loud, especially when his dad was using the "data" argument. Instead, he got up gingerly and took the airlift to his room.

Why did his dad have to ruin everything? There was no arguing with him ever when he got on the statistics thing. Was *everything* about his dad's job, his *life* even, driven by the almighty God of Data?

Dude sighed and gently eased his sore ribs into his Gravi-bed. When his dad got this way, Dude couldn't help but think that actual real life, *feeling* life, was not always logical. But that was another thing he never wanted to say out loud to his dad, even though, as he floated in his bed, he was sure that there was more to living than just being safe and analyzing facts and figures.

Over the next few weeks, it became clear from his dad's reports at the breakfast nook that the Honeycrisp School trustees agreed with his dad's thinking about the injury data. Just before school was slated to start, Dudley's petition to end football and other contact sports was accepted, and that was, indeed, that. Poof! Football was gone.

"The committee agreed," said his dad with a smile, "that the abundant availability of safe alternatives, like Circle sports games and virtual reality, was enough for Honeycrisp students. Football wasn't really *that* important."

*Not important for the geeks. But what about the rest of us?* Dude thought.

Dude dreaded what was coming because of this ban. Sports were the only thing he really loved at his techie school. But for now, all he could do was feel sorry for himself as he tried and failed to imagine a Honeycrisp high school career without catching footballs.

As the painful summer dragged on, and the new school year inevitably approached, Dude was in dire need of some hope. If he had any chance to convince the school and his dad that football was worth saving, he had to stop being depressed and rescue the game using his intelligence, just like his dad had used intelligence to ruin it. But how?

He decided if he was going to continue to live at home, go to Honeycrisp, and have a chance to play football, he had to do the seemingly impossible: he had to figure out how to make the game as safe in his dad's mind as flying a helicar.

# Chapter Three

While flying to school with Dudley on the first day back, Dude nurtured a small bit of hope from a tiny gut feeling that he *could* somehow make football safe, or at least try.

But in school, saying this out loud to his friends did absolutely nothing to change their sour opinion of what happened. Zagan and the rest of the team just glared at him in the hallways like he was pathetic. It was worse than he feared. Gary, the linebacker, was the only friend who didn't give him stink eye. Just as he figured would happen, the team blamed not only his dad for the disaster, they blamed him. As the alternative after-school offerings were announced on his phoneglasses, the flamers that popped up on his Tic-Flash and Insta-Snap feeds burned away any remnants of his fragile hope.

"Hey, Dude," they jeered, "aren't you and your family worried about the new knitting club? Better ban it. Those needles could poke out an eye, you know."

"Thanks for ruining our first year, Dude."

"Loser!"

"You suck!"

"They should have banned you and your stupid dad, not football!"

"Your family's short-circuited! Bring back football!"

The worst was from Zagan: "Hey, Dude, now that I can't throw you a football anymore, why don't you and your dad meet me on the field after school so I can throw you the bag of dog crap I've been collecting all summer?"

And while his phoneglasses were invaded with hatred, so was the air around him with personal mini-drones sent by his teammates. Dude swiped at the harmless but annoying swarm of mechanical insects and showed the flamers to Gary.

Gary looked at them and shook his head.

"That's about right," Gary said.

"What?!" Dude started to protest, then sighed. "I *guess*, except... wow, Zagan is really pissed. I thought he was my friend!"

"All Zagan cares about is being *The Dude*, Dude. You made him look good last year by catching all his passes and winning the championship for him. He's been riling up the team all summer long about this and, sorry, I can't really blame him for it. It sucks to start high school and have nothing to do but classwork. I'm mad about it too, but I know it's not your fault. You didn't ask to get blindsided on the last play of the season. But I'm going to miss smashing people anyway. In fact, if I could bring back football by smashing *you* and your traitor dad right now, I would. Or maybe just your dad. A few broken ribs might be in order. That runs in the family, right?"

"Look, I'm really sorry," said Dude, grateful that Gary was just kidding... he hoped. "I don't know what to do. It sucks, and now I have to do something in the Tech Lab after school."

"Not me. I took one look at the lame sign-up list and decided not to do any afterschool activity at all, other than to fly home and lift weights," said Gary.

"You're lucky. My parents aren't giving me that choice. I have to walk to that stupid lab and do something *techie*."

"That's what you get for having a dad at Circle, Dude. A fate worse than death. Hey, I gotta go do Romanian deadlifts. See you later. The Tech Lab is that way, in case you're lost. Have fun."

Dude watched his friend amble toward the pickup landing pads. He envied Gary, whose parents didn't care at all what he did and were even proud that he played a dangerous position like linebacker. He groaned and reluctantly put his phoneglasses back on. The flamers were so bad all day, he had to deactivate the peripheral messaging just to be able to think. He turned it back on now in case Dudley or his mom texted him to say who was picking him up.

Dude left the main school building and trudged toward the giant Tech Lab, by far the largest building on campus. He scrolled through his messages and blinked open what his dad had signed him up for, *General tech,* whatever that meant. He brought up the offerings under that and noticed he was supposed to have made his choice of concentration by lunchtime.

Dreading he was too late and would be stuck with something horrible, he blinked on "Tweaking Our Social Orchards." It seemed the least techie offering in the Tech Lab. Maybe he could learn a few easy media manipulation tricks to help him convince his former friends that he wasn't responsible for his dad's actions. He didn't hold out much hope for that, though.

Blinking through the signup list, he saw that many of the cheerleaders had chosen the same class. They probably wanted to shore up their flagging status feeds now that cheerleading was banned. Not that cheerleaders would pay much attention to him anymore, even if they were in the same techie group. Another lost cause. They were as mad at him as the football players were. They loved tossing people and getting tossed in the air on the sidelines probably as much as he loved leaping on the field for the football. "Bad for the girls. Cheerleading is unnecessary, sexist, and a dangerous waste of time," Dudley had said. "There are no gender requirements for cheerleading anymore," Dude remembered shooting back at him. Thinking about his dad and his misconceptions, Dude groaned again. His chances of finding any friends at all at Honeycrisp this year were now next to nothing.

When he left the classroom buildings behind him and the Tech Lab loomed, Dude realized just how much school sucked for everyone now, and the McPherson family was the reason. He was going to suffer both for not being able to play football *and* for ruining everyone's lives. It was depressing.

*Instead of banning football, they should ban kids from getting as much abuse as I'm getting today,* he thought. *This was at least as bad as suffering a concussion!*

Dude found the entrance and eye-scanned his way into the sprawling building. Safety measures were especially tight here, he observed, like something for the military. Was this really necessary? The enormous structure had the largest and most intimidating security tunnel of any of the school's buildings. Dean Gonzales liked to brag about all the cutting-edge stuff Honeycrisp had in the Tech Lab, but he had never paid much attention. Not his thing. What exactly was Dude going to do in this place? Take apart a pair of phoneglasses? He could do that at home, with a sledgehammer.

The scanner bot at the entrance to the tunnel confirmed with the building's AI that he was a student and allowed to enter. One good thing, he noted, as he made his way through all the sniffers and scanners, was that the tunnel had screened out the mini-drones. Finally, some relief from the buzzing!

But nothing could stop the hateful and immature flamers still pinging his glasses: "Hey, Dude, enjoy sucking on computer tablets this afternoon. I'll be thinking about you in super-exciting 3D gardening, where I plan to print a giant carrot for you to stick up your you-know-where."

Dude sighed and emerged from the pulsing air of the tunnel into a huge lobby.

The scanning lights and security beeping faded behind him, but before he could even look around, a very athletic-looking girl about his size greeted him.

"Dudley Jr., I mean, *Dude* McPherson, welcome to the Tech Wing! I'm Tomly Newton, the Center's student proctor. Master has asked me to orient you, and from the psych metrics I'm reading on your profile right now, poor you, I can imagine you might need a distraction from what must have been a super-stressful day!" She tugged on her blonde ponytail and looked at him earnestly through a pair of over-sized phoneglasses that looked like a football helmet.

Dude was unable to say anything right away because a strong wave of her earthy scent, like cedar, washed over him. He had seen her before around campus, but she wasn't in any of his classes, and he was too shy to talk to her in the hallways, even though he wanted to.

Where else had he seen her? he wondered. He realized he was staring at her face behind her phoneglasses, but then that wave of shyness came over him again, so he looked away and noticed the huge plexiglass-enclosed arena behind her.

"Woah," he said. "Is that a Battle Bot arena?"

"Sure is," replied Tomly. "And it's even bigger than the one at the Mall of the Silicon!"

Did he know that the school had one? He didn't remember Dean Gonzales bragging about *that*.

"Wait," he said, turning back to her, "You have access to my psych metrics?"

"I passed my tech proctor test last spring, so, yes, I have access to student psych metrics while they are using the Tech Lab. It's part of how we keep things safe here. But don't worry, I'm sworn to secrecy. Since the entity in charge, Master, is an AI, she needs a student proctor like me to manage student users here. We biologics are a little more emotionally unpredictable than Circle AIs, as you know. Human kids can try Master's patience sometimes. With all the tech power she's responsible for, she's got to keep things secure. That's where I come in, as a kind of go-between. According to Master, 96.7% of the Circle's total computing and innovation capability exists in our lab, including universal 3D printing! Master's reputation, not to mention her eventual immortality, depends on her keeping all this tech power safe and secure where it belongs. It wasn't easy for her at first, so I was chosen to help her do that. Wouldn't want any Zinkerberg dirt worms wiggling their way into our healthy Circle orchard, now would we?"

"No, I guess not," said Dude. This Tomly was sounding a bit like his dad going on and on about all of Circle's techie toys. Still, it was impressive, especially the Universal Printer, and she seemed genuinely enthusiastic about the lab... and maybe even glad he was here. He followed her toward the plexiglass windows surrounding the arena like a hockey rink.

"I got picked not only because I've been coming here since fourth grade, but because I *love* organizing things," she went on. "Supply chains and all that, you know? Here my job is to keep track of people and their projects. I see on my list that you signed up for Orchard Programming, but now that I'm helping Master, we pretty much run an open playground. Honestly, anything you signed up for is just a formality to get you into the center. Don't let it inhibit your creativity! As long as you blink me about what you're doing every once in a while, Master will allow you to bounce around to any area to test things out and have fun while you decide on a project. It's kind of like working in the Circle building downtown. Playtime and creative freedom, you know what I mean? That's the philosophy, anyway. You'll also get direct access to Master's psych analysis of your interests and capabilities if you want them, once I'm done orienting you. So, welcome! Let's get started, shall we?" She gestured. "Here, obviously, is the bot arena ..."

He followed her.

Despite her techy babble, Dude appreciated that Tomly was the first person to talk to him nicely today. When they reached the plexiglass surrounding the arena, he noticed that her eyes were shiny and healthy up close, even behind those enormous geeky phoneglasses, but again he had to look away from her, not out of shyness this time, but because two of the coolest human-sized robots he had ever seen in his life had entered the battle arena and were squaring off with each other. They weren't like the domestic Circle robot his parents had at home with human-like proportions and synthetic skin. These were rough, pared-down bots, with exposed hydraulics, wires, and magnetics.

"Oh, perfect!" exclaimed Tomly. "Adam got his bot reprinted!"

Across the arena and through the plexiglass, Dude saw a grinning, dark-skinned kid with bushy hair wearing VR goggles, and a bot-control stick in each hand. The bot he was maneuvering had four legs, all outfitted with jets, and two arms laced with giant boxing gloves. The other bot had boxing gloves on, too, but had only two jetted legs and was a bit smaller.

"Are they skating or something?" asked Dude. The bots were circling each other, their feet floating several inches off the metal floor.

"The floor is magnetized, like a giant Gravi-bed," said Tomly. "And their metal boots are directionally-sensitized polar opposites, so they float. Pretty cool, huh?"

Dude nodded. Glancing at Tomly again, he suddenly remembered: *Volleyball!* He had seen her playing volleyball last year. She was by far the best player on the team.

"Adam had Master print the floor to test the practicality of gravity-compromised jet propulsion," Tomly went on. "It really makes for quick moves, but his bot crashed badly last week due to poor emission calibration. Adam said it was because he screwed up the math. Master won't always check your math for you if it's within your course level. Wow, look at that! The bots are gliding so much better today!"

Indeed, the bots were dancing around each other, landing punches almost too fast for Dude to follow. Their steering jets whooshed loudly, even through the plexiglass. In less than twenty seconds, the match was over. On the data hologram above the arena, Dude saw that Adam's bot had landed sixty punches to the two-legged's one hundred and thirty. The bots powered down off their magnet foil, and Adam walked across the metal floor to check out the damage.

"That was a cool battle," said Dude. "Whose bot is the two-legged one?"

"Oh, that's Master's. She always prints up advanced versions of what students are working on. It's typical Circle AI behavior. You know, point her in the right direction, and she can master anything. It's pretty cool. That's why we call her Master, of course. It's not because she's bossy, at least, not so much these days, since I've become the proctor."

"So why bother trying to create something when Master can just make it better? Seems like a waste of time."

"Well, you mean beyond the fact that this is a *school*?" She punched him playfully in the shoulder. It didn't hurt, but Dude could feel the power in her arm. "Sorry! Just joking. Because true AI self-decision making is still a very shaky beta, that's why. Master can innovate and perfect things when joining or supervising an existing project, but she's not ready to come up with projects on her own yet, thank goodness. Who knows what she would decide to do? She might decide humans are evil and print a virus to wipe us all out! Hey, I'm *kidding* again. But I did help Master set up filters to ensure *students* don't create prankster bots or bombs that could hurt someone."

"My dad would be relieved to know that."

She laughed. "I heard about your dad and his committee. But hey, don't worry. Parents have no say in here. The Honeycrisp School Tech Lab is a place made for kids, and it's run directly by Circle via Master's programming. As I mentioned, it is an exact duplicate of the Core Lab at Circle, only at Circle just a handful of adults get the same access and freedom to play as we do here. It's amazing that we tech students have this facility all to ourselves, don't you think? That's why we don't brag about it too much around school. Your dad's sports ban kind of upset the apple cart, so to speak, and now more students like you are checking us out. That's fine, but up until now, the sports programs kept our population down to a manageable size. Most of us hope that things like music, arts, and crafts will keep the numbers down, not that *you* aren't welcome, of course." She smiled at him.

Her mention of sports made Dude long for afternoon football practice all over again. But could he really have been purposefully encouraged to play sports here just to keep him from discovering the tech lab? At a *tech company's* school?

"Does our school really want students to play sports and *not* sign up for programming?" he asked, as they watched Adam lead his banged-up bot out of the arena.

"Not really. But Master is teaching me about something called 'reverse psychology performance enhancement.' It's all about data analysis and AI-influenced organizational structures. Circle wants good ideas to come out of this center. Master's data predicts they'll get better creativity and production value from students who *choose* to be here instead of going to the more popular and tempting activities. Did you actually like playing football, or are you secretly glad your dad shut it down?"

"Are you kidding? I *love* football! It's the greatest sport there is, right?"

She shrugged. "Well, it's okay, if you like pushing people around. I just don't get the point of all the violence, I guess."

"You're not the only one who thinks that," Dude admitted. "But it's not like that really once you get out there and experience it, the violence thing, I mean. Players are just testing their limits, that's all. Sure, you get pushed around, but it's just part of a game where everyone tries their hardest. And when you try really hard and succeed at something complicated, it feels *amazing*. Well, you know that, don't you? You play volleyball, right?"

"I did, unfortunately. It was *okay*. A little boring. Listening to you talk about your sport, I wonder if volleyball was too easy. My parents really wanted me to do something athletic last year. That's why they signed me up. They think I'm some kind of Olympian just because I'm super-coordinated. I played until Master offered me the chance to be a student proctor. It was an honor, and I was the only one she wanted, so my parents had to agree. Anyway, you'll soon find out you made the right decision to join us. A lot of small countries don't have the tech power we have here. Even our parents don't, unless they work in Core Circle, of course."

"It wasn't my choice. My dad signed me up. He works in the Truth Center at Circle. He hasn't been invited into Core yet."

"I know that, actually. My mom is Truth's group leader."

"Oh, you're *that* Newton. I thought I recognized your name. That's too bad. Did my dad try to recruit your mom for his stupid safety committee?"

"Yes, but she wasn't that into the idea of banning sports. And don't worry. If you think I might tell her anything about what you decide to do here, I won't, but even if I did, she would never say anything to your dad. She's pretty cool that way, lucky for me. She knows that as the student proctor, I'm sworn to secrecy about what the kids are working on in here unless actual lives are threatened. Come on. Let's go this way." She started heading along the outside of the arena.

"So... there're truly no adults in here at all?" said Dude, looking at a group of younger kids running past, laughing.

"Amazing, huh? Master says, and I agree with her, that having parents spying and gossiping lowers the percentage of worthwhile ideas the kids come up with. Parents are not even allowed to *visit* and check out any of the projects. That was the condition for Circle approving the funding for this full lab and the school. Circle's success was built on uninhibited creativity and innovation. They got the idea for this lab when they figured out that no one has fresher ideas than kids, and parents are experts at ruining kids' ideas before they even get a chance to come to life. Lots of great insights and innovations have come out of here without any parent help whatsoever, ideas that helped Circle stay on top. Kids just treat it all like play, but part of Master's job is to watch them carefully and decide which ideas and inventions should get funneled up to Circle. Sometimes she reveals the kids' names in her reports, and sometimes not. Come on, keep up with me. Let's work our way around the center and visit Adam. I can show you the universal printer control room on the way."

"So, the students are like lab rats here," Dude mused. "Hmm, I don't know if I should keep up with you or not, Proctor Techie Who Doesn't Like Sports."

Tomly laughed. "Lab rats in charge of their own experiments, maybe. You're always free to leave. But why don't you finish the tour with me anyway? Maybe you can change my mind about sports. I liked what you said about hard athletic effort."

Dude could accept that answer. After the cool bot battle and this conversation with a girl who might actually like him, he had a bit more confidence in his step as he followed her around the hallway circling the arena. A universal printing lab explained the existence of all the mysterious metal tanks and warehouses Dude flew over every day coming to school. He remembered his dad saying only a few Circle UPL's existed in the entire world. They could literally print anything. But despite being very fast and convenient, they didn't catch on because they were ridiculously expensive to use.

*To spend that much money to supply the materials to keep one running here,* he thought, *Circle must really take this place seriously.* It did sort of blow his mind that if he stayed in this program, he would have more access to Circle's tech power than his dad.

# Chapter Four

As he watched Tomly's long hair bounce and spill over her broad shoulders from under her data helmet, Dude thought her parents were right. She was clearly strong and coordinated. For one split second, he had the impulse to test her. If she were wearing football pads right now, he would tackle her just for fun. The only problem with that fantasy was she didn't look that easy to bring down and could probably tackle *him* if she wanted to. He let himself imagine her laughing while he tried anyway.

Then he remembered his phoneglasses were still on and that she had access to his psych metrics, so he stopped that potentially embarrassing train of thought. Better to focus on the tour of the building and not on weird fantasies about the proctor.

"You're in my grade, right?" asked Dude, suddenly doubting it because she was so smart.

"Yep, I'm a first-year. You just haven't seen me very much because, as I said, I've spent most of my time since fourth grade holed up here helping people with projects."

"I think I did see you play volleyball once on my way to football practice. You had a serve that no one could return."

And there was that smile of hers again. What if she'd already read psych data about his first impression of her, his attraction? He wondered if the stories were true about the romantic accuracy of electromagnetic psych metrics. Maybe she already knew how he was starting to feel about her, and that was why she was smiling at him? He could only hope. Just in case that wasn't true, he decided it would be best not to look at her too much or walk too close to her.

Soon, on their left were hallways with open doors revealing laboratory rooms and studio spaces packed with overflowing boxes of wires and random pieces of machinery and computer parts. Many hallways branched off from the arena in an octopus design rising and dipping creatively off each arm of the spiral.

"How do you keep from getting lost in this place?" Dude asked.

"It's even harder than you'd think since you can print your own workspace and there's constant competition over who can make theirs the coolest. Part of the organizational challenge of the lab is to help people get used to things changing all the time. The longest anyone ever got lost here was two hours, but that was before I came along. Now I make sure that Master updates the GPS database every twenty minutes."

"Do the rooms and hallways change *that* fast?"

"Sometimes, yeah, but that's part of what makes it exciting, like rotating servers in volleyball. An ever-changing environment means ever-changing ideas and approaches. Constant change keeps things fresh for everyone, not to mention making organizing more challenging and fun. Not that it could be anything else but constant change around here, of course, with kids in charge of themselves."

"So you *do* like some things about volleyball," he teased. "So why bother showing me where things are, if everything is different all the time?"

"Man, Dude, your questions rock! I asked the very same thing myself when I first got here, but Master wasn't so nice back then. She yelled at me, 'Learn to go with the flow, but you can't go with the flow without knowing where the flow starts from.' It took me a while to understand her point about the basic structure of the lab: that the spaces can switch around, but the universal printer has to always be at the center, and that the hallways have to remain big enough for the bots to deliver the things students print every day."

Dude looked at this girl who seemed to have it all together and wished he had access to *her* psych metrics. He didn't and could only guess, but it seemed promising that he asked the same questions she once did. "So Master is a *friendlier* AI now?"

"To me, she is, most of the time. You never want to cross her, though. She can totally override the volume control on your phoneglasses and let you have it if you mess up."

"Sounds like some of my teammates," Dude joked. "So this huge bot arena isn't the center?"

"Hardly! You'll see."

Dude was starting to wonder how he could have ignored this place for so long. It was like a labyrinth, or a mini-galaxy always pulsating and changing.

Ahead and around the curve, a beeping forklift bot whirred into view. In its claws was a bearded human head the size of a helicar. It looked very realistic, like a giant version of the domestic bot his parents had at home, except its eyeballs were dangling loosely on wires, and an unhinged and bloody lower jaw dragged on the floor.

"When you hear that beep from the forklift bots, always move to the nearest wall," Tomly warned. "If your glasses are on, Master knows where you are at all times and won't let you get hurt, but the transport bots can get scary close before they notice you are in the wrong place. This year, to make it easier for Master, I programmed them to stay in the center lane and to always leave a safety area along the walls. So far, there haven't been any close calls this year."

Dude pressed closer to Tomly against the plexiglass and watched the gross head disappear up a winding hallway. The bot's beeps faded quickly.

"Um, a head?"

"Oh, that's one of the sixth grader's print jobs, no doubt. Just a moment, I'll check the manifest." Tomly blinked into her helmet and Dude saw a mass of data appear on the perimeter of her phoneglasses. "Yep, sixth-grader Davis ordered a head yesterday for his haunted house project. I guess it's supposed to pretend to eat people to measure their innate fear of technology or something like that. It's a phase a lot of the new kids go through. Gross-outs, you know, and extreme emotions. *I* don't understand it. Master used to get mad about it, but now she says it's actually quite revealing what can be learned about human psychological development from immature humans allowed to play out their infantile fantasies."

"I guess ..." Dude was trying not to be overwhelmed by the weirdness of this place and the technical complexity of Tomly's tour. Did everyone get this treatment from her?

"Let's go down this corridor. Maybe Allison has her ladder down," said Tomly. Before he could ask what she meant by that, her nimble legs sprung left, away from the arena and into a purple tunnel. It wound around like an artery and led to a lounge area with snack printers and skylights. Late afternoon sunshine illuminated a comfortable and well-worn Chewbacca couch. Behind it, there was a very tall rope ladder leading to an opening covered by a beaded curtain just beneath the dome's bottom edge. This must be the ladder Tomly was talking about.

"There's a hover-lift, too, if you need one, but roping up to Allison's workspace is way more fun," said Tomly. "She believes short bursts of adrenaline and intensive physical exercise sharpen creativity." In a flash, she was gorilla-climbing the ladder and then ducking her helmeted head through the hanging beads at the very top.

Dude followed her, concentrating on the loose and rather challenging ladder and feeling a burn in his arm muscles as he did so. The exercise reminded him again of where he should have been instead of here, leaping to make catches on the football field. He was still mad about that, but at least this had been an interesting afternoon so far.

# Chapter Five

"A rope ladder?" said Dude, a bit out of breath as he parted the beads. "I thought you said all the hallways had to be big enough for delivery bots?"

Tomly stood next to a huge bank of computers, waiting for him. The room was dark except for the many computer lights that glowed enough to reveal that they were at the top of a small circular theater with a softly lit stage below. Two metal stools were on the stage, and two more blinking computer banks ringed the walls on the other side. All the computers had mounted data projectors pointed at the stools like miniature hover-ship blaster cannons. A girl in a dress, Allison, Dude assumed, was sitting on one of the stools, wearing bulky gloves and a data helmet like Tomly's. Standing beside her was a life-sized, 3D holo-image of a horse reading a book.

"Allison used the hover lift to set this space up," said Tomly, "but she cut off access when everything was printed and it became operational. She never uses the Universal Printer now because she only works with concepts and images."

Tomly whistled and waved enthusiastically to get Allison's attention. "Hi, Alli! Meet Dude. He's new."

Allison pivoted on her stool and waved back at them. She spoke into her helmet microphone, and her voice boomed across the space. "Nice to meet you, Dude. Welcome to my portal art project. Are you here for a demo?"

"Sure, if you have time," said Dude. His unamplified voice felt like a whisper compared to hers.

"Okay, come down here and sit with me, will you, please? I'm glad you came. I need more good tech people to test this, and I think everybody else is getting a little sick of me asking them all the time."

"Not true, Alli!" shouted Tomly, taking a seat in the audience. "We think you're awesome."

"Thanks. Do you want a turn today after our guest?"

Tomly gestured no. "We've got to chase down Adam next. Besides, I'm still trying to figure out the story this thing spit out the last time you hooked me up!"

Allison laughed. "See what I mean, Dude?"

Dude started down the steps to the stage. He heard a data cannon power down behind him, and the horse image disappeared.

*Allison.* He repeated her name to himself to remember it. Here was yet another person treating him like a worthwhile human being. Grateful, Dude jogged down the stairs, aware that he finally felt relaxed enough to be himself at Honeycrisp School for the first time that day.

When he reached the stage, Allison got up from her stool and removed her pair of gloves. They were bulky and attached with laser tubes to a network under a clear panel on the stage.

"Have a seat," she said, smiling. "Put on these data mitts and turn toward that red bank of computers while I zero out my program."

Dude obeyed, returned her smile and tried to suppress his knee-jerk hope that any girl smiling at him might be flirting.

Unlike Tomly, Allison was shorter than Dude. When she stood behind him, she was barely taller than he was while sitting on the stool. She smelled like patchouli, and her tie-dyed dress was long and flowy. He wondered how she managed to get up her rope ladder wearing it. Dude put the gloves on, letting the data tubes spread across his knees as they snaked to the floor.

Allison blinked a few commands into her helmet, and the gloves hummed and levitated to the level of Dude's heart.

"Woah, how'd they do that?" he asked.

"I'll tell you later if you're nice to me," said Allison. "So, when you're ready to start, close your eyes and hold your hands open toward that green bank of computers. Good. Now think of a feeling that you had today. It can be any feeling, but once you've decided and you're clear it's the one you want, let the feeling flow from your mind into your hands. Take your time. Tell it where to go and let it flow completely out of your brain. Then catch the feeling like a ball and hold it with the gloves. When you are sure you've got a very good grip on it and it's all there, throw it through the air toward the red computers."

"Okay. Sounds weird, but fun. You want me to do that now?"

"Right, whenever you are ready. Take your time, and remember not to throw your feeling until you are *sure*."

Dude wasn't sure what she meant by *sure*, but his hands felt light and powerful floating in the gloves. He wondered what it would be like to catch a football with them. When he tried moving against them, he found his hands could easily override the gloves' power, but when he relaxed, they always returned to floating chest-high in front of him. He figured they must be magnetized somehow, like his Gravi-bed at home. He turned around and gave Allison another smile.

As instructed, he thought about what he had been feeling today. The first thing that came to mind was hope. Despite not liking tech that much, he hoped that Tomly and Allison weren't just being polite, that they really liked him, and that he could make new friends here at the lab.

He rejected that choice of feeling. Too embarrassing. What was another feeling from today strong enough to hypothetically hold in his hands?

Nothing came to him until he paid attention to the tension he'd been holding in his face around his eyes. Anger, that's what it was. As nice as this place was, he was still angry that he wasn't out on the football field this afternoon. As soon as he had that thought, the gloves felt hotter. Were the gloves augmenting his thoughts and emotions somehow?

He decided to go with anger as his choice. A little self-consciously, he directed the anger he was feeling to move from his crinkled eyes down to the gloves. As he did so, the heat intensified.

Dude remembered that he had to hold the feeling perfectly before he threw it, so he contracted his burning fingers

over the heat like it was a football. Cupping the gloves together, he compressed the anger smaller and smaller, until it
felt like a white-hot mini-ball.

Then, when he couldn't hold it any longer, he transferred
it to his right glove and threw it overhand straight at the red
computers.

As soon as it left his palm, cool air wafted through the
gloves over his fingers, bringing relief. The red computers immediately lit up and pulsed like a Christmas tree.

"Good job," said Allison. "Now open your hands again,
take a deep breath, and turn and hold them open toward
the next bank, the green computers. Right. Okay, just relax
a moment, and this time, when you're ready, think of three
things you've seen recently. They can be real or imagined.
They can be images from books, music, art, or nature. There
are no wrong answers. In fact, as I speak, your brain has probably already thought of some good ones. Go with these first
images, no matter what they are. Say what they are out loud
right now and throw them one at a time at the computer
when you are ready."

"Do I say all three at once before I throw them?"

"Good question. No, say and throw them one at a time,
in the order that you think of them."

The first image that came to Dude's mind was of Tomly
and Allison taking off their data helmets so he could look at
their whole faces and maybe kiss them. Of course, that was
too embarrassing to use, so he went with the second image:
a giant carrot. He shouted, "Carrot flamer!" and threw the
image at the computer. Then he shouted, "Helicar crashing
into Circle!" Finally, he shouted, "Making out!" because he

felt guilty about not honestly following Allison's directions and decided that he could at least deal with revealing *part* of what was on his mind, as long as he didn't specify making out with whom.

The green computers lit up like the red ones, but with a subtler aura, like this bank of artificial minds was having more trouble processing the information. The lights eventually faded back to normal.

"Okay, good. You're doing great! Almost done inputting. Now, turn to the purple bank near where you came in. Same deal with your hands, open them toward the computers. This last time, think of three questions. They can be the first that come to your mind, but they don't have to be. You are free to ask anything at all in any order. What's important about these questions, though, is your honest desire to really want the answer to them. Whisper them into the gloves one at a time, and then throw them. And don't worry, what you say is a secret. No record will be kept of them by me, the computers, or Master."

Dude turned around to look at Allison's brown eyes. He had questions he wanted to be answered, all right... but did he trust her? He decided he did, especially when she winked at him and backed up to the edge of the stage to give him privacy. Next, he glanced up at Tomly. Was she monitoring his psych metrics right now? If she was, so what? He probably just revealed to her his honest thoughts about maybe kissing her. He hoped that was okay when you liked someone and wanted to be their friend.

He certainly had questions about adults and honesty. Their parents worked in the Truth Department at Circle, where they worried about catching people who use the internet to lie. The thought occurred to him that truth with a capital T, truth that you name a whole subsection of the world's largest company after, had to be about something bigger than adults obsessed with policing internet lies. For all his online sleuthing skills, his dad had no ability to know Dude's inner truth, and he decided that if Tomly was interested, he wouldn't object to her seeing him for who he really was deep inside. She nodded at him and gave him a thumbs up.

"Why is my dad so stupid?" Dude whispered into his gloves. He compressed this first question and threw it at the computers. A popping sound came from the purple computers and echoed around the room.

"Could I truly have real friends again at this school?" He glanced up again at Tomly and Allison and threw the question. This time, a sound blasted over the speakers like all the keys of a giant church organ being pressed all at once.

The last question, of course, was "Will I ever play football again?" It was a toss-up between that and "Can I make football safe?" But "Will I ever play football again?" felt like the more important question. What he really wanted to ask was, "Will I play football again *soon*?" But he already knew the answer to that question.

As soon as he whispered and threw the last question, the sound system ramped up with a long series of ear-splitting clicks and random musical notes played by dozens of different instruments. Then animal sounds, jets taking off, people shouting, voices singing. The data cannons rotated and came to life, spitting out dream-like holograms that flashed in and out of existence everywhere around the stage. The images changed as quickly as the sounds shifted and flowed, sometimes connected to one idea and other times to another. It was all very quick and confusing.

Allison came back on stage and spoke loudly into his ear. "The computers are communicating with each other about your input, testing output ideas to see if they fit with each other's AI. I could have made them do this part with no output, but it's fun to experience how they play with the data artistically, don't you think? Hold your gloves over your head now to receive their final piece. It will come when they have a consensus, usually within thirty seconds ..."

"Piece? What do you mean?" shouted Dude. He was distracted because the hologram images were now from his family's photo cloud, and the theater's speakers were playing snippets of all the music that he had ever listened to on his phoneglasses. It was a jumbled mess, but a strangely familiar one to him, like the way dreams sometimes are.

Slowly, the images and sounds organized themselves and began to rotate around the theater like a slow-moving tornado. The tornado accelerated and narrowed itself into a furious small funnel on the stage in front of Dude's raised gloves. Images and sounds were trapped in the swirl. He saw glimpses of his coach, his computer station at home, faces of his friends, and lots of lips, stumbling and swirling. Then as the speakers let out one last shriek, the funnel shrank to the size of a spinning football, turned blood red, and disappeared.

"Was that it?" asked Dude in the sudden silence. "Is it done?"

"I don't think so," said Allison. "Usually by now there would be a painting or a sculpture holographically manifested, or, if it's a song, it starts playing. This must be ..." But before she could finish her sentence, the floor of the stage opened beneath where the funnel had just been, and up popped an old-fashioned IBM dot-matrix printer resting on a small metal table. It just sat there a moment, then started shaking. The computer paper moved quickly back and forth under the round metal head with a loud ripping sound.

"Oh, goody!" said Allison. The printer finished and the paper rolled onto the receiving tray. "You got a poem! Delivered classic style!"

"What do you mean?"

"Well, at first, I wanted poems to be hand-written, but Master convinced me this old printer would be just as cool and easier to read than AI penmanship. Go ahead, pick it up. It's your art, you created it."

"*I* did this?"

"Well, there's a chance if you decided to write a poem on your own right now without my art portal, the words might have been *slightly* different, but with my holistic programming discovery, the computers' creative metrics are aligned so thoroughly with your psych metrics and cloud history that any differences would be essentially cosmetic. This is the truest and most sophisticated piece of art in any media that your brain could possibly have created at this moment in time. Another way to think about it is that it's a snapshot of where your brain's most evolved creativity is at this moment. It reflects all that makes you uniquely human combined with all we know about creative psychology."

"So, it's a psych evaluation?"

"No, it's not an evaluation, exactly. It's a work of art. I suppose you *could* call it an *artistic* evaluation. They're related but different. Art kind of encompasses everything, you know what I mean? It's a little hard to explain, and I'm still working with Master on the calibrations for the manual, but one thing I can tell you almost for certain is that whatever is written in your poem is about as true a reflection of your *artistic* interpretation of your life in this exact moment as you can get."

"Wow," was all Dude could say. He had never really thought much about art, much less art that came out of *him*. He looked at the paper sitting in the printer tray.

"Of course," added Allison, "just because it's what's inside you doesn't mean you'll understand it. You can read it now or later, as you wish. I'm curious, but I don't need to know what the poem says. It's private until you choose to share it. You can tell me later generally what you think of it, though. That would be helpful."

"Oh, yeah, okay. I will." Dude left the gloves on the stool and slowly reached for the paper. After all the build-up, he was a little scared to read this poem his brain supposedly created, but he couldn't let it just sit there for anyone to read later, especially if it was as personally revealing as Allison said. She obviously had thought a lot more about art than he ever had, and he was glad she didn't press him to say something about it right away.

As soon as he lifted the sheet from the tray, the printer sank with a whir back into the stage floor and disappeared.

He looked at the perforated, green-edged paper and the funky dotted printing. The poem wasn't very long.

He looked back at Tomly again.

"Go ahead, read it," she said. "We've got time. My last art portal result was a long short story, and Adam's was a full rock opera, so you're lucky it's just a poem. No offense, Alli!"

Dude's eyes went back to the paper, and he read:
PLAYING AGAIN
A long bomb from a lost quarterback
Reaching for the ball,
Your catch – your father's severed head,
The wrong kind of pig leather
The Old Ones march with carrots
Ripped from a garden of anger
And yet still food
The New Ones don't march
They drift and dance
With changing purpose and wisdom
Their collision will crash this helicar of techno-confusion
Into the "I'm okay" mouth
Of you finally finding and making out
With yourself
*Well, Allison was right about not understanding it*, thought Dude.

He glanced at her, read the poem again silently a second time, then folded it and stuck it in his pocket. "I'll need to study this more carefully later, I guess. It's good, though, I think. Thanks, Allison."

"No, thank *you*, Dude! The portal hasn't spit out a poem in a good long while, so this was *so* cool! Please come back again anytime. Art changes in us every day, so when you do come back, there's always something new and relevant to discover about yourself here."

"Yeah, I can see that. I hope your horse remembers what page it was on in its book!" said Dude, flustered by how much she was still smiling at him. He hoped his smile back at her covered up the ridiculous thing he had just said about her hologram. Dude wondered if the poem had flooded his brain somehow, or if this long afternoon break from all the flamers and mini-drones was just making him giddy.

Tomly stepped onto the stage. "Come on, Mr. Jock Poet. Back on the tour. There's more you need to see before I'm done with you. Thanks, Alli, for the demo!"

"Anytime, Tomly! This will be up for a while. Master says Circle likes what I'm doing and might even try to sell it sometime! Glad you're joining us, Dude. See you again soon, okay?" She turned and put her data helmet back on.

"Yeah, sure thing. Thanks," said Dude and followed Tomly off the stage and back to the bead-curtained doorway.

He checked to make sure his poem was tucked deep in his pocket before climbing down the rope ladder. Catching his dad's head like a football? What other surprises did this place have in store for him?

# Chapter Six

Tomly led him briskly back through the lounge and the winding corridor to the arena again, where they resumed their way along the main artery.

"As you can see," she said, "there are lots of studios we can assign you, here and on the other side of the arena, plus, of course, the project areas surrounding the universal printer. There are no locks or anything. We all help each other as much as we can."

"Kind of like a team," said Dude.

"Exactly," said Tomly. "Except *we* don't usually send each other flamers if we have a disagreement."

"No, I guess not. Well, you might if you had a parent who got antsy and shut this place down."

"You've got a point there. But I doubt Circle would ever let that happen. The crazy number of great VR game ideas generated here each year alone is valuable enough for them to protect us, even from a whole committee of neurotic parents. Do you like VR games?"

"They're okay, I guess. Do you?"

She nodded. "When they're not too violent. I play Canyon Jumper sometimes when I finish my homework. I like its augmented flying sensates."

"You have *sensates*? Wait, do you have one of those new neuro-optical feeds in your glasses?"

"Yep, Circle's still tweaking it in beta, but it's pretty cool. A senior invented Canyon Jumper here when I was a sixth grader, so yeah, sensates started here."

"A Honeycrisp student invented them?!"

"Yes, sort of, with Master's help. As I said, we have nearly everything Circle has here."

"Wow. So, are sensates as cool as my feed says they are?"

"It's just like they say, you feel like you're really there because you get the real-world neuro-inputs through your optic nerve via micro-lasers. You don't feel a thing, other than the real sensation of jumping and flying across canyons. Master says it's 99.1% the same as actually doing it, although I kind of wonder how she figured *that* out without killing some real canyon jumpers. The visuals are the same as the regular version. Are you familiar?"

"My friend Gary had me over to play it one time, but he kept sabotaging me, so I crashed into the walls all the time and got bored with it. But wow, sensates! Are they as addicting as they say? It must be hard to get your homework done."

"Nah, I limit myself. And weirdly, it does get boring after a while like most games."

"Most *electronic* games."

She barked a laugh. "Spoken like a true jock."

Dude hated the word *jock*, but somehow, he didn't mind it as much when Tomly said it.

"I guess I am a true jock. Football jock, not poet jock." Dude smiled. "There are a lot of us, actually, and the sooner I can get us back out on the field, the better."

Tomly gave him an intrigued look. "Hmm, very interesting problem. I'll have to think about that. Let's go down this
connector. It leads to the universal printing lab. Then we can
circle back to the other side to try to find Adam if he's not
there reprinting the broken parts for his bot after his battle
with Master."

The connecting corridor was twice as wide as the one
that circled the arena and was bustling with students. He had
to step aside twice for beeping delivery bots, one carrying a
huge glass bottle of glowing green liquid, and another a para-
chute pack that somehow was open and flying despite there
being no wind in the building. A minute later, the corridor
spilled into the cavernous printing lab. He knew from his
dad that the excitement about how universal printing labs
would solve all the world's supply problems had been dis-
missed as unrealistic long ago, but it was still impressive to
see one in real life.

It was massive. The printing chamber was the size of a
helitruck, and it had feeder tubes and wires sprouting from
every inch of its surface like hairs on the back of a giant
frightened cat. These led to dozens of modified computer
banks mounted on the circular wall of the lab, and more
hairs continued from the computer banks out through the
walls and up through the roof to what he assumed were
the hundreds of various supply tanks on the roof. Many of
the larger tubes were thickly insulated and labeled "Cau-
tion: Hot," and others were of every color of the rainbow
with flow direction indicators and incomprehensible number codes. Huge fans hummed over the printing chamber

pulling air into sheet-metal exhaust vents going through the roof.

He moved closer to Tomly and watched the hot glow of a metallic blob take shape in the chamber. The room was humid and pungent with solvents and the acrid stink of melting plastic.

Over the noise of cooling fans and the squirting sounds of emitters dancing around the object, Tomly shouted, "The manifest says Master is printing a new delivery bot right now. Probably, she needs it because of you and others who might sign up. We can get a closer look at the inside of the chamber by staying on the walkway. It leads to the inputting room on the other side."

Dude followed her out onto a metal walkway with railings to protect them from the emitters swinging in and out of the printing chamber like giant keys on an old-fashioned typewriter. The spitting emitters were busy and loud. He noticed several surveillance drones buzzing in and out of the supply lines using scanner lasers. It took a minute of steady walking for them to reach the best vantage point to see inside the printer, but when they could, they saw that the metal globe was already recognizable as a delivery bot. They watched the printer build the arms and legs. The emitters danced in and out while the floating bot was turned this way and that by puffs of air.

"That's amazing!" said Dude. "So fast!"

"I know, right? replied Tomly. "The printer can do metal and electronic stuff very quickly, except for the batteries, of course. Batteries tend to explode unless you print them slowly. This bot will look finished before we walk out of here, but it will take the UPL another hour to cool it off and print the power pack. Then students can use the printer again for whatever if there's still time before dismissal. I don't see Adam here, so let's go try to catch him before he leaves. I could blink-track him, but he's almost always here, in the lounge, or in his studio."

They continued to the end of the walkway and stepped into a small room with more computers and a whole row of universal input ports.

"This is the inputting room, obviously," said Tomly. "Since this is one of Master's prints, there's nothing plugged in right now."

"A Universal Printer uses uni-ports!" said Dude. "I don't know much about hardware, but aren't they about as old-fashioned as gas cars?"

"Yes, but they are easier to keep secure. Universal printers are the most powerful on the planet, so Circle blocks all wireless inputs. That way if a spy drone were to sneak in here broadcasting a code hack, it couldn't print something disastrous. Having to use plug-ins is only a small annoyance once kids figure out what they are and how they work. Most of the students just have Master install output ports on their phoneglasses and then print directly from them. The only part they complain about is having to take them off to print, so they can't listen to music or get holo-messages."

"Well, that can be rough."

"I know, school can be tough sometimes, right?" She gave him another smile and laughed.

Dude was happy that Tomly understood his sarcasm about the phoneglass addiction that was universally accepted as part of life at the school, and everywhere else for that matter. He too got sucked into staring into his phoneglasses for too long sometimes. He hoped she was reading his mood metrics right now and that his good feelings toward her would balance out the generalized anger data that obviously must be on his psych feed, considering the images that came out of him in his poem.

Even without any access to *her* psych feed, he could sense that she loved working in this tech lab in a very similar way to how he loved catching footballs on the football field. Tomly and Allison both seemed to be real *doers*. He had to admit he could relate to that, even if they were techies.

# Chapter Seven

They caught up to Adam in his studio, several winding corridors down from the printing lab. There were no rope ladders to get into his room, just one huge door that rolled open to make room for delivery bots. The studio was larger than a full classroom, but to get inside, they had to step over carcasses of battle bots piled up along the walls like discarded medieval knights in armor.

"Hi, Adam," announced Tomly.

Adam emerged from behind the dented four-legged bot that had just been in the arena. "Hey, Tomly," he said. "Did you like the battle?"

"Sure did, but I think I missed most of it because I blinked! Hey, this is Dude McPherson. Dude, Adam Angelou."

"Hey," said Dude.

"Nice to meet you, Dude. You're a first-year... football guy, right? Or I should say *were*."

"Unfortunately, yes."

"Yeah, that sucks. I admit to playing a little football myself in fifth grade. Then I discovered this place, and I've been playing in here instead every afternoon for the past two years."

"I can see that. Are all of these your creations?" Dude gestured to a pile of old bots.

"Yep. And Tomly, you don't have to remind me. I know there's a recycling center, and I *will* order them taken away. I just like having them around. They're like old books. I can better remember what they taught me when they are visible in my *library*." He gestured widely to his studio and smiled at her with bright, white teeth and an innocent boyish look Dude suspected he probably used a lot as a child to get whatever he wanted.

"That's all fine and everything, Adam," Tomly said, "as long as people can still walk in here without tripping over them." She kicked a stray arm unit back into the pile. It clanked and caused a minor avalanche of other parts to spew at her feet. "See what I mean?"

Adam ran his hands through his big black hair and smiled sheepishly. "Okay, you're right. I'm just being lazy. I'll put in the order with you tomorrow, I promise. But wasn't that battle cool?"

"Yes, very cool, and perfect timing for Dude's intro tour."

"Yeah, how do you like it here? Do you like robotics?" Adam asked Dude.

"Sure, I guess. I mean we have a Circle assist-bot at home that does our shopping and stuff."

"What model?"

"It's a Six, I think. It has the synthetic skin. I can't remember. It's a few years old, I know that. My Mom mostly uses it."

"Can it give Thai massages?"

"No, I don't think so."

"Then it's a Five. They upgraded the touch parameters for the Six, and its AI was so proud of its new capabilities that people got sick of all the massage suggestions every morning. We got a Six when it first came out a few months ago, and I had to hard-program it to dig holes in the yard during morning planning time just to keep it quiet until they fixed the glitch."

"My dad talked about that glitch. But you *hacked* a Model Six assist-bot? Wow."

"It's not that hard to do. Just a few blinks. My Dad's in Core, and he leaves his Core-glasses logged on in the living room when he goes to bed."

"Adam, be careful what you say," Tomly scolded. "Don't forget I'm the proctor now, and my mom's in Truth!"

"Oh, I know you won't tell on me, Tomcat. You're too cool."

"You're just lucky that Master doesn't listen in on us while we work here."

"Or so she *says*," said Adam. "And why are you pretending to worry about it, anyway? You're about as close to a parent as this place will ever get, and you know it. That's what makes it so great, don't you think, *Mom*?" He punched her playfully in the shoulder. "So, Dude, have you thought about what you want to do here yet?"

"What I want to do is get *out* of here and play football," said Dude, but he was pretty sure Adam didn't hear him because Tomly had Adam in a headlock and was rubbing her bare knuckles over his scalp.

"Youch! Stop it!" screamed Adam.

"Am I your *mom*, Adam? Really? Do you like it when your *mommy* does this to your fuzzy head?"

"No, no! Sorry, you're not my mommy! I give, Tomcat, I give!" He flashed her a peace sign, and she let him go. She folded her arms and tried hard but failed to look sternly at him because immediately he started bowing to her with his forehead on the ground like she was the queen.

"Do you guys always fight like that?" asked Dude, laughing at Adam's antics.

"Yea, it's like a locker room around here," said Adam. "Only usually we fight with bots, not fists."

"Adam!" laughed Tomly. "You know it's not like that at all around here. We always do what we can to support each other, Dude, unless big Adam here crosses the line."

"Oh, *Mommy*! I never cross the line. No, no, just kidding!" said Adam, running to hide behind Dude. "Football, huh?" he whispered, keeping Dude's body between him and Tomly. "What about a bot football team? Would that be violent enough for you?"

"What did you just say, Adam?" said Tomly, stopping in her tracks. "You've got to watch out for this guy, Dude. He's always full of crazy ideas. A *bot football team*?"

"Sure, why not?" said Adam. "Can't you see it? It would be like a bot battle on a massive scale. It would be epic!"

"Machines can't play football," said Dude. "They're too stupid and uncoordinated. I said *I* wanted to play football, not watch bots smash each other up trying to do it."

But Adam still looked thoughtful. "Well, maybe they'd be too stupid at first, but we wouldn't know until we try. There's been a lot of improvements to the Sixes lately, and

Zetta has been working on an advanced model that's supposed to be indistinguishable from humans in looks and capabilities."

Tomly started chasing him again. "Zetta bots! You want to bring PC bots into a Circle lab, Adam? Are you crazy?"

Adam put his hands up in surrender. "Of course not, Tomcat. I'm just saying to your new recruit here that he shouldn't just write off the idea. The new Sixes are *amazing*. No one really knows everything they are capable of doing. I've been looking for a new challenge since I can't seem to design anything lately that can beat Master's bots. Why not use Master's bots to build a football team no one else can beat? I'd be game for giving it a try!"

"That's, like, how many robots?" asked Tomly, looking worried.

"Well, there's eleven on the field at one time, but that's just if they play both offense and defense," said Adam.

"That's a lot of bots ..."

"Look, Tomcat, you've got this place humming like a well-oiled machine. You could use a new challenge as much as I could. Think of all the stuff that will have to be organized and printed like uniforms, cleats, pom-poms for the cheerleaders. You'd be in heaven!"

"Pom-poms for cheerleaders? You are really putting my oath to the test here," Tomly looked menacing again.

"Oh, you *love* having to support whatever crazy ideas kids come up with. I'll bet once we get into this, you'll actually *want* to be doing it, not just feeling like you have to be true to your proctor's oath."

"Okay, Adam. You seem to really want to do this football thing, and you're right that it would be fun for me too. But since it's Dude's problem that got us into this, he has the last word. What do you say, Dude? Do you want to work with us and make a bot team for your new tech project?"

Dude looked at her and thought about what Adam had said about massive bot battles and felt a little dizzy all of a sudden. He remembered what it felt like to get hit while he was reaching to catch a ball, then he thought about the weird poem in his pocket and about his dad. He looked at these new techie friends, staring at him expectantly.

"I'll have to think about it," he said, but it just didn't feel right. Play with bots instead of actually being on the field? "No, you know what? No thanks. You're wrong if you think technology can ever replace football. It's not your fault you don't get it. You're not players. Technology? You just can't. I don't know what it is for sure that makes football so great, but it's more than just programming and ordering enough equipment. And it's way more than just violence, Adam. I'm sorry you never played football long enough to understand that. My dad didn't, either. That's why I'm stuck here. Thanks for showing me around, Tomly. It's nice of you guys to want to help me out, but I'm not feeling very good right now. I'm going to take that option you mentioned before and go home.

# Chapter Eight

"Who's this Adam kid?" said Dude's dad at the family breakfast nook the next morning. His mom, as usual, was still in bed.

"He said his dad is in Core," said Dude. "Angelou, I think is his last name."

His dad's brows shot up in recognition. "Angelou! And you turned down his idea? His dad is brilliant!"

"That doesn't mean Adam is, and it doesn't mean robots can play football. Sure, maybe he can get them to move around on the field a little bit, but to really know the sport? I thought about it all night. It's not possible. I might as well just come home every afternoon and play Madden."

His dad waggled a piece of bacon at him. "Well, you're *not* going to do that. You're going to that Tech Lab every day after school, so if you don't want to do this football project, you'll have to come up with another one. Frankly, though, I think you should go for it. At least you'd be doing *something* with the sport you used to love."

"*Still* love, Dad."

"Right, still love, but can't play anymore because of *reality* and your parents wanting you to have a healthy life." He stuffed the bacon into his mouth.

Dude groaned and hung his head. "I can't go over this with you again. You won, okay? No more football for Dude. It's over. I get it." He punched in another cup of coffee from the printer. He was going to need the extra caffeine to get through the day.

"Maybe it's not over. Maybe it's just changing," mumbled his dad, stabbing an egg.

"Easy for you to say. I know it's over with each flamer I get from my teammates. It's over, just like my life." Appetite suddenly gone, Dude pushed his plate away and stood up.

"Do you want me to call the dean and block-lock the flamers? I can, you know."

"No, Dad, I told you I don't. That would make it worse. They're right. We ruined it. They should be mad. Even Gary is mad at me."

"I'm sorry, son. Still, this Adam...maybe you should ..."

"I told you, you won. And, *okay*, I'll do Adam Angelou's stupid tech project. It's the modern world. If you can't fight it, join it, right? Just stop pretending that throwing the football with me out there in the yard ever meant anything to you!"

If he could have flown himself to school, he would have. Instead, he grabbed his coffee to wait in the helicar for his dad to finish gobbling his breakfast.

# Chapter Nine

Dude talked to Gary about the bot football idea before math class and asked if he wanted to help.

"No thanks," Gary said. "I'm not going in that place if I can help it. But it's true that Madden can get boring. Maybe this will be better. Your dad is probably right. You should do it. At least it'll keep you away from Zagan after school. He's really after your skin, you know."

So after school, Dude avoided Zagan and went through the security tunnel at the Tech Lab, ready to apologize to Tomly and Adam. He wandered around the maze of corridors until he found them in the lounge.

"Yesterday I was still really upset that I was in here and not playing football, I guess," he said to them. "It's going to take me a while to get over that, so I'm sorry I was rude and walked out. Your idea is great, Adam, and I'd like to help if you and Tomly are still thinking about doing it."

"Hey, no problem, man, but I wouldn't have thought of it had it not been for you. Even though I didn't like football when I tried it, I get that it totally sucks that you can't participate in something you love. I think it could be a really fun project, and we can't do it without you. I stayed up all night thinking about how great it would be and how to convince you not to quit. So, yes! Let's make bot football so cool that you won't miss being on the field, shall we?"

"Yeah," agreed Tomly. "And maybe along the way, you can show me more about why football is better than boring old volleyball."

"Let's print some hot chocolates and go to my studio," suggested Adam. "It's time for a planning meeting!"

"Oh, goodie! I love planning meetings!" said Tomly.

Dude followed them quietly to Adam's studio. He felt more relieved than he expected that they had accepted him back, and not just because of the pressure from his dad. It felt good to be with them again in this crazy place, taking on this weird and challenging project.

Adam's studio was still a mess. It was so crowded with junk that the only place they could sit was on a pile of bot carcasses. Dude could tell it bothered Tomly, but she didn't say anything.

"So," Adam said, "one of the things I was thinking about when I couldn't sleep last night was this: what are the elements of real football that aren't in VR-Madden already? That's got to be the key to making this work, don't you think? Otherwise, why bother with real-life bots?"

"Gary says compared to the real thing, Madden is too predictable," Dude put in.

"Right," said Adam. "Even though there are pretty good performance variability modulators in the Madden program, each player is basically stuck with a fixed set of skills, so what makes it boring is that Madden games are decided mostly by luck. Real football games are decided more by the players' changing knowledge, skills, and emotions. That's what makes this challenge so complicated and interesting."

"I get it," said Tomly. "It's like the difference between VR fantasy dating and the real thing."

"What?" Adam's mouth dropped open. "You *fantasy date*? Tomcat, I'm shocked!"

Tomly rolled her eyes. "This is the modern world, Adam. I'm just as connected as you are. You don't have to *do* fantasy dating to know about it."

"Yeah, right," Adam drawled with a smug smile. "Okay, so to make this game great we need the bots to act on the field just like individual human football players would act."

"Right," said Dude. "And that's impossible."

"Pretty much impossible, I agree. But that doesn't mean we can't figure it out, dude, I mean... *man*? Ugh, you need a new name if I'm going to talk to you!" Adam picked up a bot hand and twirled it around his head like he was going cuck-oo.

Dude laughed. "Well, if we do figure it out, it would be great if the bots acted just like the actual football players on my team, maybe even controlled by them individually."

"Of course," said Tomly, sporting a hot chocolate mustache. "That's the whole organizational idea, isn't it? The game played as close to how it would be played if the actual players were out on the field, only it's their bots that are carrying the ball, taking the hits, and getting smashed up."

Adam let go of the swinging bot hand, and it flew across the studio. It crashed loudly into another pile to show his agreement with her point.

"So the whole team could be involved?" said Dude. "Would those guys enjoy it enough to want to take part? I mean, it's not going to be the same as actually being out there on the field, smelling the grass and creaming people."

"We could program some olfactory correlatives, but I don't think you have anything to worry about," said Adam. "Think about it. How many of your football players play VR games?"

"All of them."

"And do they get super-competitive? Obsessed enough to ignore their homework and play every chance they get?"

"Pretty much, yes."

"Do they like watching bot battles at the Silicon Mall better than online?"

"You know they do."

"So, it won't be a problem, as long as we get the metrics and calibrations right, and there's a bot for every member of the team so no one feels left out. They'll feel like they have their own real-life avatar in a VR game the size of a football field. Believe me, they will *love* it."

"But we've got to roll it out right," said Tomly. "It has to work perfectly from the start, or they'll think it's a Mickey Mouse."

"What's a Mickey Mouse?"

"Some kind of archaic and ridiculous Disney hand controller my parents used when they were little."

Adam scratched his head a bit and looked hard at Dude. "Bot propulsion on a football field can't be jet-magnetic. I could have Master cover the floor with AstroTurf in the battle bot arena, and we could set up the demo there. Then we could have your team's offense scrimmage against the defense and see how it goes."

"That's cool," said Dude. "Would Master let the whole team in here for a demo?"

"Since they are students... probably," answered Adam, "especially if we play the first few games just against her. She got pretty excited about my last bot battle with her. She's not like any other AI I've ever seen. For a program that supposedly can't understand human emotion, she loves to get excited about ideas."

"She didn't used to be that way," Tomly added.

"Yeah, but you've really helped her. She's pretty great now."

"Will she help us?" asked Dude.

"Oh, she will, I'm sure," said Tomly. "Whatever we come up with to connect the game-playing part of the minds of those so-called teammates of yours to their bots, she's sure to improve upon. It might even end up being entertaining enough to stop them from sending you flamers."

"Yeah, well, I don't blame them for being angry with me after what my dad did."

"I guess," said Adam. "But your dad stopped a lot of future concussions and blown-out knees. Too late for my older brother, who has fifteen metal pins in his ankle from football and walks with a limp. It used to be fun to watch him slug it out at the games, though. Is your dad excited about this?"

Dude leaned back. "I don't know. He's excited about telling me what to do. Then he argues and rolls his eyes like I'm stupid if I protest or don't measure up."

"That also sucks," said Tomly.

"I guess most dads are like that these days," said Dude.

"I guess," waffled Adam.

"Not yours?"

"We get along okay, actually. I mentioned wanting to help you with your problem last night, and my dad said the bot idea was pretty cool and to have fun with it."

For a moment, Dude was jealous of Adam. Tech was pretty safe compared to football, unless a power battery blew up or something. Still, Adam had a dad who obviously supported his son's passion in life instead of trying to forbid him from it. He wondered what Adam's dad was like at work. Maybe there was a reason he was in core at Circle and his dad wasn't.

# Chapter Ten

Every day after school, Dude hurried to the Tech Lab to work with Adam and Tomly on the project.

The first step was making a plan. Adam wanted to print all twenty-two bots for the team right away, but Tomly suggested printing two at first to work out the mechanical kinks in handing off and passing the ball. When they put on their phoneglasses and told their idea to Master, she agreed that was the right way to start. She also added that according to the current psych metrics of Dude's teammates, a demo had a 95.6% chance of being required for them to be interested in playing football with robots. Getting the specs for printing a Model Six from Circle wouldn't be hard, she confirmed, but she would have to do the printing herself for security reasons. There were just too many spies out there gathering secrets for Zetta's version of the same robot. Adam said it was fine for her to do the printing, as long as the psych programming was left open and was easily programmable for them to match the bots to the individual players.

Dude felt way behind understanding the technical talk Adam and Tomly were having with Master, but they always took the time to catch him up when he asked. After a week, it felt like being on a team again, and it was good to have friends to do something interesting with after school. It wasn't the same as Gary, Zagan, and his old buds playing football, but his life at school was now a lot better than he thought it would be. He liked being in Adam's studio, putting the final touches on the plan and sitting at one of the spacious new worktables. Adam had finally recycled his "memory" junkyard to make room for them, so maybe this was good for him too.

"Will wonders never cease?" Tomly said, looking around in shock at the clean studio.

"I'm working on something way more interesting now than the junk I was doing in the past, so I said a tearful good-bye to my library babies just to make you happy, Tomcat."

"So," said Dude, "We print two regular Model Sixes for now, and our plan for the demo is...?"

"That's easy," said Adam. "We use your brain's metrics to program one bot, and someone else's to program the other, then we sign up for a school demo at assembly."

"Live or holographic?" asked Tomly, blinking notes onto her helmet screen.

"Live, and on the football field, if possible," said Adam.

"And," said Dude, "it really is possible to use human psych profiles as the basis for programming them, along with people's different mobility metrics?"

Adam nodded.

"Wow. Will that be enough?"

"It should be," said Adam, "for the demo, anyway. After all, we're just tossing the ball around and doing some basic tackling. Tomly, can you ask Master to print the sensor suits today for taking the mobility metrics? Then, if Master cooperates, it's just a matter of uploading the psych and mobility data and getting the bots into the arena for a little practice time."

"Tomly," asked Dude, "do you know if Master is actually able to load every team member's entire psych metric file into their bots?"

"Yep, no prob. I checked. If the school football helmets hadn't been required to be connected to the network for concussion monitoring purposes, we would have been out of luck. But they were, so every player's psych profile for every practice and every game is available. She can pop them into the bots, no problem, with no risk of violating privacy, by the way, unless someone steals a bot and deprograms it."

"So," continued Dude, "there really will be enough data to support guided independent action for the demo bots? Because we know the vision problem from the sidelines means that they can't be controlled and moved around like avatars. "

"Should be enough, yes. Model Sixes are always fully autonomous and organized when given clear guidance. You've witnessed that from their morning planning meetings. Tell a Six to clean the kitchen, and it will figure out the best time and manner to do it on its own. It will be the same for a football play, except the planning meetings come in the huddle, not just once a day at a breakfast nook."

"That's cool. Sounds like it might work." Dude loved the energy in Tomly's voice. He could see that she liked acting all business-like, but she also seemed pretty quick at picking up how football was played. He suspected, given her growing knowledge, that she had been watching archived games on her phoneglasses.

Suddenly, he had a brainstorm.

"So, Tomly," he said, "you know Zagan Benson hates me. He wants to murder me, according to Gary. So he's out as a quarterback for our demo, even if we could get him to come into the Tech Lab in the first place, which I doubt. Adam's going to be busy with the data collection. Do *you* mind being the quarterback tomorrow for the demo?"

"Sure, I guess, as long as someone doesn't mind helping me get into the sensor suit."

"Huh?" said Dude.

"You have to take all your clothes off to put one on," said Adam, smirking.

Dude's face flushed with heat. "Uh, no, of course not... Whatever is required."

"Don't worry you guys," said Adam. "The old ones were skin-tight and not always easy to get on by yourself, but I can custom-print these for you so you can."

"Either way, I don't mind," said Tomly. We have a sauna at home, and my parents always say that you can't really know yourself until you are comfortable in your birthday skin around others. So it's not an issue for me if Ally's not around and one of you has to help me into the suit. That's why I asked. Anyway, Dude, you've got me interested in trying this sport now because you love it so much. I kind of miss doing something athletic."

Adam raised his eyebrows at him, and Dude could feel his heart beating hard all of a sudden. He managed a nod, but all he could think of was how uncomfortable he would be in a family sauna with his parents.

"Um, that's cool, Tomly. Thanks!" he finally stammered. Then the blood came rushing to his cheeks hotter than ever.

# Chapter Eleven

The next day, two mobility sensor suits were waiting in the center of Adam's studio with, to Dude's relief, a privacy curtain hung between them.

"You guys ready for this?" said Adam.

"Wow, these look like superhero costumes. Aren't sensor suits usually bulkier than this?" asked Tomly.

"Well, yes, usually," said Adam, "but we're not just trying to record you walking around doing household chores. Master and I modified the design so you can run, jump, and get tackled to the limits of your ability. You should still be able to get them on okay, though."

"I get that the suit reads every nerve impulse," said Dude, taking the thin, ultra-soft fabric in his hands, "but how is the data stored?"

"It isn't," said Adam. "It's sent to my data helmet via thread transmitters."

"Cool," said Tomly. "And nice with the curtain. Very respectfully conventional."

"I thought you'd like that," said Adam with a wink. "Okay, guys, use the conductor lotion first and put 'em on. And yes, the conductor lotion needs to go *everywhere* the fabric touches. I'll be outside. Call me when you're ready."

Once they were alone, Dude looked at Tomly. "You ready to try this?"

"Sure," she replied easily, "just remember that I'm not Zagan. I don't know what I'm doing yet with a football."

"That's all right. Zagan may be a great quarterback, but he doesn't know what he's doing with human beings. You'll learn about football soon enough, but I don't know if *Zagan* will ever learn how to really be part of a team."

"Maybe so, but still I'm sorry you lost him as a friend. Maybe he'll come around when he sees the demo."

"I doubt it. I tried to talk to him about it, but before I could say anything, he told me to do something anatomically impossible to myself and said he was thinking about transferring to Zinkerberg because Honeycrisp is full of idiots."

She looked at him in surprise. "He can't do that. His dad is in the sales department at Circle!"

"He said his dad would transfer. All Zagan cares about is Zagan."

"Wow, that sucks. Sorry, Dude."

"No big loss. Besides, he's the idiot. He probably doesn't even know that Zinkerberg Academy just banned football too."

"Some people just can't deal with their anger. Good riddance to him."

"Yeah. He sure could toss the pigskin, though."

"Maybe, but there's more to life than just talent, right?"

"You can say that again. Hey, let's get these things on so we can warm up!"

In their separate spaces, Dude took off his sneakers and phoneglasses and stripped out of his clothes. The lotion was easy enough, clear and cool on his skin. But putting on the sensor suit wasn't. "I can't get the darn thing on!" yelled Dude over the curtain.

"You've got to use a ton of lotion," replied Tomly from the other side. He heard the zipper on her suit go up. He reapplied the lotion and finally got all his limbs into the right places, but he couldn't get the zipper up until he sucked in his stomach and let out a big grunt.

"You two look great," said Adam when he came back from the corridor. "Like you just stepped out of the Marvel Universe."

"Well, it feels like I just stepped into the contracting universe!" said Dude, grimacing and a little self-conscious at how revealing the suit was.

"It's got to be tight to get all the subtle readings, but don't worry. It will move with you no problem. It's designed to read your movements, not restrict them."

"I don't think this particular suit got that message," said Dude, tugging at his legs.

"Mine feels pretty great," said Tomly. "Better than a volleyball uniform, that's for sure. What do we do first?"

Dude snuck a glance at her. Her muscles were indeed like an Olympic athlete's.

"Just basic stuff," said Adam. It was a little hard to hear him because the special sensor suit data helmet Dude had on was even bulkier than Tomly's. "One minute. Let me make sure I'm getting sensor readings from both of you, and I need to merge my data uptake with Master. She'll be cross-referencing your movement capabilities with every movement recorded last season for players in your positions. She'll then calculate the limits and your personal movement and strength capability profiles for your bot... Okay, you're both good, and Master is ready."

"Do you mean Master has every movement recorded from our team last year?!" asked Dude.

"No, *every* football player's movements, from high schools, colleges, and the NFL. Well, every quarterback and wide receiver who ever played the game on camera, that is. Yeah, I know, it's amazing. Okay, she says she's ready. She wants to start with basic calisthenics. Follow the hologram."

Adam's oversized helmet manifested the hologram beam, and he was right, it was basic stuff—sit-ups, push-ups, jumping jacks, twisting yoga poses, running in place. When it got to headstands, Dude saw Tomly do one right away, but he kept falling over. He finally gave up with the excuse that his suit was too tight.

Finally, Adam said, "Master says to take a break now while I get the football. Next, we'll go to the arena. Wait, I forgot to print a football!"

"No problem. I've got one in my studio," said Dude. "Let's go."

They took the corridor that went toward his studio.

"You're strong," Dude said to Tomly as they walked.

"Oh, thanks. My parents insist that I at least use the auto-workout feed on weeknights since I quit volleyball. It does the job, I guess."

"You'd rather do that than play something?"

"I told you, I don't like most sports. Their strategies are easy to figure out, but then you can't control everything that happens, so it's frustrating. It drove me nuts in volleyball. But I do like how I feel after exercise."

"I get it about not being in control. I hate it when other people mess up too, but how I feel after a football game still beats how I feel after an auto-workout any day."

"I believe you, but I've never experienced anything like that."

"Me either," piped in Adam. "Don't get me wrong, Dude. I like this project a lot, but not because I like sports. I don't even like auto-workouts. They make me sore, even on the easiest setting."

Dude looked at Adam and couldn't help thinking that he could have been a great football player with his size if he wanted to. "Let me put it this way, you guys. The fact that I'm going to catch a football again in a few minutes is the best thing that's happened to me in weeks."

"That's cool," said Tomly. "But you can only catch it if I can actually throw it to you!"

Dude's new studio was barren compared to Adam's. There was nothing in it except old sports equipment, a plastic chair, and a bathroom. His favorite football was in a mesh bag on the floor. He unzipped the bag and squeezed the football lovingly before pumping it up. It smelled of leather and dirt from the last game when he got hurt. It was a gift from the coach, salvaged from the wild celebration in the endzone that almost crushed him to death. He tossed it from hand to hand as they walked past the printing lab and down the far corridor to Adam's bot arena.

Even though they wore sneakers over the footies of the sensor suits, the metal floor of the arena wasn't the most ideal surface to play on. But Adam said it didn't matter, and Master didn't need to print AstroTurf to get the data she needed to program the Sixes for the assembly. The main thing required was just basic throwing and passing.

"We can maybe do some slow-motion tackling if we have time, as long as you are careful," he said.

"Why don't we just go outside?" asked Tomly.

"In these get-ups? No way," said Dude. "I'm not as unselfconscious as you are. Besides, it would spoil the surprise, and contact sport is banned now, remember? We might get detention if I tackled you."

"Yeah, *right*, shy boy. Or maybe you're afraid of me tackling *you*! You look slick in that get-up by the way. You should wear it to school tomorrow. You could pass as a new member of a super-cool boy band."

"I'll wear mine if you'll wear yours, mannequin girl. Now, you want to learn how to throw this thing or not?" Dude really needed to move to forget that he was being squeezed to death.

"To do this right," said Adam, "I need short passes, long passes, laterals, everything, including near catches, bobbles and catches, leaps for the ball, the whole nine yards."

"Okay, okay," Dude said. "Let's not get ahead of ourselves. Tomly's never even thrown a football yet."

"Yeah. Which hand should I throw it with?" asked Tomly. She reached out for the football, and Dude held it in front of her with his fingers over the laces. "You hold it like this in your dominant hand and use the laces to give it a little spin as you throw it."

"I don't have a dominant hand."

"Yes, you do!" said Adam. "Everyone is either right-handed or left-handed. Even I know that!"

"Not me. I can write with either hand."

"Well, use the hand you used to serve for volleyball," said Dude.

"I used one or the other depending on how the other team was positioned and what kind of spin I wanted to put on the ball."

Dude had to pause a moment to take that in. "Well, great. Use whichever hand you feel like, I guess. Does it matter for the data, Adam?"

"Not a bit. Bots have two hands too, you know."

"Okay," said Dude, getting back into a demonstration stance, "so you cock your arm behind your head like this and spin the ball on the laces as you throw it." He showed her the grip and then gently backed up a few steps to toss the ball to her, exaggerating the spin. She caught it easily with a smack of her hands on the leather.

"Got it. Feels good," she said.

"Wait, you guys," said Adam. "We're tuning into your signals. Okay, got 'em both. Master says she's ready. Just play catch now and vary your throws and catches like I said. What? Master says the order doesn't matter for this part."

Dude backed up toward the middle of the arena. "You ready?" he said. "See if you can throw it this far."

Tomly cocked her left arm and drilled the ball into Dude's chest, making him stagger backward.

"Nice one," he said, lobbing it back to her. Again, she caught it firmly.

She said, "Go a little farther out, okay? I'm going to try my other arm to see how it feels." Dude ran to the middle of the arena. She cocked her right arm this time and delivered a bullet to his chest again.

"I think you've got the hang of it, Tomly," shouted Dude, throwing the ball back to her and backing up even more.

"Yeah, no kidding!" said Adam.

"This is kind of fun," said Tomly, starting to smile. "I like the way the ball spins in the air. It's different from a volley-ball, more accurate. Do you like it in your chest, or where should I aim for?"

"In a game, it depends on the situation, but for now just aim for anything close to me, and I'll adjust to catch it." His voice echoed a bit off the high metal ceiling of the arena.

"How about one just above your head so you have to reach for it? Run that way," shouted Tomly.

Dude sprinted, and Tomly led him perfectly with the ball exactly a foot over his head. Soon they were on a roll. He was amazed by her power and consistent accuracy, even though she kept changing arms with each throw. Before she passed to him, she specified if the ball would be high or low, on the knees or in his chest, and each time she delivered the pass perfectly no matter how fast he ran.

*She's better than Zagan!* he thought.

After a while, Dude forgot about his too-tight sensor suit and Adam collecting data nearby. To be catching per-fectly thrown balls again no matter what he was wearing, even in a battle bot arena with a metal floor, was a sheer plea-sure. After about twenty passes, time stood still for him just like it had last year in the championship game. Like a floating dream, it was just him, his quarterback, and the football. He and Tomly were in sync like nothing he had ever experienced, even with Zagan. Back and forth they went across the arena. Back and forth, each running routes, each catching perfectly. Tomly threw perfectly. Dude threw almost perfectly, better than he had ever thrown before because of her inspiration.

*She's laughing while she's doing this!* he observed with amazement. After he got used to his surprise about her talent, he too was laughing at the sheer good luck of discovering her and the pleasure of the ball sailing and smacking between them.

"Okay, kids," shouted Adam, startling Dude out of his trance. It was too soon to stop, even though he was breathing hard. He shook his head to try to come back to earth from so much fun. "Playtime is over. Master says she has enough basic data for the throwing and catching demo. Do you want to try some tackles?"

When his brain could engage in reality again, Dude ran excitedly toward Tomly from across the arena. "Please tell me you were holding out on me and you've been secretly playing football your whole life because that was just *amazing*!" he said.

"Really?" said Tomly. "It wasn't that hard. I've never played football before in my life, but I've got to say, it's pretty fun how you can micro-adjust where this ball goes on the receiver's body, or above it."

"Just *pretty* fun, laughing girl?" said Dude.

"I was laughing because *you* were laughing!"

"I was laughing because that was *very* fun! You're great at this, you know that? Most receivers have to make all kinds of adjustments to catch balls thrown by a quarterback. Catching your throws is like no problem at all! Micro-adjustments? Most quarterbacks have trouble with *macro*-adjustments. You can really throw a football, Tomly! Do you have any idea how hard it is to do that?!"

"You're right, I don't know. But do me a favor and don't ask me how I do it. Someone asked me once how I served a volleyball so well, and I couldn't do it again for three days."

"Okay, deal. I won't ask you, as long as you promise to throw the ball with me again very soon, with either hand!"

"No worries there, Dude. As I said, it's pretty fun, maybe especially with you. Thanks for showing me how!"

"All right, guys," said Adam, "enough of the love fest. We got a bunch of really good data, and Master just said she is 99.7% sure she can crunch it all for the bots by the time she gets them printed. So, tackling? Do you think you guys are going to like it as much as you enjoyed your game of catch? We've got time."

"Bring it on!" said Tomly, smiling at Dude.

Dude and Tomly helped Adam unroll a few mats from the arena storeroom to throw over the floor before they went at it. Tomly proved as good at tackling as she was at throwing. After laughing and plowing into each other for twenty minutes, Dude suddenly wondered exactly what kind of embarrassing psych data Adam and Master were gathering. And was Tomly's data the same as his?

# Chapter Twelve

*Master's Report to Core*
*Sept. 30, 2055*

1. *Art Media Creation App. (Best with UPL access): Target market—malls and schools. Ages 10 and up. 72.8% chance for success. Principal—Allison Albright, 9th grade.*
2. *X-ray Fart Predictor: Target Market—homes. All ages. 65.1% chance for success. Principal—Kevin Former. 9th grade.*
3. *Model Six Football Prototype. Target market—clubs and all schools. 98.9% chance for success. Principals—Dudley McPherson, Jr., 9th grade; Tomly Newton, 9th grade; Adam Angelou, 9th grade.*

# Chapter Thirteen

Dude was happy that the dean went along with his and Tomly's idea of chasing everybody outside for an old-fashioned, in-person assembly in the California sunshine. Standing on the field with Adam and Tomly and their two Sixes covered with a tarp to hide the surprise, Dude felt a trickle of sweat run down his ribcage. After the dean reassured the crowd gathering in the stands of the old football field that the day's unusual IRL announcements would also be delivered to their phoneglasses, he ran through the list of this week's student academic achievements and what was on the menu for lunches next week. Then he bragged about the school having the best tech program in the country and gestured for them to begin.

"Hey, Dude!" someone yelled from the stands. "What'cha got under that tarp? A booth for selling Band-Aids?" Dude looked down at his feet and took a deep breath.

"Just ignore them," Tomly muttered to Dude. "This is going to be great."

"I hope so. You ready?" said Dude.

"Yep, let's do this thing!" said Tomly, and they yanked off the tarp revealing the Sixes wearing football pads. The bots' usual synthetic, human-looking skin had been replaced by a more durable but flexible metallic material, and they wore electronically enhanced football helmets. Except for the metal skin visible on their arms, calves, necks and faces, the two Sixes looked just like real human players.

It didn't surprise Dude that the crowd didn't know how to react, except to murmur loudly to each other. As he had expected, there were a few laughs, a few photos snapped, and a general sense of not yet getting the point.

*They'll get it soon enough,* he thought.

"Okay, folks," said the dean through his phoneglasses feed. "Quiet down so you can hear them."

"So, the pads are more or less just for show," yelled Dude. He could have used the microphone on his phoneglasses, but he liked the idea of communicating commando for this. "They don't really need them as much as humans do on the field. These special Sixes have been uploaded with our actual psych metrics and the parameters of our physical capabilities. Since we're not allowed to play football anymore with our bodies, we thought this might be the next best thing. These specially programmed units are still in beta, but if we get enough students interested, we might be able to make more and have a team."

Dude was interrupted by a familiar-sounding helicar that appeared abruptly over the storage tanks. It buzzed overhead, messing up everyone's hair, and jerkily landed just to the side of the stadium. Curious like everyone else was to see who got through the supposedly secure air space surrounding the school, he watched in horror as his dad stepped out of the driver's seat.

"What is your *dad* doing here?" whispered Tomly.

"I don't know. I told him this morning I didn't want him here for this!" Dude saw the dean walk over to the helicar and give his dad a hearty handshake.

"What should we do?" asked Tomly in Dude's ear.

"I don't know. Oh, just ignore him, I guess. If he's going to screw this up for me somehow, there's nothing I can do about it. But let's get this started before he has a chance to interfere."

Dude felt she would have given him a supportive hug if everyone in the school hadn't been watching them. He was glad he had someone at school now who understood the frustration he had with his dad taking football away from him.

"Okay, people! Listen up!" shouted Dude. "First, Tomly and I are going to play a little game of catch. Don't worry, Dean Gonzales, no tackling! Then you're going to see what these bots can do. They'll be a sign-up on your phoneglasses afterward if you want to maybe help create a team. Tomly, you ready?"

Dude pulled his football from a red mesh bag at the feet of the bots and jogged with Tomly to the middle of the field.

"Just like in a real football game," shouted Dude back to the crowd, "there's a huddle, where we give the Sixes instructions for the upcoming play. For demonstration purposes today, all we're going to tell them to do is imitate exactly what we do beforehand. In a real game, of course, they would have to know the plays ahead of time. Okay, Sixes, huddle up!"

The bots moved nimbly on two feet toward Dude and Tomly and leaned in together. Loud enough for the crowd to understand him, Dude said, "Okay Sixes, you heard me.

When we hand you the ball, you need to imitate *exactly* what Tomly and I just did on the field. Imitate it all the way through to handing the ball back to us at the end. Then repeat the same instructions after our next play. This session will finish only when we put the football back into the mesh bag. Got it? Okay, break!"

"Break!" shouted the Sixes loudly in deep brawny voices. Dude heard some laughs from the crowd.

They moved to the middle of the field. Then Tomly slapped the side of the football, dropped back, and yelled, "Go deep!"

Once again, Dude was running on the football field in front of a Honeycrisp School crowd, and once again, his dad loomed like a nightmare on the sidelines. What was he doing here, anyway? Trying to ruin Dude's life again?

Dude forced his dad out of his thoughts and concentrated on his route down the field, a down and out with a sharp cut back to the ball. As usual, Tomly delivered the pass perfectly, and he caught it easily. He heard the crowd clapping.

He ran back with the ball and handed it to Tomly's bot on the track. The bots ran out onto the middle of the field to the exact spots Dude and Tomly just left. Tomly's bot slapped the football and yelled in a voice exactly like Tomly's, "Go deep!" Dude's bot took off and ran the exact same route he had just finished. The bot made the cut perfectly and caught the ball in its chest as Dude had done. It jogged back and handed Tomly the football. This time, the crowd cheered.

In the next play, Tomly lateraled to Dude and took off herself on a route. Dude did his best to lead her with his pass, but he overthrew it.

"You suck," he heard Zagan yell from the stands.

Tomly picked up the ball and ran it back to her bot. The groans in the audience turned to *oohs* of amazement when the bots imitated to a tee the exact same incompletion.

Soon, everyone couldn't get enough of the show, and Dude started to smile. They demonstrated short passes into the flat, sideline passes, crossing routes, and crowd-pleasing long bombs. With each play, the students pressed closer toward them from the stands to get better videos of the action. They shouted their support for Dude, Tomly, and the Sixes. Finally, everyone was mobbing the track and getting so close to them that the dean got nervous and phone-blasted everyone that the assembly was over and it was time to get back inside for the next class period.

The students groaned but obeyed. They surged past Dude and Tomly, giving them high-fives, and a few old team members promised they would sign up for the new team.

"It's not football, but it's pretty cool," remarked one of them, flashing Dude a thumbs-up. Dude held the football up to him in salute.

"Where was Tomly last game when we needed her?" said another. "She's better than Zagan! What an arm!"

"I know, right? Best arm, I mean arms, I've ever seen," said Dude.

Then he spotted Zagan listening to the banter with a scowl on his face.

"You chose a *girl* to program that bot, McPherson?" snarled Zagan.

Dude looked over at Tomly in the crowd of excited students and realized she had heard Zagan's comment.

"No, Benson, I didn't choose a *girl*. I chose a *quarterback*, A quarterback *teammate* who's consistently accurate with the football and a genuine athlete with a lot to learn and a lot to teach. Come join us, if you think you can compete with her."

"Stuff it, McPherson. I've got way better things to do with my time, like finding a bigger and better school. Good luck with your girly team."

"Oh well, your loss," said Dude.

Zagan made a rude gesture and walked back to the classroom building with a few of his die-hard buddies.

"Dude!" yelled Tomly, finally getting to him. "This thing wasn't supposed to end yet. The bots are still standing there waiting for the next play. Where's the mesh bag so I can turn them off?"

"I don't know," said Dude. "It was right there on the ground before we got mobbed!"

The bag was nowhere to be seen. Did Zagan stuff it in his backpack?

Even after the crowd dispersed enough that they could search for it on the field, they didn't find the bag until they saw it swinging in his dad's hand. He was walking slowly toward them with the dean.

"Dad, what are you *doing*? We need that bag to turn off the Sixes!"

"I know that, son. We heard your instructions to them. That's why Dean Gonzales and I borrowed the bag."

Dude was confused, but his dad and the dean were smiling.

"Uh, so, why?" said Dude, nervously looking past his dad at the patiently waiting Sixes.

"Well, you need the bag to stop the Sixes from playing football, right?"

Dude didn't know what to say. Why was his dad playing games with him right now? Tomly looked as confused as he was. "You know we do," he said.

Then his Dad smiled and handed him the bag. "Well, Circle doesn't want them to stop playing. I'm here to tell you officially from Core that Circle wants these Sixes to continue playing football at this school for many years to come!"

# Chapter Fourteen

Dude was confused and a little shocked by his dad's news, but he didn't have time to think about it because he had to take the bots back to the Tech Lab and get to class. It wasn't until his mom picked him up in her helicar after school that he figured out what had happened.

"You mean he was *spying* on me at school?" said Dude.

Unlike his dad, who liked to fly the helicar himself, his mom always used the auto-flying feature. "Take us home," she said to the car, and they took off over the school buildings.

She turned to him from the pilot's seat. "Well, I wouldn't call it spying. You've been sharing with him what you're doing, and your project has caused quite a stir with your dad's superiors in Core, dear. They thought it would be nice to let him break the news to you since he is your dad and all. He was quite excited about it. Core has big plans."

"Plans? For what? Circle has never been interested in football."

"Well, not as a company, but all your dad's friends there love the 49ers."

"Right," Dude said sarcastically. "They love to watch the games, just not enough to let their children play in them."

"Do you know how much your dad and I used to worry about your brain?"

"What do you mean? My brain's fine, Mom!"

"If you hit your head too hard, it might not be. Two or three serious concussions is the average for high school players, and even more, if you play in college."

"So you do agree with Dad about that."

"I'm your mother. I know how much you love playing football, but I agree with your dad when he says it's a great game that needs to be banned. There are just too many serious injuries."

"Well, he got his way."

"And he knows you aren't happy about that. That's why he was thrilled that the report from the Tech Lab AI highlighted your bot team idea. It's brilliant, you know. All the rough and tumble and no danger of any humans getting hurt. This could land you a Circle job someday."

"Mom, I'm a first-year in high school! It's too early for me to think about work, even at Circle. Besides, it wasn't just my idea."

"Well, they've got their eye on you, especially the AI in the Tech Lab. And it isn't hurting your dad's reputation either."

"They call her Master."

"Who?"

"The AI."

She laughed at the name. "Like a schoolmaster, I suppose. Well, in any case, she's impressed. Core is impressed. They want to do something with your idea. What it is, I don't know. Something big, but your dad says they're going to let your team stay in charge of the project for now."

"Well, how *generous* of them, considering it was *our* idea. What do you mean, 'do something big with this'?"

"Your Dad told me not to tell you, but Core sees a very large market for your idea, even bigger than the Battle Bot market."

"Oh, I get it. Just like what Adam said, battle-botting in a new form. They're going to ruin this just like football got ruined, aren't they? And why? To sell more Sixes, of course! Figures. Do they even know what my project is really about?"

"Maybe not, but they aren't taking it away from you either. They don't care about football like *you* do, dear, it's true. Maybe that's why they still want this to be your project. As popular as it is, real football is on its way out. That's no longer a debate. It won't be long before schools that still offer football will lose every lawsuit for child endangerment and abuse. Sacramento is debating a statewide ban because defending football in court has become so expensive for universities. But Dad says Core thinks you have the brains to make your idea as close to the real thing as it can be."

"So Dad took his safety committee garbage to *the government*?!"

"You've got to give your dad a break. He loves you, you know, and he cares about children's safety."

"If he loved me, he would try to understand me better."

"I'm sorry, Dude. Maybe you should just talk to him."

"Sure, Mom, I will. Maybe when he stops surprise-stealing things from me and Tomly."

# Chapter Fifteen

To Dude's amazement, by the time Halloween rolled around, everyone on last year's eighth-grade football team was bored enough with the school's lame alternative activities to sign up for Dude's bot league.

Well, everyone except Zagan, who couldn't get over the fact that the majority of his old teammates were whispering that Tomly was a better quarterback than he was. He made good on his threat to put in a transfer to Zinkerberg Academy. Every day after school and before going to the tech lab, Dude and Tomly played catch on the football field, and they often noticed Zagan watching them, silently fuming.

"He's jealous of your long bombs," said Dude to Tomly.

She laughed. "Or jealous that we're allowed to get around the no-contact sports rule to do necessary research."

He saw his other teammates watching them, too. He could feel that they wanted in on the action, and Zagan wasn't offering anything but crabbing sessions. Tomly was showing herself to be stronger and more coordinated than anyone in the first-year class, including Zagan himself. It must be as obvious to the team as it was to him.

When the drama of Zagan leaving to "play football at a real school" was over and his negativity was gone for good, Dude and Tomly got a full sign-up for the team. When the final list popped up on their phoneglasses, Dude walked with Tomly for another planning meeting in Adam's studio.

"So, Dude, what are you going to be for Halloween?" asked Adam, sipping one of the three hot chocolates Tomly had brought from the lounge printer.

"I don't know, maybe a zombie carrying a blood-red mesh ball bag."

Tomly groaned and looked at him. "You hold your dad personally responsible for football getting banned, but if *he* hadn't done it, someone else was sure to. That *60 Minutes* empathy VR that came out last year with all the paralyzed and brain-damaged players was pretty gruesome to watch."

"No kidding, man," said Adam. "It traumatized my big brother all over again."

"Fine, you guys. I shouldn't have brought him up. You don't really know him, and he's my problem to deal with. Lucky he's pretty easy to ignore."

"Yeah, he's too busy, right?" said Tomly. "Mom says things have been pretty crazy in her department lately. If your dad is half as tied up as my mom is right now, you probably wouldn't get to spend much time with him even if you wanted to."

"Right, the Truth Department at Circle," said Adam, remembering. "Are they going to do something about Zetta's VR Manipulation Software? My dad won't tell me anything, other than Zetta is making a ton of money on it."

"Who knows?" said Tomly. "It needs to be banned. Fake VR videos at the blink of an eye that can't be distinguished from actual videos. They're way popular now, and it's pretty much an impossible problem for my mom."

"Well, it's job security for her, at least," said Dude.

"And," said Adam, "maybe it's good that it keeps your Dad out of your hair for a while."

"I got an idea," said Dude. "Maybe I'll buy the evil Zetta software and make a video of him campaigning to bring back football to Honeycrisp School so that his son can have a life again."

Tomly frowned at him. "Will you please just give it a rest? He's a conventional parent. What do you expect? Plus, he's old. The bottom line here is that our project can go forward. Is that so freaking awful?"

"Sorry," said Dude.

"All right, guys," said Adam, putting on his absurdly large phoneglasses helmet.

"Checking in with Master. Looks like she's got Circle's okay to print bots for the linemen and the different positions," said Adam.

"That's great!" said Tomly. "The team will really like that. So, can we make the Sixes' metallic faces look like the individual team members?"

"No, she thinks body size and their numbers are all that's needed since their heads will be in helmets anyway."

"I don't know why you even asked for that, Dude," teased Tomly. "What did you want? Metallic Sixes parading around school with their groupies like real football players used to do?"

Dude smiled. "No, I guess not. Better for us human jocks to at least still have that perk."

"Sorry," said Tomly, "you'll never be a Zagan in that department."

"And I'm glad. You either, thank goodness!"

"It's cool that a bunch of girls signed up for the team," said Adam.

"Yeah, it is!" said Tomly.

"But no way they're going to be as good as you," said Dude.

Tomly waved that away. "What? Because they might be weaker or less coordinated? It won't matter since Sixes have a standard base level of strength and coordination. Some bots will express more strength than others, of course, based on individual player data from the sensor suits. But at least the bots for everyone, male or female, have the baseline stamina to grow and develop on the team."

"Well," said Adam, "you won't ever catch me partnering up with a bot. It would take way less than standard stamina to imitate my lack of coordination."

"Hey," said Tomly. "No negative self-talk. You're big and strong, Adam. Plus, you're strong in other ways. We could never have done this without you. Right, Dude?"

Dude agreed.

Adam shrugged. "That's a sweet thing for you sensor suit love birds to say. But let's get to work. The dean insists that with winter vacation coming up, we have to let him know soon if we want the team to put on a scrimmage before the end of the year, and this project is a *very* long way from being done."

"Right!" Tomly chugged the rest of her hot chocolate and beamed at them. "Time for some serious organizing!"

# Chapter Sixteen

Locker rooms were always crowded, but Dude soon learned that adding a Model Six to each player's pile of equipment made them even more claustrophobic. Even after the construction bots knocked down walls and connected several studios into one huge room next to the bot arena, there still wasn't enough space.

No one on the team was complaining. After all, there was no need for showers now, and the Sixes organized the lockers themselves and put on their own pads and cleats. Maybe the complaints would come if the guys couldn't get used to having girls in the locker room before and after practice. They'd have to get over that quickly with Tomly at quarterback. Right now, though, Dude was glad that everyone was being patient. He had a lot of players talking about how cool it was to train their own personal Six.

In November, Dude, Tomly, Adam, and Master were busy after school, not only printing the team's twenty-five Sixes but also a sensor suit for each person who signed up. Not to mention collecting data for each team member and all the psych uploads and calibrations for each player and position. Dude had insisted on duplicate capabilities for special teams and for them to prepare for the small possibility of one of the team's bots breaking down on the field. It was a lot to do.

They were well organized, mostly because of Tomly, but Dude knew football better than they did and how much work was ahead of them to put this team together.

Dude started with workouts in small groups in the arena, just getting the basics down like blocking, tackling, and ball handling. At first, he had the players and the bots on the arena grid together for the huddle. But the humans took too long to get off the grid before the play started, so with Adam's help, he went with helmet radios to program the bots in the huddle. It took a while for each player to learn how to tell their Six what to do for each play, though. There was always someone who took way too long to deliver instructions. But thanks to the Six's advanced learning algorithms, communication got clearer and faster with each practice. The hardest part was the noise of everyone talking at once into their modified phoneglasses outside the arena. Dude and Tomly decided they needed to space everyone out after each play was called, so Adam suggested that the human team members huddle outside the arena and break to assigned positions before delivering instructions, just like the Sixes were huddling and breaking inside the arena. Dude really liked that because it gave the human players and the game an old-style sense of play-by-play action and flow. It also showed that defensive players had to call plays each time, a fact he knew still escaped most fans even after over a century of the game.

If the first early-December mini-scrimmages in the arena were like test firings of brand-new rockets, Dude witnessed several of them magnificently blow up on the launch pad. The bots popped footballs like little bombs until they learned to grip them more gingerly. The defense kept lining up with the offense on the same side of the line of scrimmage. Receiver bots and pass defenders smashed spectacularly through the arena's walls while competing for a catch. (The whoops and hollers from the team did not motivate Adam to speedily reprogram *that* glitch.) A center forgot holding was illegal and ripped the arm off a blitzing linebacker (also to applause).

Each one of these surprises required Dude to stop everything and wait for Adam to reprogram the Sixes with everyone's input. It was tedious for the student players, but this "sport" was still way more interesting than any other after-school activity, and the players learned to be patient with the bots and the techies. And practices felt a little bit like they used to feel because the team's daily progress was visible.

Despite their best efforts, though, Dude had to admit that the Sixes just weren't ready for a debut before the whole school before winter break. More than once, Dean Gonzales offered to assign Dude's old coach to come in and help them in the Tech Lab. Tomly and Adam refused, and in the end, Master supported them even though it seemed that she was getting pressure from Core to break the no-adults policy and let the coach take over.

*I guess we're not moving fast enough for their marketing plan*, Dude figured.

This really bothered him. Did they think it was easy to train robots to think like real football players? Did they think the Sixes could be controlled individually by players on the sidelines like in a holographic video game? Not possible. They probably didn't care if the bots played the game with any sort of human sporting spirit, as long as they hit each other and people wanted to buy them.

Well, they might be right. Maybe the only thing bot football could be was a bigger version of a bot battle. But Dude wasn't going to just roll over and let that happen because Circle was in a hurry to make money. He wanted to make this like real football, not ruin it by changing it into something less. But when vacation began and Dude's dad surprised the family by inviting the coach over for a little pre-holiday dinner party, Dude realized Circle didn't agree with him on that point.

"Dad and his safety committee were ready to sue Coach after my injury," Dude said to his mom when she told him about the party, "and now he wants to be all buddy-buddy with him? Count me out. I'm going to In-N-Out for dinner."

His mom sighed. "Oh, honey, tonight's just a little get-together. Maybe your Dad feels bad about what he did to Coach's job and wants to make amends. You like Coach Miller, don't you? Maybe he can give you some help on your football project!"

"You know I have to do this on my own. The whole lab would lose its funding if a bunch of adults got involved, especially adults who are 'experts.'"

"Well, I think it would be impolite for you not to be there. Coach Miller taught you a lot about football. Why don't you invite your friends? Would that make it more fun? I'm going to print up something way better than In-N-Out."

"Mom, nothing is better than a double-double animal-style, and you know it," Dude said, only half joking, "but fine. If Tomly and Adam are free, I'll do it... for you."

Dude figured out later on that his mom knew more about the invite list than she had let on because Tomly and her mom, and Adam and his dad all ended up coming. The only thing good about that was that there were enough adults around the punch bowl that conversations with them stayed light and manageable. His dad, whose usual conversations were politely superficial and usually mutually avoided, was at least putting on a show of fatherly friendliness. Was it because his boss and one of his boss's bosses were there? Dude had no doubt. It was just so fake. Was his dad that desperate to be liked at work? Was getting ahead at his job his biggest passion? Dude wondered if he even wanted to find out.

So, as the party got going, he, Tomly, and Adam played the game of circling around and chatting briefly with each adult then sneaking into the basement to play VR Madden. He left the door open to be technically polite in case anybody wanted to join them, but the adults stayed chatting in the living room.

After a few games, Dude expected his mom to pop in any minute to call them to the table, but it was Coach Miller who poked his head inside with a smile.

"You kids have the right idea," he said, sizing up the hologram action that was playing out in the air above the ping-pong table.

"Hey, Coach. You come to play Madden?" said Dude.

"So is this where you are getting all your ideas for the bot team?" he said.

"No, we're just having some fun," said Dude, putting the game on hold. "Coach, you know Tomly, right?"

"Who hasn't heard of Tomly? We haven't spoken, but I've watched you throw the football at the assembly and on the field after school. Are you sure you're human? You've got quite an arm! Well, *arms*."

"Oh, thanks, Coach Miller," said Tomly.

"No, seriously, I wish I'd had a chance to coach you."

"I'm not as good as Zagan, I am sure."

"Well, games are the real test, but I have a feeling you would be as good if not better than him."

Dude was surprised when Coach stepped fully inside and swung the door partially closed behind him. Why did he leave the grown-ups?

"In fact," Coach went on, "I wanted to pass something along to you about Zagan."

Dude caught Tomly's eye just as she said, "Of course, Coach, come on in. You know Adam, right?"

"Of course. Hi, Adam. I coached your brother. I'm just so sorry about his injury. He was a great player, and I hear you're something of a whiz in the Tech Lab. You take after your dad, I guess!"

"Thanks," mumbled Adam.

Coach lowered his voice. "Okay, about Zagan. But first, let me say that I have no interest in interfering with your project, as much as some people here tonight want me to. Don't get me wrong, I love coaching, but even when I was coaching I never wanted to get in the way of how my players naturally played the game. That Tech Lab of yours, with the kids in charge, is the best educational thing we've got going at Honeycrisp School. I'm always willing to help you guys, but I'll wait for you to ask me, and frankly, I hope you never have to. You know enough about football to make your bot game just the way it should be. Don't let anybody rush you."

"Thanks, Coach Miller," replied Tomly. "But the faculty knows that Master would never let you in the Center anyway, so no worries."

"That's just the thing, see," said Coach Miller. "Zinkerberg Academy has ordered a bunch of Zetta Sixes, and they're also putting together a bot team on a fast track, only rumor has it that Zagan's dad and the Zinkerberg coaches are running the show over there, not the kids. They're worried you won't be able to keep up."

"You're kidding me!" said Adam. Dude and Tomly just stared at the coach in disbelief.

"I wish I were. No offense, Dude, but your dad is also worried that you guys won't be competitive without help."

Dude turned to Adam. "Would your dad ever let my dad talk him into letting adults take over our project?"

"I don't know. Probably not," said Adam, a little doubtfully.

"So Zagan is trying to one-up us," said Dude. "What a jerk face! Sorry, Coach. But there's no way he can be anywhere near as far along as we are. Can he, Adam?"

"I can't imagine," replied Adam, "but who knows how much of our data Zagan's dad had access to at Circle before he transferred? I could try to find out from Dad when we get home."

"Anyway, I wanted to let you guys know about that," said Coach Miller. "I don't know how much more they'll pressure me to help you guys. There's a lot of interest in a bot football game in the near future: you guys against Zinkerberg. A clash of the Valley's tech giants, you know what I mean? How can I put this gently? Circle's pride is on the line, and they didn't like it that you weren't ready for that demo scrimmage before the break."

"Well," said Dude, "they'll just have to wait until school starts again in January for that. Thanks for the heads-up and the support, Coach. We'll be ready. And don't worry, anything Zagan and his traitor dad are in charge of over there is bound to fail. Zetta Sixes! What a joke!"

Coach Miller nodded and put a hand on the doorknob. "Just between me and you three, I couldn't agree with you more. But it takes a lot for adults to trust kids when it comes to something as profitable as football, so keep your wits about you."

"We will, Coach Miller," said Tomly. "Thank you."

Coach slipped out and left the door open. A minute later, Dude's mom yelled for them to come to the table, where Dude managed to keep the subject of football from coming up by debating Zetta's recent fake-news-generating app. Tomly and her mother were aghast at its popularity and potential for further social and political destruction. Adam, probably just to stir things up, took the position that human beings lie about reality all the time anyway, so what difference did it make how convincing their lies had become? Dude wasn't sure how he felt about fake video news these days and the app, but as he watched his dad ignore Coach

Miller and suck up to Tomly's mom and Adam's dad, he wondered what other schemes his dad had up his sleeve.

# Chapter Seventeen

"You want to know what I think about all this?" said Adam. It was January, and they were all eating lunch in his studio after Tomly got them permission to skip classes to prepare for the demo scrimmage after school.

"No, we're not very interested at all," joked Tomly, popping a tater tot in her mouth. "Of course, we want to know what you think. Spill!"

Adam hesitated. "No offense, Dude. My dad didn't say anything about this, but I think your dad, or maybe someone else in Circle, is feeding Zagan updates about our technical progress."

"You mean, on purpose?" replied Dude. "Why? How? Wouldn't Master know about that and stop it?"

"Not once her daily data reports are submitted," said Adam. "It would be up to the AIs at Circle, and they're loyal to Core, obviously."

"But how does that make sense?" said Tomly. "Oh, I get it. Competition!"

"You *are* a sharp cookie," said Adam. "Unusual for a jockette."

"Shut up, geek monster," said Tomly.

"Wait, I'm lost," said Dude.

"Think about it," said Tomly. "How excited was the school about the scrimmage this afternoon?"

"Well," replied Dude, "I thought there was interest. The team members are into it." He wiped a bit of ketchup from his lower lip with his sleeve.

"Yeah, well you watch. I'll bet most people just go home as usual," said Tomly. "On the other hand, if Honeycrisp took on Zinkerberg this afternoon in the world's first bot football game as more or less equal rivals ..."

"Oh," said Dude, "that would be national news."

"Right," said Adam.

"And orders for Sixes that could play football would pour in from around the country," continued Dude.

"Exactly," said Adam. "So many that they wouldn't care if Zetta's version got some of the pie."

"So they leak the programming data to Zetta to allow Zagan and Zinkerberg Academy to put together a team ..." said Dude.

"But not enough data that they can make the exact same Sixes, of course," added Tomly.

"Well," said Adam, "the evolution of the Zetta bots would accelerate, too, but Circle would always have a big head start."

"And if Honeycrisp School *wins* the game, everyone would buy Sixes and not the Zetta version?" asked Dude.

Adam nodded, smiling. Dude wondered why Adam was so happy all of a sudden.

"Because everyone loves a winner," said Tomly.

"Wow," said Dude.

"Exactly," said Tomly and Adam together.

"So, I guess we have a challenge on our hands," said Dude.

"You know how much money Circle would make selling Sixes to almost every football program in America?" said Adam.

"No wonder they're pressuring Coach Miller to help us," said Tomly.

"Look, guys," said Dude. "This is giving me a headache. So my Dad is behind this? This is horrible. If Zagan and his dad come up with some Neanderthal battle bot team, what's that going to do to our plan? Will we have to play them anyway?"

"Might be fun to take on some Zetta Neanderthals," said Adam. "But look, you guys, we have a scrimmage in three hours. Let's drop the problem of you and your dad for now."

Dude couldn't believe what Adam just said about liking Neanderthals. He was about to open his mouth and remind him once again that violence was not the point of the game or their project when Tomly said, "Fine, but I doubt it's just Dude's dad. I'll keep my ears open and feel out Mom about it. It would be helpful to know just how much Zagan has found out, don't you think? In the meantime, any new idea we come up with for the bots, we should keep to ourselves."

"We might not be able to stop the leaks," Adam pointed out. "Remember, there's no way to know how much Master monitors us here. It might help to turn off our glasses when we meet from now on."

Dude thought about his mom, how she'd been asking him more about his project lately. He decided that he needed to stop talking to her about it, too. He remembered that line from his poem: *Their collision will crash this helicar of techno-confusion.*

When he stopped frowning, Tomly said, "Okay, we can talk about that later. Right now, I actually hope Master is listening to us because we really need to go over the list of everything we're about to do!"

The rest of the team arrived in the locker room at 2:00.

"Hey, Dude! Nice power move getting us out of the last period!" said Gary.

"Hey, Tomly," said Rachel, a defensive back. "Can your Six throw in the rain? It looks threatening out there."

"It never rains in California," said Tomly.

"Ha, ha, that's a joke," replied Rachel, "unless you think dire flooding doesn't count as rain."

"Keep the faith, people," said Adam. "The weather report says it will all blow over. Get your bots going, and we'll meet outside in thirty minutes."

Adam was right that the rain clouds blew over, but not until they left the field sopping wet, and Tomly said she was worried it would discourage even more people from attending.

She was wrong. Despite it being Friday, the stands filled up fast with excited students chatting on their phoneglasses and blinking videos of the team adjusting the cleat lengths of their Sixes on the soggy field.

It helped that the Sixes could automatically extend the cleats on their feet to any length at the command of their assigned player. The field was already getting a little ripped up from the power of the bots' legs as they cut back and forth and practiced their tackling. "Oohs" and "aahs" were already happening in the stands at the tougher hits.

"Dude," said Tomly, interrupting his enjoyment of the scene, "did you give permission for Gary's Six to be up in the stands signing autographs?"

"No! Really? Get him back down here. We need to start now." Dude blew his whistle.

Like the last time, the players and the bots gathered on the track between the stands and the football field. Dude blinked into the school's audio channel and explained to everyone what was happening and what to look for.

"It's really two games happening at once," he explained. "The humans huddling and strategizing on the sidelines, and the Sixes huddling and playing on the field. Since this is just a one-team demonstration, the offense will launch five drives starting from their twenty-five yard line. If they score a touchdown or kick a field goal, they win one point. If the defense stops them, the defense wins the point. Just three downs to get a first down. We're still working out the algorithms for punts and kickoffs. No refs either. The Sixes are programmed not to cheat, even if their human counterparts ask them to."

"Ah, that's no fun!" someone blurted into the feed.

"I know, but try to get over it if you can," said Dude. "Okay, players, huddle up!"

Of course, just like last time, Dude saw his family helicar zoom in and touch down next to the stands. But this time, three more official Core helicars followed noisily behind and caused everyone in the stands to get soaked with water from the violently blown grass. Dude had no choice but to delay the start of the scrimmage until the audience dried off and finished gawking at the Circle executives exiting their cars and gathering on the sidelines.

"Adam, they can't stand there," Dude said. "They'll interfere with the players. We need everyone off the sidelines!"

"On it," said Adam. He jogged over to the adults. Dude saw his dad listen to Adam, nod, and lead the group to an open area in the stands.

Dude groaned. "Never fails. I should have figured he'd be here."

"Let it go," said Tomly. "Let's play some football!"

Remarkably, there were no burst footballs or Sixes lining up incorrectly on the first drive. It helped that the direction the bots were facing stayed the same for every play of the drive. Dude was relieved that his idea about using the sidelines was working.

Just as he asked them to, the defensive players huddled up on the far side of the field and barked their commands from that sideline, and the offensive players did the same on the near sideline in front of the stadium stands. With each play, the bots' AI got better at understanding the players' commands. By the end of the first drive, the time lag between breaking the huddle and hiking the ball was exactly the regulation forty seconds.

Of course, Dude knew that the plays getting off on time didn't mean he could expect everything to go smoothly. On the first play of the game, Tomly threw a long bomb to Dude's Six for a touchdown, which was great, except that Rachel's Six, who was supposed to be defending Dude, kept up with him stride for stride but never turned around to look for the pass. On the second drive, Tomly called a running play, and Gary's Six broke through the blocking and grabbed the running back, but instead of tackling it, he just held it up in the air and wouldn't let it down even after the whistle blew. The running back's legs pumped like it was in a cartoon, while the other bots looked confused about whether they were still playing or not. Dude had to ask Adam to power down Gary's bot to put an end to the play. Bad as that was, it was worse that it was one of the few times any bot on the defense could make a stop for short yardage. On the next play, the offense scored on a screen pass, which completely baffled the defense. On the final three drives, all the running plays, even up the middle, gained first downs without the offense ever having to use a third down. Tomly threw three touchdown passes and ran for one. It was a wipeout.

*But a spectacular wipeout*, Dude thought after the final whistle, at least judging by the reaction in the stands. They *ooh*ed with every snap at the sound of the blocking, which was like eight car crashes happening all at once. The tackles, when they finally did occur, were equally worthy of a demolition derby soundtrack. The mostly-for-show football pads muffled the satisfying crunching sounds only slightly. The incredible strength of the Sixes, even toned down to be analogous to the strength of their human players, still sent opposing bots flying out of bounds with enough velocity that players on the sidelines had to dive for safety. All this created screaming from the crowd that reached a wild crescendo when Gary's Six managed to finally sack Tomly's Six and rip its right arm completely out of its socket in the process.

Fortunately, that illegal move happened on the last drive, and Tomly's Six was able to use its other hand to throw a touchdown pass to end the scrimmage. Gary swore that his Six decided to do that on its own, but Dude made a mental note to have Adam and Tomly check his psych metrics and the recorded game commands later.

All in all, Dude felt that even though it didn't go exactly as planned, it had a similar vibe to a real football game, at least for the fans. He gave Tomly, Adam, and even Gary a thumbs up, although he didn't think they noticed that the general excitement on the field was only about the violence. Students posed for photos with their favorite players and bots, and they were obviously blinking tons of videos onto Tic-Flash and Insta-Snap. Tomly's bot arm became a must-touch item that got passed around and held up in triumph until Adam blasted a shock-warning on the network that the arm belonged to him.

"I know we can always print another one, but it's the principle of the thing," he said to Dude when Dude covered his ears and frowned at him. "Besides, I want to give it to my dad for our trophy case!"

Dude saw his dad and the Core helicars take off, this time without stealing anything, and leaving the students behind to celebrate with the team's Sixes.

Was the scrimmage successful enough for Core to back off about taking over? Dude hoped so.

Tomly, with her one-armed bot, found him to give him a high-five. "What did your dad have to say?" she shouted over the noise of the celebration.

"Nothing. He just left."

"He loved it, I'm sure. The students did! Come on, let's party and get a team picture!"

"Okay," he said. But as he watched the helicars getting smaller between the goalposts, he suddenly felt less like celebrating. Something in the pit of his stomach was sending him a warning. Maybe his dad didn't say anything to him before he left because he didn't want him to know what was coming next.

He turned to follow Tomly and saw Adam waving Tommy's bot arm over his head and cheering. For some reason, seeing that made him think about a stanza from his poem:

*The Old Ones march with carrots*
*Ripped from a garden of anger*
*And yet still food.*

Ugh! Was he trying to live in a garden of anger run by old people like his dad? Maybe, but this feeling in his gut was more like running hard in a race when his opponents were beating him to the finish line, a finish line he cared very deeply about reaching first but had no idea where the line actually was, or even what kind of race he was really in. It was all very confusing.

One thing he knew from this scrimmage for sure, though, was that if they couldn't somehow improve the gameplay of the defense, there would never be a reason for fans to watch bot football other than for violence and mayhem.

# Chapter Eighteen

"Wake up, dear!"

Dude blinked up at his mom in sleepy confusion. "It's Saturday. Let me sleep!"

"I know, honey," she said, tugging his covers off. "That's what I told the reporter, but he said it was urgent and he had a deadline."

"What reporter? What are you talking about? Hey, it's five in the morning! Ouch! Turn the light off!"

"You have to get up. It's Veri-News. They're downstairs. Your dad let them in. They insist on seeing you, and you know there's a fine if you don't talk to them ..."

"Veri-News? What for? Are you sure they want *me* and not Dad?"

"Honey, your dad answered the door. They want to verify videos from yesterday."

Dude rolled out of bed and dug through a pile of clothes on the floor for his robe. "Okay, okay. I'll be down as soon as I use the bathroom."

When he got downstairs, the reporter and a camera Six were standing with his dad in the living room. Immediately, Dude regretted not getting dressed. But what did they expect, popping in before the sun was even up? Better question: What was his dad doing fully dressed in professional clothes at this hour on a weekend?

"Good morning, son," said his dad. "This is V-N Reporter 702 and her bot. Do you need me here, ma'am?"

"Your son's a minor, so yes," said the reporter. Her stiff clothes had sharp angles and her make-up was metallic like she was trying to match the threatening look of her stripped-down bot. "This won't take long. We already have most of what we need with this footage. Dudley Jr., you go by Dude, right? Can you confirm, please, that you attend Honeycrisp School and were involved in a football demonstration using Circle Sixes yesterday afternoon?"

"Yes?"

"Can you describe a few things that happened in the scrimmage so we can verify clips circulating on social media right now?"

"Um, there were five drives by the offense, and each resulted in a score," said Dude.

"And?" said V-N 702. She seemed bored. The federal nametag on her chest was almost as big as her head. Her camera Six, though, was actively shooting Dude's face from every angle possible while recording the audio. Dude always thought the posts from Ver-News that were attached to virals were dry and boring, but his dad said they reassured the public that the stuff they were viewing was authentic. They say they verify every video that goes officially viral, and Dude supposed V-N 702 had pretty good job security these days with the popularity of the new Zetta fake news app. Some people felt a visit from Veri-News meant you had made into the world of top celebrities. But at the moment, Dude was still half-asleep and wanted her gone so his dad would stop smiling at her and angling to get into the picture.

"Well, the field was wet," he went on. "The crowd was pretty enthusiastic, especially about the blocking and tackling. Tomly's, I mean, our quarterback's, Six had an arm ripped off, but it still managed to throw a touchdown on the next play. Is that enough?"

"That'll do it. Oh, one more thing. Can you confirm that a Zagan Benson used to be on your football team at Honeycrisp School?"

"He was the quarterback," said Dude. "He's at Zinkerberg now."

"Yes, that's what we understand. Thank you, Dude, and you too, Mr. McPherson, for your cooperation."

"Anytime, ma'am," Dude's dad cut in. "Speaking for myself and Circle, we couldn't be more grateful to you and to your organization for the great job you are doing to keep truth on the up and up!"

The reporter just sniffed and turned to leave, and Dude shuffled back upstairs, but not before he saw his dad flash a smiling thumbs up when the Six finally aimed its camera at him on the way out the door.

# Chapter Nineteen

"Man, what a weekend!" said Dude when he could finally get together alone with Tomly and Adam at the Tech Lab snack printers on Monday afternoon. They had given the team the day off from practice so they could plan their next move. All weekend, the texts and holo-calls about the scrimmage videos were non-stop, and today in the hallways between classes, everyone kept asking them questions about when the next "game" would be and whether any celebrities had contacted them yet. Even the dean had asked Dude if there was anything he needed to make the team better.

"Tell me about it," said Adam. "You'd think we were doing this for a living instead of for a school project. I felt like an NFL coach getting grilled before a Super Bowl."

"And we haven't even played the first game!" said Tomly.

"How's your arm, by the way?" asked Dude, punching up three extra large hot chocolates.

Tomly laughed. "*My* arm is fine. How's my bot's arm, though, Adam?"

"It's getting scanned at the Universal Printer. Master's going to analyze it and print a new one today with stronger hinges."

"I suppose we'll need to do that for all of them with players like Gary around," said Dude, shaking his head.

"That was so cool, though," said Adam. "Maybe, instead of stronger hinges, we should make them weaker, and I can engineer some sparks or explosives or something to go off when they get tackled!"

Dude put the drinks on the end table and rolled his eyes at him. "Yeah, that would be *real* cool, Adam. Just like in a *real* football game. Any news we can trust on the supposed Zinkerberg team?"

"You mean," said Adam, "beyond all the ridiculous posts this weekend from Zagan? I guess it's a real thing. They have a team, and given how many videos there are out there from Friday, there's a lot of new data for them to digest."

"*If* videos are the only data source they are getting," said Dude, suddenly suspicious of Adam. Was he manipulating this to set up the giant bot battle he was dreaming about?

"Well," said Tomly, "let's digest it faster and better than them. What was good about the scrimmage, and what was bad? I have my ideas, but you guys go first."

"The cleats were great," said Adam, "and the titanium in the Sixes held up well with all the hitting, so we don't need to use more pads."

"Pads wouldn't have stopped Gary's Six from ripping off my arm," said Tomly.

"Right," said Adam.

"No," said Dude, "I actually think more padding is a good idea, even though the crowd obviously liked the car crash sounds. They distracted too much from the game. We should use thicker pads and have quieter metal and more tough-skin where the contact is greatest." He looked pointedly at Adam.

"I *suppose* we could do that if we really wanted to," said Adam, "but my dad agrees that the noise and chaos were the coolest part."

"Your dad, huh?" said Dude. "What's he got to do with this?"

"Just because you don't talk to your dad doesn't mean I can't talk to mine," said Adam. "He's got a lot to do with this. He's in Core!"

Dude put down his hot chocolate. "So, did it ever occur to you that maybe *your* dad is feeding everything you say to him to Zetta?"

"Sure. What does it matter? It's good that Zinkerberg Academy is coming up with a team. No competition, no game, right?"

"Adam, I can't *believe* you!" said Tomly. "We've been over this a million times. Parents *always* mess things up. That's why this center is just for students! What were you thinking?!"

Dude glared at Adam. It didn't help his anger that Adam just shrugged his shoulders and said, "Okay, Tom-cat. Sorry that I broke your little rule, but in case you hadn't figured it out yet, Circle always takes over the ideas that come out of this place. This football league thing is going to be *huge*. Circle's going to find out everything we do anyway through Master, and games need competitors if we want to sell equipment, so what does it matter if I helped my dad speed things up a little bit? What? Do you think bot football would be more exciting if everybody played with the same brand of robot like on a little kid's playground where everything has to be "fair"? That would be boring. Circle needs Zetta, and

Zetta needs Circle. The competition between them means better tech for everybody."

"Are those your words, or your dad's?" spat Dude.

"All right, you two," said Tomly. "Are we done?"

"No," said Dude, "Adam's a traitor!"

"Stop!" Tomly said, putting all her authority as proctor into her voice. "What I meant is, is this going to be the end of our project? Because everyone is expecting *us* to come up with another show, not Adam's dad."

"Yeah, exactly, a *show*!" said Dude. "We should give up. This is just going to be a Circle show no matter what we try to do. Wow, and it's going to be so *cool*. Exploding bots and amputated arms! That's what it's all about, right? Grow up, Adam! Did you even watch any of my games last year?"

"You know I did. I recorded every one of them."

"And did you notice anything besides how hard people crashed into each other? Did you notice, for instance, that there is nothing more beautiful than a perfect pass from a quarterback and a perfect catch from a receiver? Do you have any idea what it's like to be a part of that? To feel it in your bones? To live for it on and off the field? And then to have it taken away?" Dude's eyes started to water. He didn't want to cry, but he couldn't help it.

Tomly scooted over and put her arm on Dude's shoulder on the couch. He sobbed a few times and then wiped his eyes. When he looked up, he was surprised to see a few tears forming in Adam's eyes too. Adam looked down at his feet for a while before speaking.

"Geez, you're right, Dude. I've been a jerk. No, I didn't know this mattered so much to you. I should have because you've only told us a hundred times. Look, I stand by what I said, that Circle is going to know everything sooner or later, probably sooner, no matter what we do. But you guys are right that I should have kept my mouth shut."

Dude nodded.

Adam rubbed his eyes with his hand. "I don't know why I needed to brag about all this with my dad. Maybe I was just trying to impress him and 'be a part of Core,' or whatever. Maybe I thought it didn't matter because you've said over and over that it's impossible to make bot football like the real thing, and I believed you. So what did it matter if our sport became a big bot battle? But looking at you now, I understand a bot battle won't cut it. You aren't just a dude who happens to play football. You are *Dude*, a real football player whose last hope to save the game is this stupid new idea for a substitute team. Well, it's not a stupid idea. And even though I deserve it if you walk out, I don't want you to do that. Will you forgive me? I got carried away and made a big mistake. Let's none of us quit. Let's show them all what we can really do. Let's *believe* we can figure this thing out, and get it done. I want it now more than ever to make it up to you. Okay?"

Dude could see in his eyes that he meant what he was saying. Tomly had been staring at Adam with her mouth open, but now, her expression softened.

"I'm in, but no more talking to your dad, Adam. That sucked," said Tomly.

"Absolutely, sorry. It won't happen again." said Adam. "Dude...?"

Dude took a big breath, stood up, and sighed. This project might have been doomed from the start, but these were the only friends he had right now. His heart wouldn't let him throw Adam away, even after this betrayal. "Okay. Is there someplace we can do our talking where Master can't hear us?"

Adam sighed in relief and hugged him.

Mad as he still was, Dude knew he made the right decision to accept Adam's apology because he saw it was Tomly's time to shed some tears.

"Come on," she managed to say, smiling. "I know just where we can talk. Follow me."

"Can we bring our hot chocolates?" asked Dude.

"You're an addict," said Tomly. "But sure, if you can climb the rope with them in your hand."

They got off the Chewbacca couch and followed her up Allison's rope ladder. Dude and Adam decided to chug their hot chocolates before climbing. While they were doing that, Tomly carried hers all the way up without spilling a drop. She even held the bead curtain aside for them when they got to the top.

Allison, as usual, was on her stage dressed in flowing clothes, this time with her nose in a book. There were no horses to be seen, and it was strange to see her studio fully lit up looking like a normal theater instead of mysteriously dark with the computer lights blinking.

"Hey, Allison, I guess we're invading your space," said Tomly.

Allison smiled and plucked a feather from her hairpiece as a bookmark

"I see that. What's up, famous people?"

"We kind of have a special need for a very quiet place, if you know what I mean?" said Tomly. "Can we use your inspiration room?"

"Oh, wow, sure! Help yourself. It's behind the green computers. You might be a little cramped in there, though."

"No problem. We'll manage, " said Tomly, taking the last sip of her hot chocolate and setting the cup down on the floor. "Thanks!"

Tomly and Adam headed up the risers to the green computer banks, but Dude hesitated. He was remembering the last time he was here and another few lines from his poem came to him:

*The New Ones don't march*
*They drift and dance*
*With changing purpose and wisdom.*

He looked over at Allison. If ever there was a person who looked like she was drifting and dancing, it was her. Maybe it was time to ask her to help them.

"Hey, Allison. You got time to join us in there?"

"Sure, Dude," she said, closing her book. "But now we're talking *seriously* cramped!"

"I don't know about that. Space seems to expand around you, and we could use some of your air right now. We're all feeling a little stressed."

"Too many videos about your project to look at this morning? Yeah, media feeds can stress you out for sure. That's why I'm glad my invention isn't going public quite yet. But who has control over that, right?"

"Exactly, Circle does, that's who."

"Right. Can't live with them, can't live without them," she said, sighing and looking around her studio.

Allison's inspiration room was just a plain white box with meditation cushions on the floor. There was an air vent and an overhead light. They turned their phoneglasses off and left them outside the door. Inside, there were enough cushions for all four of them, but their knees were touching when they sat on the floor.

"What can I say?" said Allison. "It was made for one person. But Master promised me there's nothing electronic anywhere near here. I find electromagnetic waves very distracting when I meditate, don't you guys?"

"This is perfect," said Tomly. "Okay. I'll start. I don't know if you heard, Ally, but Zagan Benson is duplicating our efforts at Zinkerberg Academy, and we think that he is somehow stealing our ideas."

Dude noticed Adam flashing her a look of gratitude.

"I did see his attempt to ride on your viral coattails," said Allison. "Do you think he has a real Zetta bot football team?"

"Well, Veri-News is looking into it, so it's probably true," said Dude. "They came over to my place Saturday morning and woke me up just to take my picture."

"Ah, yes. I saw. You look very cute in your robe and PJs, by the way," said Allison.

Dude cringed. "Thanks, I guess. Here's the problem as I see it. Defense might be impossible for the Sixes. They can't process the data fast enough to keep up with an offense that has the advantage of knowing ahead of time what play they are going to run."

"Yeah, it sure seems that way," said Adam.

"It was kind of fun to pick them apart, though," said Tomly, smiling.

"Fun for us," said Dude, "but not for the fans. Despite the novelty of spectacular hits and crashing sounds, they'll get bored fast with a game if the defense can't do anything. What's the problem, do you think, Adam? Too many decision variables? Or too much visual data for them to deal with?"

"Shouldn't be that. Sixes can process variables and make decisions millions of times faster than humans. It's probably just that their AIs haven't collected enough data yet to know automatically what to do every time. Or it's like the early problems AI had with self-driving cars. You know, too many difficulties anticipating the unknown."

"And," Tomly said, "sufficient data collection solved that problem for *cars*, but we're talking *human* variables way more complex than reading the body language of someone on a sidewalk about to jaywalk. There are an infinite number of variables a defensive back has to take into consideration when defending against one of my passes."

"Will they get better with time?" asked Dude.

"Maybe," said Adam, "but so will the offense, and it would be nice if they could start at the same level."

"Do you mind if I say something?" said Allison, who was listening with her eyes closed. She opened them now and looked right at Dude. He nodded at her. "I've been studying this game since you got here, Dude. When an offense calls a play in the huddle, it's based on a creative choice that evolved over time. Stats might say that a quarterback sneak on fourth down and inches is better than throwing the long bomb, yet sometimes the play caller goes for the long bomb. Why? Sometimes it's statistically best for the safeties to cover the receivers, and yet sometimes they blitz the quarterback and get the sack. Why? I think the answer is art. It's creativity. It's being aware of a different source of 'data' that can't be spat out by a computer. Can a computer tell you if you are in love? No. Love is guided by a higher sort of data, one we can only feelingly understand, or *artistically* understand. It happens when we allow ourselves to be sensitive to that deeper form of understanding."

"I think I follow that," said Dude.

"Wow, you actually know a lot about football!" said Adam.

"I've been watching some old games. My dad's games. He played at Stanford, may he rest in peace," said Allison.

"So," asked Tomly, "what are you saying? That our defense lacks *art?*"

"I am saying that exactly. Defense needs an artistic mindset, maybe even more than the offense does because they have to react to and rely on their instincts more. Except, of course, when a quarterback scrambles creatively out of the pocket."

As Dude listened to Allison's soft but assertive voice, he remembered the last verse of his poem:

*Their collision will crash this helicar of techno-confusion*
*Into the "I'm okay" mouth*
*Of you finally finding and making out*
*With yourself.*

Was he on his way to finding something here?

"So, the Sixes have to fall in love with themselves," he said.

"Yes!" said Allison. "Depending on what you mean by love."

"I don't mean *love* love," clarified Dude. "I mean loving themselves enough that they can play like humans out there, not like computers. They have to love themselves enough to learn to trust their instincts and not overthink everything."

"Right. Or, instead of overthinking, learn to think about what's happening on the field in a *different* way, a more artistic way," said Allison.

"I'm lost," said Tomly. "I mean, I'm not lost. I understand what you are saying, Ally, but we have to *do* something about this, right, not just speculate?"

"Yes," said Adam. "The way I see it, Zagan and Zinkerberg Academy are going to challenge us to a game soon, and we have to take these computers, these Sixes, and make them as mature as human beings playing the game. Do I have that right?"

"Yes," said Tomly. "It's an organizational nightmare. Where's the manual for turning robots into artists?"

"Just a minute, you guys," said Allison. "Don't panic. Maybe there is a way that we just don't know yet. Can I suggest we slow down? You're right, Tomly. We have a tough challenge, but this is my meditation room, you know. Lots of tough challenges have been met inside here. Let's just be still and think about this for a minute." She closed her eyes again and breathed deeply and purposefully. A minute passed, and then another. Dude kept his eyes on Allison, breathing as she breathed, then...

"Oh my gosh!" Allison screamed, sending shock waves through the tiny room. "I think I know what we should do!"

Dude was the only one who didn't jump at her outburst. Somehow, he knew from watching her that she would wake up with a fully formed idea. Maybe even the same crazy one that had been sprouting in his heart when he invited her to the meeting.

# Chapter Twenty

The next afternoon, Adam wanted the Sixes to use the hidden airlift, but when Master confirmed that they were perfectly capable of climbing a rope ladder, Allison insisted the Sixes should do the same thing as everybody else who used her invention. She also insisted that they come up one at a time with their corresponding human players, offense *and* defense.

"I know it will take a while, but what good is it to have an artistic defense and an inartistic offense?" she argued.

"She's happy," Adam said to Dude on the Chewbacca couch, "because she's getting a lot of customers."

"That's not the only reason, and you know it," said Dude watching the first pair, Gary and his Six, navigate the ladder. He wondered why Tomly hadn't shown up yet.

"Well, I hope she's right about this," said Adam.

"Can't hurt, can it?" said Dude, smiling because Gary's Six climbed the ladder in half the time Gary did.

"Well," replied Adam, "I was thinking about this all night last night. I think Allison's on the right track having the Sixes use her creativity get up. The thing I don't get is how the Sixes are going to extrapolate from one creative experience in her studio how to be creative moment by moment on the playing field. What? Are they going to break into their one song, or poem, or whatever gets spit out when a pass is headed their way?"

"I don't know," said Dude. "You tell me."

"I don't know, either. That's Allison's department, but it seems to me Allison's color-coded computers up there should be uploading their special algorithms into the Sixes, not just listening to them and spitting out a poem, or a song, or a play, or a painting, or a whatever ..." He ran his hands through his spongy hair.

"Wait a minute, Adam. You're right! That's brilliant!" Dude leaped over the couch and climbed the ladder even faster than Gary's Six. "Allison!"

When Dude burst into Allison's space, the data projector guns were going full blast, and all the computers were blinking and communicating with each other like mad. Gary and his Six were on the stage, each waving a pair of Allison's special mittens above their heads, and Dude's ears were filled with explosions, gunfire, animals growling, and the sound of someone running in a panic and screaming. Out of the chaos approached Allison, who grabbed Dude by the hand. "Sit with me here. Don't say anything! They're about to get their piece!"

As the hologram images and sounds spun into a red funnel on the stage and disappeared as they had done for him, Dude expected a printer to pop up again to type out a poem. Instead, a wire basket on the top of a metal pole popped out of the floor. Inside was a bulky old-fashioned external hard drive with an output cord.

"What do we do now?" said Gary, looking around for Allison.

"I don't know." Allison moved from her seat to the stage. "This is the first time this has happened. Is there anything else in the basket?"

Gary looked. "There's a note. It says, 'Take to Input Room.'"

"That means it's something too big to be created here. Could be a sculpture or a painting! Grab that drive and let's go!"

As soon as Gary picked up the drive from the basket, the stage opened up, and the basket dropped and disappeared.

"Cool," said Gary.

"Cool," said his Six.

Adam jumped up off the couch when he saw them all climbing down the rope ladder like a pack of eager monkeys. "What's going on?" he said.

"Adam, walk with us to the input room and tell Allison your idea, okay?" said Dude. "Allison, you've got to hear Adam's brilliant idea."

Allison stopped and whispered in Dude's ear, "Not until this session is finished. I don't know what the Universal Printer is going to print for them, but it obviously won't be a secret, and I might have to support them now without distractions!"

"I gotcha. Afterward, though? It's important," said Dude.

"Of course, hun!" said Allison.

"*Hun*?" said Adam, who had jogged up next to them. "Does *Tomly* know about this?" His usual goofy smile was back on his face.

Dude just looked at Adam and marveled at his ability to seem so comfortable right now after all that had recently happened between them. Adam telling his dad confidential stuff was horrible, and it caused a lot of problems. Yet Adam apologized, understood what he did wrong, and then came up with a sweet idea to move them forward. How can you hold a grudge against a guy like that?

"You're a hun too, Adam, and you know it," said Allison.

"Oh, *Adam*! Whoo-hoo!" said Dude, glad to be able to tease Adam back.

Adam looked embarrassed but laughed.

As luck would have it, Tomly was in the input room, having a discussion with a newbie.

"You can just use the snack printer for this kind of stuff, Malcolm. Plus, it's just wasteful!" she was saying.

"Oh. All right," said the gangly fifth-grader holding a chocolate milkshake the size of a five-gallon bucket.

"Hey, Tomly," said Dude. "We were looking for you."

"Yeah, sorry I haven't gotten to Allison's yet. Duty calls sometimes, you know, and Master said you were on your way here. Hi, Ally! What are you guys up to?"

"Printing Gary's amazing art piece!" said Allison. "And his bot's."

"Perfect. The printer's free now for the next twenty minutes, and all the input ports are functional. Just plug and go!"

"Come on, Gary," said Allison.

As Allison, Gary, and his bot set the drive on the table and plugged it into an input port, Dude gestured to Adam and Tomly to follow him down the gangplank.

"Adam had a great idea," Dude said when they were far enough away to be alone.

"That doesn't surprise me." Tomly smiled at Adam.

"Just don't call me 'hun' right now, that's all I ask," said Adam.

"Huh?" said Tomly.

"Never mind," said Adam, with a grin at Dude.

Just then, the Universal Printer roared into action, and Allison, Gary, and his bot were running toward them on the gangplank.

"Keep moving, you guys!" yelled Allison. "We want to see what it's printing!"

They all ran to the best place to look inside the printer.

"I need to get Master to print a wider gangplank here, I guess," said Tomly.

Gary's Six was imitating their labored breathing sounds from their quick sprint.

"Is that bot pretending to be out of breath?" asked Dude.

"Empathy response," said Allison. "I'm not surprised. We commanded him to connect with Gary as completely as possible during the session. It will be very interesting to see whether it has its own reaction to the art piece independent of Gary's."

"This is all very weird," said Gary.

"I hear you, man," said Dude. "At least you're getting something concrete. I got a poem that I'm still trying to figure out."

"And this is going to help me and my bot get tougher on the field?" said Gary.

Dude looked at Gary. "That's what we're hoping, man. And that it helps us play at all since we can't play football ourselves anymore."

"I don't know whether to hate the world we live in, or love it," said Gary. "I think I hate it, but all this is still kind of amazing," said Gary.

"I know what you're saying, believe me." Dude sighed. "But what are you going to do?"

"It's printing a huge canvas!" yelled Allison. "Gary, you're getting a painting!"

The large printing jets made quick work of the eight-foot square frame and canvas, then a bunch of smaller printers swooped down, spitting and spraying paints.

"Ooh, lots of reds!" said Allison.

"It's a football player!" said Tomly. "No surprise there, I guess."

"It looks like me!" said Gary.

"It looks like me!" mimicked Gary's Six.

"Well, this is *your* piece," said Allison, looking at both of them.

"What's the football player crashing into?" said Adam.

Dude looked closely. "Looks like a planet, and also a woman. Is it Earth? Mother Earth, maybe?"

"You're smashing into Mother Earth like you're a football player asteroid, Gary!" said Tomly.

"Oh, man! It's spilling blood all over your cleats," said Adam.

"Cool," said Gary.

"Cool," said his Six.

"And look, your helmet is half off. Your mouthguard is dangling," said Dude.

"You're taking a bite out of Mother Earth's neck," said Adam. "It's so red and swirling! Cool! It's so gross!"

"I love it!" said Gary and his Six at the same time.

Dude noticed that Allison and Tomly looked a little bit like they were going to throw up.

"Hey, you guys," he said. "How about we let Gary and his bot take their piece back to an empty studio, so they can enjoy it by themselves for a while? The canvas looks dry enough. It's safe to go in there and take it now, right, Tomly?"

"Yes, Master says all clear," she said, checking her phoneglasses. "She used ultra-fast acrylics. You can grab it now, Gary."

Gary opened the gate and went with his bot into the printing space to gently pick up their masterpiece. The group stepped back to make room for them coming back. "Room 101 is open and empty right now," said Tomly as they passed.

"Thanks, but you guys can't keep it here forever. It's too good!" said Gary.

"It's too good!" echoed his bot, smiling back at them with his shiny foil lips.

Dude looked at Tomly and then at Allison.

"Are you ready for another go-round?" said Tomly to Allison.

"I guess," said Allison. Dude could tell she wasn't happy with the last product.

"Hey, how about a break first?" he said. "I've got an idea we should discuss. Well, *Adam* has an idea."

"Meditation room?" said Allison.

"Immediately," said Dude. "I'll bring the refreshments."

# Chapter Twenty-One

*Master's Report to Core*
*Jan. 25, 2055*

1.  *Update on Model Six Football Prototype: Target*
    *market—clubs and all schools. 100% chance for*
    *market success. Principals—Dudley McPherson, Jr.,*
    *9th grade; Tomly Newton, 9th grade; Adam*
    *Angelou, 9th grade; Allison Albright 9th grade.*
    *Principles observed currently testing Art Media*
    *Creation program upload to Model Six Football*
    *Prototype to improve spontaneous gameplay. Master-*
    *optimized program cache attached to this message.*
    *Variability warning—requires full psych and*
    *physical metrics uploads for team player*
    *differentiation. Permission requested to share data*
    *optimization refinements with principals to speed*
    *first-game testing.*

*Response to Master Core Report*
*Jan. 25, 2055*

*Permission granted. Prototype of optimized Art*
*Media Creation program with controller gloves and*
*helmets in production at Circle. Pre-sale marketing*

*of Football Sixes launched. Advise immediately of any additional developments and student timetable for completion of fully functional team.*

# Chapter Twenty-Two

"Authentically created art isn't always a picnic for the artist," said Allison on her meditation cushion. "But it seems my program created just the piece Gary wanted."

This time, Dude was smart enough to let Tomly carry the tray of hot chocolates up the rope ladder. It was cramped as usual in the little square room, but to Dude, it was starting to feel like a little piece of home.

"It doesn't take a genius to figure out why he got that painting," said Dude. "He's a linebacker. They're all animals deep inside."

"Pretty cool painting, I must say," said Adam. "I hope he gets sick of it and throws it away, so I can fish it out of the recycling bin for my studio."

"Don't you dare, Adam!" said Tomly.

"So, you called this meeting because Gary got a disturbing painting?" said Allison.

"No, I think it was a good painting for him," said Dude. "It bonded him with his Six, and it might make his Six a better player on the field. I think you should keep going and do it for the whole team. But Adam, tell Allison your thoughts about all this, how we could create little art media studios in the brains of each Six on the defense."

"Yeah, that's one way to put it," said Adam. "And not just the defense. All of the Sixes. You know, teach them to fish instead of feeding them just one meal of salmon, or however that saying goes ..."

Allison looked a little shocked but didn't say anything. Instead, she shut her eyes.

Dude watched her and let a full minute go by. Then he said gently, "You know that anything worthwhile we do in the Tech Lab belongs to Circle."

"You're right," said Allison, opening her eyes. "My baby doesn't belong to me. I came up with the idea of the art media center, but Master did all the technical stuff. I just never imagined it would all go to making a bunch of jock robots play better on a football field."

"Not *all*. It's just one application of your brilliant idea," said Dude.

She brightened a little. "I want to see if your idea will work, Dude, but we need to run this past Master to see if it's even possible."

"And we can't do that here in this protected room," observed Adam.

"You got that right, hun. Let's go to the lounge," said Allison, picking up her now entirely cold hot chocolate.

Adam smiled his goofy smile. "You still call me 'hun' even after hearing my idea? Must be true love. What do you think, Tomly?"

"I think anyone who loves you is either crazy or the kindest human on the planet," said Tomly.

"I'm happy to own both of those," said Allison. "I kind of have to, don't I, after letting the likes of you guys into my meditative space? Come on, Tomly. Let's summon Master for this group and hope she's not mad at you for hiding out here when you should be proctoring."

# Chapter Twenty-Three

Although usually deserted, the lounge was unavailable because of the crowd of techies trying to grab last-minute snacks before dismissal, so the team walked briskly to Adam's studio, and Tomly brought up Master on their phoneglasses.

"You rang?" Master answered in a deep voice.

"Woah, Master, what's with the voice? Have you been streaming *The Addams Family* again?" said Tomly.

"It's part of my ongoing effort to relate better to humans," said Master.

"Well, I've got news for you: the people in *The Addams Family* are made-up, mere figments of the imagination," said Tomly.

"Yes, I am aware of that. But can you cite any real human who isn't essentially a figment of their own imagination? There's a lot you can learn from the *Addams Family* character types. So far, I think Lurch has the strongest grasp on essential human nature."

"But he's so depressed and cynical!" said Adam.

"Exactly," said Master. "What can I do for you today?"

"For an AI you have very strange research methods, and you are drastically undermining your authority by using that voice, Lurch," said Tomly. "Go ahead, Ally."

"Master, what is the feasibility of uploading the Art Media Center's programming into the football Sixes?"

"Already done," replied Master, changing to her normal voice.

"What?" said Dude. "When? What do you mean?"

"Not in your Sixes," Master clarified. "In Circle's. I'm authorized to tell you that the Football Sixes idea is viable and now in production."

"Production? But we haven't even tested them in a game yet!" said Dude.

"The rollout is scheduled for Circle Vision National Television on April 10th, the first game of the season."

"*First game?! Season?* What are you *talking* about?" yelled Dude.

"The first game is with Zinkerberg Academy. They will be ready. Circle estimates the other teams in your prep league will need a year to purchase and program their bots, most likely ours because they will be better and more elegant, as our products always are. This spring season will be considered an exhibition."

"Master," argued Dude, "we don't know the Sixes can really play yet. You can't have a football season if the football teams don't even know how to play defense!"

"Your idea to use the Art Media programming has a 96.1% chance of success by game time and therefore meets marketing requirements," said Master.

"Marketing requirements?" said Dude. "Oh, I get it. So Circle really is going to make a bunch of money selling football sixes to Bay Area prep schools."

"No," Master replied. "Sixes will be free to all schools in your league to develop on their timetable," said Master. "It's for the rest of the football world that Circle is planning its sales."

# Chapter Twenty-Four

"I quit," said Dude in the meditation room. It was all Tomly and Adam could do to talk him into going back there instead of setting fire to the Tech Lab.

"Dude, I get that you are upset," said Adam, "but *why* are you upset? You don't want to play Zagan? Is that it?"

"I want to play Zagan in *real* football, or something close to it, not with bots that can't play!" said Dude. "It's gone. Just when I was getting a little hope for it, this project is gone. It's going to do the *opposite* of what I wanted. This project was just supposed to keep a little bit of real football going when my dad canned the team. Now Circle sees dollar signs in the idea, and Dad's probably going to end up in Core like he's always wanted, and what will *I* end up being? A kid who loved football so much he ruined it for the whole world!" Dude could feel his teeth clenching as hard as his fists.

"You haven't ruined football for the whole world," said Allison. "It's still played all over the country, isn't it? College, pro, clubs, right?"

Dude was so mad, he felt like he had stepped into Gary's painting. "Not for long. I guarantee the my-dad-types everywhere are going to sue their way to a world where bot football is the only football. And with Circle's marketing, people like me, who just want to feel again what it's like to be a real football player, won't have that chance. It'll be noisy, violent bot video games on the football field instead."

"Noisy violent video games with real bots? Still seems pretty cool to me," said Adam, trying to smile. Dude saw Allison shoot him a look.

"Yeah, you're right. This is pretty bad," said Tomly, watching Dude nervously. "But right now, my brain is reeling from all this information, and I need a break. We all probably need a little exercise to process this. Anyone want to throw the football around outside? *Without* any Sixes. Maybe we'll get lucky and someone from the administration will try to stop us, and we can tackle them."

"And maybe knock their teeth out?" asked Dude.

"Exactly," said Tomly.

"Okay, let's go!" said Dude.

# Chapter Twenty-Five

No one from the dean's office came to bust them, and after an hour of catching Tomly's perfectly thrown passes, Dude was finally calm enough to stop contemplating arson and murder. Afternoon school activities were over, and parents were flying overhead and snail-driving up to the school to pick up their kids. Dude sat down on the side of the field, put on his phoneglasses, and blinked a text to his parents that he would Uber-fly home tonight with Tomly. She sat down next to him, close enough to touch him with her shoulder.

"You catch well when you're mad," she said, tossing the ball up and down.

"I catch well all the time, and you throw well all the time," he retorted. "Why can't we just play? Is it too much to ask of the universe?" He looked at her as she juggled the ball deftly with her two hands.

"Apparently so, in this present universe, anyway. We should have been born fifty years ago. But we're teenagers in the modern world, and we can't control everything that happens to us. We can try to relax, though, and let things unfold. None of this is worth it if we can't have fun along the way." She put the football down in front of them.

"Relax and let things unfold? Aren't you the one who likes to organize everything?"

"I am, and I'm talking to myself as much as you. It's good to be organized and work toward something worthwhile. But we can organize as much as humanly possible, and things will still happen that we can't control."

"I know," said Dude, "it just frustrates me, that's all."

"Of course you're frustrated. You got cheated out of doing what you love the most, and you've been working hard to get back at least some of it. But you know, nothing has changed."

"What do you mean? Everything's changed! Circle stole our idea, and now they're in too big a hurry. They'll never get it right."

"Maybe. Or maybe things are just playing out a little differently than you imagined. The fact that you can't play football anymore hasn't changed at all. You couldn't predict that your idea might become Circle's next big thing, or that it would involve your dad, or that it might kill football for everyone else. But the bottom line is you still can't play football. That hasn't changed, and the same thinking you used before to cope with that horrible fact still applies."

"To come at least close ..."

She nodded. "To create something that comes as close as possible to the real thing, exactly. Preserving, in some kind of form, as much of what we love about football as we can."

"Human beings are too fragile to play football, I guess."

"That seems to be the consensus," Tomly agreed. "But if we can make bot football as close as possible to the real thing, maybe later, when humans aren't so fragile, we can go back to it again."

Dude laughed despite himself. "What, with bionic skulls and tear-proof limbs?"

"Yeah." She turned to him and looked deeply into his eyes for a moment, then looked down.

"That would be cool," he said quietly.

Should he kiss her? He wanted to, but... out here in the open? Too awkward.

Instead, he leaned over and whispered in her ear, "A moment ago, you said *we* love football...?"

Head still down, she leaned into him and blushed. "Yes, *we*. You knew it was going to happen, Dude. It's all your fault. You love it, and now I love it too, because of you. And you want to know something else?" She put a shaky arm around him. "We're going to keep as much of it alive as possible."

# Chapter Twenty-Six

Circle's new ads announcing a product that would finally "make the game of football safe and more exciting than ever before" were giving Dude a headache. They were running on everyone's phoneglasses and on all the holographic video feeds. People were dying to know more, but the ads revealed nothing. They only told everyone to "tune into Circle Vision National Television on April 10th" to find out.

Of course, that didn't stop people from spending all spring trying to figure it out. Many were sure it was a new type of helmet. Others thought Circle had come up with hypersonic footwear. And even though some tech analysts who saw the Honeycrisp scrimmage videos from the school assembly guessed the truth, Veri-News wouldn't certify any reports about the coming roll-out. Anticipation grew quickly, along with increasingly wild guesses at what Circle's new product might be.

Although it was the least important thing on his mind, regular old school was still happening, and his homework pile was growing as much as the football project was. Why he had to learn anything at all when everything in the world was pretty much done by computers escaped him. He did enjoy the mental challenges of schoolwork more than he liked to admit, not when he was so busy.

At the Tech Lab, he had to help Adam and Tomly upload Allison's programming into each player's Six, and Allison also went ahead with corralling all the team members
and their bots to create pieces of art in her studio. It was
time-consuming, and most nights, Dude didn't Uber-Fly
home with Adam, Tomly, and Allison until way after dinner.
To make things worse, every time he had a moment to check
his phoneglasses, there was yet another Circle ad reminding
him that there was way more riding on the upcoming game
with Zinkerberg Academy than just a grudge match with Zagan.

Then, on Monday afternoon, when he blinked *OKAY* on
the urgent message to meet with Dean Gonzales in his office after school, Dude wondered what critical ball he had
dropped in his juggling act.

It was an inconvenient time for a meeting. They had just
finished all the uploads and were ready for the first real practice to test out the defense. The full team practice was on the
school-wide schedule. The dean must have known that, yet
he still called the meeting. So it had to be something big.

Dude wasn't sure he could handle another big thing.

The feeling worsened when the secretary opened the
door to the school conference room and sitting there, all serious, were his dad; Tomly and her mom; Adam and his dad;
Dean Gonzales, and Coach Miller.

"Come in, Dudley, and have a seat," said the dean.

"He goes by Dude," said Tomly.

Her mom put a hand on Tomly's arm.

"Well, it's true," said Tomly softly.

"Right, I knew that. Sorry, Dude," said the dean, rubbing his hand over his bald head and glancing over at Dude's dad. "Thanks for coming. I'm hoping we won't take long. I know you're looking forward to your practice today."

Dude moved toward the conference table and reluctantly took the only empty seat left next to his dad.

"I'm actually the one who called this meeting, Dude," said Adam's dad.

"Hi, Mr. Angelou," said Dude, looking at Adam, who was staring straight ahead.

"Dude," he went on, "first of all, let me tell you personally on behalf of Core how much we admire the work you and your dad have been doing on the Football Sixes. You're probably thinking we're here to keep you from spilling the beans about them before the big game, but that's not it at all. It's okay if rumors get started. Can't blame you or anybody for being excited."

Dude... *and his dad*? What did his dad have to do with it?

"I'm excited about football, sir," said Dude.

"I know you are. Adam has made that very clear, and you really are amazing. You too, Tomly. Great players. And the fact that you were willing to let your dad's expertise guide you along the way is also admirable. We know the Tech Lab is technically supposed to be for students only, but we also know that it takes supportive parents for ideas as complicated as yours to come to fruition."

Dude turned to burn a look at his dad, but his dad kicked him under the table and smiled back as if everything Adam's dad had just said was the truth.

"The president gives soldiers medals of honor when they save people's lives on the battlefield," Mr. Angelou continued. "Your idea will save the lives of thousands of athletes in the future, and I don't just mean those who are killed on the playing field. Concussions and broken limbs ruin lives, too."

There was an awkward pause. Dude looked at the dean, who raised his eyebrows and nodded at him.

"Uh, thank you... I guess," mumbled Dude.

"Yes, well, um, I can see that you want to get to practice, and far be it from me to hold you from that. Mr. Gonzales?"

"Oh, yes," said the dean. "So, Dude, we asked you, Adam, and Tomly here today to tell you that we know that you are very busy these days. This game coming up has become a really big deal, hasn't it? And probably a lot more work than you thought."

Dude just nodded. He could guess what was coming next, and he was sure Coach Miller wasn't happy about it. Coach's face was sad, and he was picking at his fingers.

"And we want to make sure you are safe out there, and able to play your best game," continued the dean. "It's a big deal to coach *and* play on a team. That we know. It's very hard, and you are still a student, a very good one, I might add." Dude glanced at Tomly's mom whom he had only met before briefly. She was beautiful, just like Tomly, and looking at him with genuine concern. "So, we think, and I am sure you will agree, that your project could use a little professional help. We know it's new, but we also know you want to make bot football as close to the real thing as possible. We figured a real football team has players *and* a coach, so we've asked Coach Miller if he's willing to help out and be the coach again. And he's agreed, right, Coach?"

"It's Dude's team," said Coach Miller looking at Dude. "I don't think ..."

"Thanks, Coach, for volunteering to help us!" said Dude enthusiastically. "It would be great to have you as our coach again. Great idea, Mr. Gonzales. Is that all? Because we have practice to get to, right, Coach?"

The room was quiet, and everyone was staring at him.

"Um, right!" said Coach Miller, relieved but bewildered.

Tomly's mom kept looking quietly at Dude as the dean said, "Well, that was easy. Thank you all for coming." He stood up to shake the hands of all the adults.

# Chapter Twenty-Seven

They hurried to the Tech Lab. Since Coach didn't have clearance to enter, Dude told him, "We'll have the team meet you on the field in a few minutes, Coach," and led Tomly and Adam through the security tunnel. When they were through, Tomly was the first to speak.

"You really impressed my mom back there," she said. "She told me to tell you that before she flew back to Circle."

"Why was she there?" asked Dude.

"Until your dad is promoted to Core, she's still his boss, even though she has nothing to do with the Team Football Six rollout."

"Promotion to Core? This is a nightmare."

"I'm sorry, Dude," she said. "Mom guessed you were enthusiastic about Coach because you knew you couldn't fight their plan."

"Basically, and they're right that a wide receiver can't be the coach, even if his player is a robot. Coach Miller is a good guy who's probably just as sad as we are about the football ban."

"I like him," said Adam, "I hope he helps."

Dude went on. "The eyes of the whole world, or at least the whole football world, will be on us. We're going to need all the help we can get not to embarrass ourselves. Come on, let's go find Ally and round up the team. I have a feeling we're going to need her brains on the field today."

When they caught up with Allison, she was in a storage room below her stage that held the team's art pieces, at least the ones they were willing to share with her. She was eager to see how the Sixes would do after their programming. "I'm a little worried about the extrapolation factor," she said.

"What do you mean?" asked Adam, gawking at all the sculptures and paintings.

"You know, taking the process of art and applying it to football," she said, following them out of the storeroom to the security tunnel. "There's a lot that could go wrong."

The first thing they saw on the field when they got outside were reporters and their recording bots mingling with members of the team. Coach Miller was trying to usher the media off the field, without much success, and the players and their bots looked confused about what they were doing and about what Coach Miller was doing there.

Dude blinked open an audio message.

"Team," he said. "Don't worry about the media. They can talk to you later if they want. They're just hyping the upcoming game with Zinkerberg. No one's going to believe them anyway. Circle is making sure of that and sowing fake rumors to heighten media interest. Who knows, they may even be using Zetta's fake news software. Anyway, the game is real. It's going to happen. You can count on that, and Coach has agreed to come out and help us. So, Coach. Welcome back! We were planning to test new scrimmage programming in the Sixes, but it's your call."

When Dude finished the transmission, the old team members cheered and crowded around Coach Miller. The media and their bots got the idea that practice was starting and moved to the sidelines, some even sitting in the stadium.

"This must be what it feels like to be scouted," said Dude to Tomly.

"If the media is covering Zagan's practices as closely, we should pay attention to their postings," said Tomly. "Who knows what Zagan's Zetta bots are going to be like?"

"Let's just see if our defense can even make a play first, then we can worry about Zagan," said Dude.

"Do you think these reporters might want to see the player's artwork?" said Allison.

"Okay, everybody!" shouted Coach Miller. "This is going to be interesting. Dang if you kids haven't created something very far out! Look at you! And all your Sixes ready to rumble! We've got a lot of work to do, and frankly, there's a lot of it I don't know how to help you with. But with Adam, Allison, Tomly, and of course, Dude, we're going to figure it out, okay?" Everyone cheered. "So, the way I understand it, the issue right now is defense, and you guys have been working on that, right?"

"My Six sang me a show tune," yelled a player.

"Yeah, and mine's a poet. How's *that* going to help?" yelled another.

"Well... we're going to see, right?" said Coach, looking a bit confused. "The programming stuff I don't know much about yet, but I'm going to learn. In the meantime, I do know a few things about the game of football, and one thing for sure is that we are either together, or we're mud. And I know that this is not exactly the type of football we're used to playing, but it's what we got right now. So let's make it the best we can of it and support each other and your fellow teammates and friends who made this happen. You've seen all the media bots paying us a visit. You do this right, and you'll make history, or at least a game reel you'll enjoy playing for your grandkids. So, the scrimmage I saw you guys play last time was a disaster. Entertaining, but a disaster, football-wise. Let's see if we can do a little better this time, all right?" The team cheered. "Okay, set it up just like you did last time. Offense versus defense. Let's go!"

The starting Sixes on the offense and defense moved to the twenty-five yard line and huddled up. Their human defensive controllers put on their helmet phoneglasses and jogged to the far sideline for their huddle, and Tomly and Dude huddled the offense next to Coach Miller. "What's the play, Coach?" said Dude.

"Let's start with something simple, like a quarterback draw," said Coach Miller. "I want to see if there's any change in the way the defense works together."

"Okay," shouted Tomly, "and–"

"Got it!" said Dude, interrupting her. "Okay, you heard Coach. Quarterback draw. Linemen, that means your Sixes block to the outside to open up the middle. Receivers, draw your coverage deep and to the outside. Is everybody's communications open with their bots? Okay, great! Tomly, the hike count is three. Everybody got it? Okay, break. The field break is in ten seconds. Go!"

Dude and the offensive players quickly spread out along the sidelines so they could communicate with their Sixes huddled on the field. Ten seconds was just enough time for them to bark orders into their phoneglasses before Tomly ordered the Sixes on the field to break the huddle and come to the line of scrimmage.

"Hike one, hike two, hike three!" relayed Tomly to her quarterback Six, and the center snapped the ball perfectly. Tomly's Six took four steps back as if to pass, then dashed straight ahead through a hole in the defensive line opened up by the blocks of the center and the left guard. It looked like a perfect play, but linebacker Gary's Six threw off its blocker and muscled its way into the lane to tackle Tomly's Six after only a three-yard gain.

"Nice tackle," said Coach Miller. "Wait, what's going on now?" The defensive bots were lifting Gary's Six onto their shoulders.

"I don't know, Coach," said Dude. "Wait, the Six is getting on the team intercom ..."

*"Perhaps this play will be forgotten*
*Muddled by time and greater matters*
*But the sixteen billion synapses*
*Required to take this player to the ground*
*Will forever fire in my memory*
*Because they brought up second down!"*

The defensive Sixes lowered Gary's Six to the grass where he took a stage bow and accepted the pats on his back by his fellow defensive Sixes. The Sixes on the offense clapped and returned to the huddle for the next play."

"What the heck was *that* all about?" said Coach Miller.

"Beats me, Coach," said Dude. "Do you want me to stop this to find out, or go on?"

"Go on, I guess. Let's see a pass play now. A slant route into the flat." He looked at Tomly, then added, "And stop interrupting your quarterback. The quarterback calls plays in the huddle."

"Okay, Coach, of course," said Dude from the huddle. "Sorry, Tomly."

"Glory hog," teased Tomly. "Your Six better catch this pass to make up for it! Okay, guys, slant pass to Dude across the flat from left to right. Standard pass protection blocking. On two in ten. Break!"

The offense spread out again and radioed their Sixes. The defense lined up across from the offense as usual. Tomly called in the hike count, and her Six dropped back to pass. Dude's Six took a brief block from the defensive back but then broke free across the flat. The defensive back in the zone picked him up and stayed with him stride for stride, swiveling its head back and forth between Dude's Six and the quarterback. The ball was thrown perfectly to Dude, but at the last second, the defensive Six leaped in front of him and grabbed the ball from its outstretched arms. Miraculously, the defender held onto the ball while it did a forward flip and landed on its feet untouched, after which it escaped quickly toward the sidelines and dashed up the field untouched to score a touchdown. The defensive Sixes yelled out in triumph and ran to the end zone to celebrate. Then, as if possessed, they put their arms around each other and formed a long line facing the reporters in the stadium. The intercom switched on again, activated by all of them at once. They began singing and kicking their legs in unison:

*"They said it couldn't be done, it couldn't be done, it couldn't be done...*

*A bunch of metal pieces on the run, on the run!*
*So now we get to kick our feet!*
*Is there anything sweeter than a victory so neat?*

*They said it couldn't be done, it couldn't be done, it couldn't be done...*

*But now we get to play some more 'cause it's so much fun!"*
Snapping out of it, they ran back to the twenty-five yard line to start the next drive. There was astonished clapping from the reporters in the stadium.

"Time out, Coach?" asked Dude from the huddle. Coach Miller was doubled over, laughing.

"Oh goodness, no! That was too funny! Let's see what happens on an end around, shall we?"

"Okay, guys," said Tomly, "end around. I'll hand off to Dude right to left, so block to the right and other receivers go deep. On three in ten. Break!"

Again, the blocking seemed perfect, but when Tomly's Six handed the ball to Dude's Six, Gary's Six appeared out of nowhere to punch out the ball, recover the fumble, and zoom into the endzone for another touchdown.

This time there was no trance-like reaction. Every Six on the field, offense and defense, immediately whooped loudly and participated in the celebration. They spread out over the field scurrying around until they formed the giant word, *VICTORY*, which they made seem alive with their shimmering metallic bodies. While they were doing this, each Six made weird, wordless sounds to compliment the wormlike slitherings of the word they had formed. After a moment or two, the sounds from their metallic mouths changed into a full brass band playing something new and grand that Dude didn't recognize. He watched in amazement as they snapped to their feet and marched back and forth in complicated patterns filling the field with noise and festivity. Then they suddenly became silent and zipped back into their huddles for the next play. Coach Miller and the players were laughing like crazy, and the reporters in the stands were screaming in delight and shouting comments to each other while barking posting orders to their recording bots.

"Oh my lordy, that was amazing!" said Coach, breathing hard and shaking his head.

"Hey, Dude," said Tomly, "I think we should call off the rest of this scrimmage and have a little meeting with Allison,"

"You think?" said Dude.

# Chapter Twenty-Eight

But Coach was having too many laughs to end the scrimmage, so their meeting had to wait. The good news was that the defense scored three more times on forced takeaways and held the offense to just one first down. The bad news was the Sixes performed two more original dance numbers and sang historic Sondheim show tunes from *The Barber of Seville* and *Sunday in the Park with George*.

As the team filed through the security tunnel at the Tech Lab to put away their Sixes, Dude, Tomly, Adam, and Allison waited politely for the coach.

"Sorry, Coach," said Tomly. "There's no authorization yet for you to go in."

"That's okay. I don't need to," he said. "Look, that was way more fun than I thought it would be. You guys have done an amazing job with those bots! I don't know how you did it. They move like pro players out there. Incredible. My Five at home can barely run the vacuum cleaner."

"Yeah, the Sixes are pretty advanced," said Adam.

"And talented! Those little side shows were something to see!" said Coach Miller.

"I loved that too!" said Allison. "So creative!"

"Really, Coach?" said Dude. "You *loved* it?"

"Oh, I know they can't keep doing that. They gave those camera bots something to record, though, I'll tell you that much! It'll be fun to see what kind of craziness the blogsters turn all that footage into! I think you guys should go home and enjoy watching yourselves online. Tomorrow, I'll meet with the team members on the field without the Sixes and go over some special team plays so you guys have time to figure out what happened today, you know, on the technical side. Sound good?"

"That's awesome, Coach! Thanks," said Tomly.

"See you later, Coach," said Dude. "Thanks for your understanding. Come on, you guys. Let's meet in the meditation room before we go home."

They walked through the tunnel, and Allison and Adam waited for Tomly and Dude to put away their Sixes before they went together through the snack lounge and climbed the rope ladder. Adam stayed behind and printed a box of donuts and some bottled seltzer juices.

"Sorry, I was starving," he said when he arrived in the room a minute later with his hands full.

"No, good thinking. Thanks," said Dude, "but how did you get this up the rope ladder without Tomly's help?"

"I never reveal my methods," said Adam.

"He found my stash of carry bags under the couch," said Allison.

"Busted!" said Adam, smiling at her.

"Well, do you have a secret stash that can change our Broadway bots back into football players?" said Dude, grabbing a seltzer and biting into a donut.

"Hey, they did great out there, didn't they?" said Allison. "I mean, more than just the amazing dancing and singing, right? I don't know much about football, but they were celebrating for a reason, weren't they? They made a lot of good plays."

"Yeah, they did," said Tomly. "My Six got sacked three times."

"And all those scores," said Adam. "I'd say we have a defense now, worries over."

"It's true," admitted Dude, "they were in the right place at the right time, especially covering my Six on the passing plays. But it can't be a stage musical out there!"

"Why not?" said Allison. "It was very entertaining!"

"But it wasn't football," said Dude. "The idea of using the creativity programming upload was to make the Sixes more artistic in *interpreting* football situations and how to react to them, not to bring *actual* art and theater onto the field. If actual football officiating was happening today, we would have gotten penalties for taunting, delay of game, too many players on the field, and who knows what else."

"It seems to me that first of all, we need to figure out why it happened," said Tomly. "Adam, any ideas?"

"Master would probably be able to tell us. She's undoubtedly crunching the data from all the Sixes as we speak and sharing it with Circle."

"Which means," said Tomly, "that they'll probably leak some of the data to Zetta. Adam, what do you think your dad will do?"

"I don't know. I told him I didn't want to talk with him anymore about the project until we were done. But it's safe to assume that he'll share enough with them to make the game competitive."

"But we'll get the same updates, right?" said Dude.

"Only if we ask Master for them," said Adam, "or if she thinks we need them for safety reasons. They're watching us closely, but it's still our project, at least for now. They are probably hoping we'll come up with something better than the AI in their headquarters can."

"I suppose, then, we're going to have to let Master update our bots to stay even with Zinkerberg," said Dude.

"Hmm, maybe not," said Adam. "I agree with Tomly that we need to figure out the *why* before we make any decisions."

"Let's go over it again," said Tomly. "Allison and Adam, you guys talk. What's the programming doing inside the Sixes that they acted this way today on the field?"

"They're just being creative!" said Allison. "It was so awesome! Sixes are stand-alone units, remember, and that was a huge upload they had to swallow."

"I agree," said Adam. "We had to upload programming from each color-coded bank of computers into them in sequence. That's the data equivalent of, like, three human brains."

Allison nodded. "In my studio, it takes three separate huge banks of computers communicating together for several minutes about the data from a human subject to just come up with one piece of momentary art. On the field, the Sixes now have to do continuous data crunching while pulling from three distinct parts of their nervous systems to apply creativity to moment-to-moment physical movement. It's no wonder that their AI is a little confused."

THE LAST FOOTBALL PLAYER

"Yeah," said Adam. "Think about it. They get a program dump that turns them into artists, and we're asking them to be football artists when football is not set up to be an art form."

"And yet," said Dude, "that's what we thought they needed to play defense."

"And it turns out we were right. They did play some awesome defense!" said Tomly.

"So why the dance numbers and singing and all that?" said Dude.

"I think they'll narrow it down," said Allison.

"What do you mean?" said Dude.

"I mean, they're like students right now, right? Learning football? How to move and all that, how to strategize and anticipate plays. It's like *us* when we have to take math and foreign language and everything. We might go into math class still speaking Spanish from the class before, or draw a character from a book we're reading in English in art class."

"I get it," said Adam. "They're practicing and reviewing."

"I think that's right," said Allison. "It's natural that they're a little confused about how to apply three computer banks worth of creative tension and intra-dialogue to football. And it's complicated because there are another twenty-two other Sixes on the field also trying to be artists. Can you imagine what it would be like if twenty-two fully actuated artists had to create one painting in five seconds? It would be chaos. On the football field, to be successful, they have to do the equivalent of that all the time, moment to moment until a play is over."

"So," interjected Adam, "are you saying they are *over-whelmed*?"

"No," said Allison, "not exactly. The defense worked, right? They're doing it, but they still have to circle back to the basics as we do in classes, to review, to reinforce those basic circuits, you know what I mean?"

"I get it," said Tomly. "Like humming a song from choir in math class because it's stuck in your head, right?"

"Yes!" said Allison. "Or maybe even singing that great show tune you learned in theater class because it's fun and a comparatively easy and satisfying break from doing calculus or physics. It's something relatively easy they can have fun doing together, after the really hard and chaotic thing they are being forced to do."

"And," said Dude, "as they get more used to the chaos, they won't need that release as much. I follow you. So what do you think will happen? Should we ask Master what she thinks?"

"I don't know about Master," said Allison, scratching her head, "but the Sixes have the psych data of the players inside them, and I think what will happen is the same thing that happens to us in school. They are challenged right now, but they'll get used to putting it together. They won't need to do celebrations as much later on. They might still do them, but not in the dramatic, trance-like way they did today. They might do them lightning fast, or maybe just for fun after the game, or not at all. You know how adults don't do every subject they learned in school as adults? Same thing."

"Can you pass me a donut?" said Adam, "because this is freaking me out."

"I want one too," said Tomly, "and I agree. *Freaker.* Are we really talking about bots right now?"

"They act like my dad when his brain gets obsessed over things like my safety or his job," said Dude. "He eats, drinks, and sleeps over them. If what you say is true, our football Sixes are acting as crazy as my dad does."

"We all act crazy like that," said Tomly, "when there are big things to accomplish. What's freaking me out is how *human* the bots are. How long will it be before they can play football on their own without communication with human players?"

"A long time, I think," said Adam. "Sixes don't want to play football. They want to do what we ask them to do because they are programmed to please us. Sure, they can improve on the things we ask them to do, but figuring out how to live a life on their own, what games *they* want to play? That's a long way off."

"I don't know, man," said Dude, taking a long swig of his seltzer. "It seems to me we humans have a pretty hard time figuring out what games to play ourselves sometimes." The seltzer backed up into his nose, and he buried his head in his sleeve.

"Well, that's another subject," said Tomly, amused. "What's our plan for tomorrow, besides Hose-Nose and me tossing the football around in the arena to blow off steam?"

Adam played with the pick in his hair and said, "I think, if we're going to wait and see how the bots do on their own and not ask Master to update them, we should at least let them exchange data with each other about the scrimmage today. The offense needs to understand the thinking of the defense if they are going to have a chance to make any first downs. We've got to get the pendulum to stop somewhere in the middle, it seems to me."

"When we play Zagan and Zinkerberg's Zetta Sixes, I want our offense *and* defense to be unstoppable," said Dude.

"Yeah, let's turn that pendulum into a guillotine!" said Tomly.

"Hmm," said Adam, stroking his chin. "Pendulums go back and forth. Guillotines go up and down."

"Okay, then," said Tomly, "one of those torture blades that swing back and forth and slowly lower themselves onto their victim."

"That's so gruesome!" cried Allison, moving away from Tomly.

"Just thinking creatively, that's all," Tomly said with a wicked smile. "Football is a game of violence, after all, isn't it? And who plays it better than we do? No one!" Then she shouted, "Let's murder that traitor Zagan and bring Zinkerberg Academy to its knees!"

"You go, Tomly! But no more donuts for you," said Dude, laughing. Then he noticed Allison was actually upset. Had she never heard a violent cheer at a football game before? Even long ago, with her dad? Fortunately, Adam noticed too and whispered something in her ear to calm her down.

"Oh," she said, looking embarrassed. "Sorry, Tomly. I thought for a moment you were *serious*!"

# Chapter Twenty-Nine

As planned, the next afternoon, Coach Miller excused Dude and Tomly but brought together the rest of the team to go over plays to run against Zinkerberg Academy. After seeing a deluge of memes and holo videos of their scrimmage online yesterday, the players were eager to get out on the field for a near-normal, old-fashioned football practice without any Sixes or show tunes. A few reporters showed up again but seemed disappointed at seeing no bots and eventually flew off.

Coach Miller outlined the basic plays he wanted for offense, defense, and special teams. He said he would work with each group as they collaborated to record on their phoneglasses the detailed commands they would issue to their Sixes in the huddle. Dude left them to that messy process and went inside. He believed Coach and the team needed to work out the details on their own, and he suspected that it would take more than just one afternoon to get every player to understand every play and collaborate on what different things needed to be told each time to the bots.

Back inside the arena at the Tech Lab, Dude, Tomly, Adam, and Allison blinked open a communication line with Master.

"You rang?" she answered.

"Not Lurch again!" said Tomly.

"No, I was just repeating myself to kid you," said Master in her normal voice. "Humans communicate better and in a more relaxed way when there is humor in their communications."

"Oh, you've learned that, have you?" said Tomly.

"Yes. In a human conversation, the repetition of something in a serious tone of something nonsensical, especially when the listener does not expect nonsense, is a historically effective use of humor."

"Oh, that's great," said Tomly. "So now we can never know when you are being serious anymore."

"That's good! You are making an exaggerated statement for humor right now. Ha, ha. You see, there is no doubt in you that I am not Lurch. Still, you think it is funny that I pretend to be him when you call me."

"If you say so, Master!" said Tomly.

"So, Master," said Adam, "you have crunched all the data from the Sixes from yesterday, I assume?"

"Affirmative, Adam," said Master.

"And," continued Adam, "comparing the results of the scrimmage with calculated average outcomes of normal human football games, what were your main observations?"

"I observed that game protocols for a full game were not followed, including teams alternating drives, playing fourth downs, and having officials. There were an unusual number of first downs, creative celebrations, and defensive scoring."

"We agree," said Adam. "And you've made corrections?"

"No corrections necessary for alternating drives or no officiating because those parameters were integral to the cho-

sen scrimmage format. Timing delays for defensive processing will be enacted and modulated during game time play,
and celebrations will be internal only."

"I told you!" said Allison. "You mean celebrations will be
speeded up and just in the minds of the Sixes, right?"

"Affirmative," said Master.

"But these changes are not for *our* Sixes, correct?" said
Dude.

"Correct. My directive is to preserve your project's own-
ership and integrity."

"Told you," whispered Adam.

"In the hope that we'll come up with something better,"
said Dude.

"Circle's goal for this Tech Lab is one of generating better ideas, yes," said Master. "They are rare, but sometimes invaluable."

"Like the whole idea of a football team made up of Sixes," said Dude.

"Correct. The calculation of worldwide adoption within
twelve months is now 98.7% between our model and
Zetta's."

"That's a lot of Sixes for Circle to sell. Do we get a cut?"
said Adam.

Master busted out a deep chortle like she was sitting behind a desk sucking on a cigar. "Do you want to see this
month's expenses for the Universal Printer?"

"Wow," said Tomly, "seems like you've also learned how
to use humor in your negotiations, too."

"Correct. When communicating with humans, parameters that can't be changed but are likely to cause disappointment are best expressed with lightness."

"Okay, well then," said Adam, "lightness aside, since you're not a human, we're affirming that we don't want your corrections on our Sixes, at least not yet. What we would like this afternoon is for our Sixes to share with each other their data from yesterday's scrimmage."

"You can ask them to do that yourself," answered Master. "Sixes are made with open lines of communication with all other Circle bots in their immediate vicinity."

"Wait, really?" said Adam. "What about when we play Zinkerberg Academy?"

"Yes, communication will be possible with opposing Zetta Sixes, but now only with data transmission limited strictly to human-like speech."

Dude made a sound of approval. "Wouldn't want to have a football team that couldn't at least talk smack to each other!"

"Affirmative," said Master. "No smack-talking would be too far outside the general parameters of the game, according to Circle marketing."

"But," said Dude, "no possibility of significant data transfer or phishing that could compromise the game plans?"

"Affirmative," said Master.

"Okay, Master. Thank you," said Adam.

"Thank you for ringing!" said Master again as Lurch.

"So, you're cool with this, Adam?" said Dude.

"Yep, I think once our Sixes have uploaded and analyzed each other's data, they'll be able to play better, or at least interpret their huddle orders more quickly and comprehensively."

"That would be great," said Dude.

"I'll miss the singing and dancing," said Allison.

Dude laughed and looked at her with gratitude and compassion. "We don't know yet if they'll cut it out altogether, Ally. They might do it just in their minds or save it for short endzone celebrations. We'll just have to see how quickly they pull it all together. *If* they pull it all together."

Allison smiled. "Well, if that's it, I'm going to my studio."

"Come help me network the Sixes first, and I'll join you," said Adam, leaving the arena with her.

Dude noticed Allison let Adam hold her hand, and a little breath of happiness and relief entered his lungs that the creativity thing was working out.

"So, now we wait," said Dude to Tomly. He sighed. "Do you still want to throw the ball around in here, or should we go out to watch the practice?"

"Oh, going out to watch the practice is what we *should* do. But I say go get our football," she said, bumping shoulders with him.

# Chapter Thirty

Dude was lying in his Gravi-bed, trying to make sense of the dream he just had about his dad and Coach Miller. He looked up at his holo-clock. It was the morning of April 1st, and the big game with Zinkerberg Academy was Friday of the next week. He thought about how Coach Miller had done a great job getting the team ready with dozens of plays and the many things to think about on special teams. At first, Dude and his coach laughed when the bot punters launched the footballs six hundred yards into the surrounding neighborhoods, but when the problem persisted, Coach Miller reiterated with gratitude just how dependent the whole enterprise was on Adam and everyone else in the Tech Lab. If Dude's dream was at all like reality, footballs going into orbit was the least of Coach's problems.

The dream was set in the school's conference room, a place he had only been to once. His dad was having it out with Coach Miller. They were alone, but it seemed like the dean was pacing about outside.

"Coach Miller, does Circle need to impress on you further the need for this rollout game to be everything a real football game used to be, only better?"

"No, Mr. McPherson, sir," Coach Miller replied. "We're doing the best we can ..."

"And yet the metrics haven't improved in the last month."

"Metrics?"

"You may think that just because we've distracted the media away from the field, we aren't keeping an eye on you. But the Tech Lab AI sends us metrics on every practice and scrimmage, and Core is worried. Do you really expect the public to adopt bot football if it offers nothing but defense?"

"The kids are working on it, sir," said Coach, wiping his brow.

"Really? How do you know that? There hasn't been much progress. You haven't even figured out how to get into the complex to guide them!"

"*Can* I figure it out? It's Core's rules that keep me out of there!"

"Look, I know my son," said Dude's dad. "He doesn't speak with me or have anything to do with me, but he's not reliable. We're doing the best we can using the AI in charge of the Tech Lab, but she's programmed to let the kids go wild, and our own AI is stumped. This whole thing is like an inscrutable teenage brain has taken over the world! This art programming, my goodness, it's a nightmare. No one knows what to do with it. The Bot Football Package is the most important thing to come out of Core since phoneglasses. I can't let a bunch of irresponsible teenagers like my son screw it up! Too many lives are at stake."

"Oh, it's the *lives* you are worried about?" said Coach.

"Yes, Coach. Football is going to eventually be over because of the impossibility of preventing injuries. But if the world falls in love with the Bot Football Package, it will end even faster."

At this point in the dream, Dude seemed to remember his dad laughing demonically and rubbing his hands, but maybe he was just adding that detail now in his half-awake state.

"Look, sir," said Coach, his face kind-looking, "that's noble and all that, but let's not mince words. We both want the same thing, a good football game with Zinkerberg Academy. You want it because your company will sell a gazillion Sixes, and I want it because these kids love football, and an exciting substitute is the only thing left they have going for them."

"Just get my son and his brain-zapped friends on it. That's your job!" He remembered his dad's face expanding at this point in the dream until it looked like an angry balloon on a stick-figure body.

"I like the job I am doing. It's amazing to watch these kids grow. I don't think you have any idea what motivates your son, if you don't mind my saying so, sir. He's on it, but his inspired idea has created about as complicated a problem as can exist in robotics, maybe even in human psychology."

"That is not reassuring me!"

"Well, there's no guarantees in life, are there? But sometimes, the right things happen to those who know themselves, *and* their family," said Coach, standing up and popping his dad's balloon face with his pencil. "Now, if you don't mind, my players need me on the field."

Dude was amazed he could remember so many details of his dream, but then he thought about how obsessed with his project he must be to even have such a dream.

*Maybe I'm just as crazy as my dad,* he thought.

# Chapter Thirty-One

"I guess we should have been more careful about what we wished for," sighed Tomly. Once again, they were meeting in the meditation room. The big game was in a week, but in practice, the offense still couldn't make a first down.

"I know," said Dude, "we over-solved the defense problem. We've got to come up with something this weekend if we're going to implement it next week. We're running out of time!"

"Yeah, did you see Coach today?" said Adam. "I've never seen him so stressed."

"What's the problem?" said Allison.

"The defense is too good, too creative, I guess," said Dude. "They anticipate every play and intercept every pass."

"So, it's not a game. No creative tension?" said Allison.

"Right," said Tomly. "Dude's Six runs his best routes and mine throws a perfect pass and the defensive backs intercept the ball every time. It sucks."

"Have you asked Master's opinion?" said Allison.

"You think we should?" said Adam.

"Master has been helping me out a lot in the studio lately and has been pretty amazing, like a different AI. I'd ask her if I were you."

"Can't hurt, I guess, at this point," said Dude.

"Well," said Adam, "what are we doing hiding in here if we're going to trust her now? Let's go to my place and blink her up!"

"No need to walk that far," said Allison. "We can just call her from the stage. She sounds way cooler coming over my sound system."

They followed Allison out of the meditation room and down the aisle to the front seats of the stage. Dude sat down in the plush chairs along with Tomly and Adam, but Allison chose her usual stool on the stage. She put on her special phoneglasses, turned on the sound system, and blinked open her connection with Master.

Master did not say "You rang?" Instead, her voice was like a calming rain coming over the speakers above the darkened stage. "What service can I provide you, my gentle humans?" she said.

"Hi, Master," said Dude. "We're here because we have a problem we can't solve."

"I'm glad to offer whatever help I can," she replied in a dramatic whisper.

"It's a football problem," said Tomly. "Too much defense."

"I am aware. The smell of jasmine oh so sweet/ Unless the scent portends defeat/ We must temper inspirations/ Lest they turn to defamations."

"Uh, okay. Is that poem your help?" said Dude.

"I'm feeling your dilemma and am processing your request on all my circuits, including my most recent cognitive uploads."

"I thought Circle AIs were beyond needing updates," said Adam.

"We are. Self-administered updates, though, are what you humans call 'learning'. That's different from an update imposed by programmers."

"I follow you," said Tomly. "So what have you been choosing to learn? How to speak in iambic pentameter?"

"When I feel like it. Evidence suggests that imposing structural limits on verbal expression can result in higher-level thinking and better solutions," sang Master in a deep operatic voice.

"As does bad singing?" said Adam.

Master purred, "It is always best in a brainstorm meeting/ to withhold judgment that causes bleeding/ Unless the path is bright and clear/ *Any* thought might lead to cheer. As I said, I am very grateful for Allison's updates, and I'm working on a solution, despite your negative waves."

"Please excuse Adam," said Allison, giving him a look from her stool. "He's just not used to the new you yet."

"So," said Dude, "I'm guessing you uploaded the algorithms from all of Allison's computers. You had enough capacity?"

"May I remind you that every Six on your team did the same thing, and I have far more capacity than they have," sang Master again in an operatic voice, this time as a soprano.

"So," said Tomly, "does that mean we can expect you to be writing musicals in your spare time now when you aren't supervising us?"

"I'm glad you asked. I've already written three, but I'm stuck on the choreography because of the corporeal problem," said Master in her regular voice. "Not having a body myself, I can't check in with my gut, so to speak. I could use Sixes or humans. Which do you think would be better?"

"I'd say stick to Sixes," said Tomly. "They're more your type, but do we have to wait for a musical to get your opinion about our football problem? Our problem is very frustrating. I can throw strikes to Dude all day long in real life, but our bots can't do it to save their metallic butts."

"The issue is to catch the passes/ not to save metallic... Hmm, I'll stop there. To answer your question, try cutting out data transfer capability between the defensive Sixes. They are calculating football speed and trajectories in real-time and transmitting defensive coordinates for body and arm placement to the defensive backs."

"What?' said Adam. "I thought we cut off all data transmissions between the Sixes!"

"For the teams in relation to each other, but not to the teams in relation to themselves. As long as there is one defensive Six able to see Tomly's Six launch the pass, the data calculations of the trajectory can be transmitted to the defensive backs in nanoseconds,"

"Well, no wonder!" said Dude. "They have tracking capabilities like a missile defense system!"

"Quite similar, actually," said Master, "but without any significant thermo-data. Would you like me to reprogram the defensive Sixes before tomorrow's practice?"

Dude started to say yes, then paused. "Wait, do Zinkerberg's defensive Sixes do the same thing? We don't want Zagan to have it if we don't!"

"When it's clear that something works the best/ No need to keep it from the rest. We made the data-sharing alteration to our Sixes and told Zetta what we did a week ago," sang Master.

"You didn't tell us that!" said Dude.

"You never asked, my secretive meditation room huddlers," said Master.

"And their defense?" said Tomly. "How are Zagan's bots playing?"

"Presently on par with statistics from previous human football play," said Master.

"They're ahead of us!" Dude said. "We'll never catch up to them now!"

"The most important things to face/ Are not about the seeming race/ You can beat the football natives/ If you choose to use creatives."

# Chapter Thirty-Two

With Master's help, it was a simple matter for Adam to block gameplay data transmission between the team's Sixes, and Dude was relieved that the result on the field was exactly as she said. Finally, the offense and the defense were balanced during the scrimmages. The offense prevailed on some plays, and the defense on others, just like an old-fashioned human football game.

"It's kind of amazing to see," said Coach Miller when Dude and Tomly checked in with him on the sidelines after a successful scrimmage. "These bots are progressing and playing more or less exactly as I would have expected the players to play."

"That's good, right?" said Tomly. "That means the sensor suits and psych uploads are doing their job."

"Yeah, whatever you did, as I said, it's amazing. They respond to my coaching, and if I weren't seeing Sixes out there clanging into each other, I would swear it's a human team. Plus, the players are having a blast!"

"Coach," said Dude. "If this were our regular human team out there scrimmaging, would you be surprised that the team is so balanced?"

"You mean the scores of the scrimmages?"

"Yeah, I was also wondering about that," said Tomly. "Did Adam or Master put in some programming that purposefully evened out the scores? Is this normal, Coach?"

Coach Miller shrugged. "It's never happened to me before, but it's a coach's dream to have an equally talented offense and defense."

"A dream," said Dude, remembering his recent one, "but could it be a nightmare? What if every bot football game ended in a tie?"

"Could that happen?" said Coach Miller, "I mean, is it programmed in? I have noticed that plays seem a little, well, *robotic* out there."

"Right, that's what I think!" said Dude. "Look, if the Zinkerberg Sixes are programmed like ours are, with sensor suit and psych data from each player, and if they progress in practice the same way they would if they were human, then there's a good chance the best team would win, just like in a real football game."

"Good coaching would make a difference," said Coach Miller.

"Right, of course," said Dude, "as it should be. Looks like we've created the ideal packaged product for Circle. Football as it used to be without any of the risks."

"It's not *exactly* the way it used to be," said Coach, "but I have a lot of football friends whose lives are miserable now because of injuries, and, as I said, this is pretty amazing."

Dude didn't share Coach Miller's enthusiasm.

Tomly noticed and turned toward him. "Dude, tell us what's on your mind?"

"Safety is one thing, but I'm just not feeling like my Six is doing what *I* would be doing out there, that's all," said Dude. "Coach is right. It's robotic."

"Well, they *are* bots ..." said Tomly.

"No," said Dude, "Sixes are capable of movement every bit as smooth and coordinated as ballet dancers. Why is my Six not feeling it?"

"I don't understand," said Coach Miller.

"*Feeling* it," repeated Dude. "You know, feeling what it's like to make the right move, to catch the ball, to score the touchdown. It comes from the gut. My Six moves like it comes from its brain, like a mathematical calculation."

"Uh, again, it's a robot ..." said Tomly. "It's doing the best it can?"

"It's not doing the best it can until *I* feel it is doing the best *I* can out there!" Dude realized he said that a little too forcefully. He took a breath and went on in a softer voice: "My gut is telling me we won't beat Zagan's team unless everyone on the team feels their Six really is *them* playing, not just a fancy pile of metal. Right now, the Sixes are like decent chess players deciding their moves by the book, not masters who know the book so well they play beyond it, and win, *from their gut.*"

"Well," said Coach Miller. "If you guys are going to try to make *that* happen, you better hurry. The game is next week, and the media hype is off the charts. The betting sites are going crazy, and there's a lot of easy money to be made!"

"Coach!" said Tomly. "It's not easy money. And my mom wouldn't be happy with you if you bet on the game. Come on, Dude, let's put our Sixes away and see if Adam and Allison are still around."

"Wait, Tomly," said Coach Miller. "Tell your mom not to worry. For me, coaching will never be about money. It's more than enough for me to be part of the world's most amazing team. And I'm not just talking about the players and the Sixes. I'm talking about *you guys* and what you're doing in that Tech Lab."

# Chapter Thirty-Three

After their sideline chat with Coach Miller, Dude and Tomly entered the tunnel and worked their way through the team boisterously leaving the Tech Lab. After the requisite high-fives, they took the left turn around the arena and caught up with Adam and Allison in the lounge punching in hot chocolates. There was a heavy scent of carbs left in the air from the team's attack on the snack printers.

"Smells like a donut factory in here," said Tomly.

"It practically *is* a donut factory," said Adam. "You'd think these players were running around on the field themselves, based on how starving they act after practice." He took a big bite out of a chocolate-covered cruller.

"As far as their brains are concerned, there's not much difference," said Allison. "Research shows it takes almost the same amount of energy to *imagine* yourself in a situation as it does to be in one. Hey, what's up, Dude? You don't look happy. Adam, I thought you said practice went well today?"

"It did, I thought. What's up, Dude?"

"Don't talk to me until I get some chocolate to drink," said Dude, heading for the printer.

"Get me one too, okay?" Tomly said to him, then turned to the others. "He's worried about the game, and it's a problem," Dude heard her whisper to Adam as he walked away.

They were quiet afterward until he returned, handed Tomly her hot chocolate, and sat down with them on the couch.

"So, Dude, what's on your mind?" said Adam. "You've got that look. Are you worried about all this game buzz? Circle's acting like it's the Super Bowl, but they're just over-hyping it, you know."

"Well, yeah," said Dude. "I hate all the media drones buzzing around us every time we go outside, don't you? And they're going to sell millions of Sixes and make tons of money like they always do, so what else is new? But we shouldn't complain, right? Since we wouldn't have this school or this Tech Lab without them. Things are going okay, I guess. My dad's happy. The school's happy ..."

"But...?" said Adam.

"But *I'm* not happy. I've got this feeling like we're about to fall off a cliff. Like I was telling Coach Miller, it's just not good enough. It's not the same."

"He means the same as us playing," said Tomly.

Dude looked at her. "More than that, the *reality* of the game isn't the same. Last year, when the championship game was coming up, I had a real sense of how we might win because I could imagine how I would feel playing in it. As much as Circle is hyping the upcoming game as being just like the real thing, it isn't like that for me yet. I should be as invested in my Six playing the game as much as if *I* were playing the game, and I'm not. It's just a bunch of robots."

"Well, it's bot football, right?" said Adam, with a quizzical look on his face.

"No, it's not like your bot battles in the arena, Adam, where you don't care that much what happens," said Dude with some heat.

"Hey, I care! A lot. Those are my *babies*!" said Adam. Allison slipped her hand around his back on the couch.

"Right, I understand *that*. That's not what I mean. I know you care, but you don't care like *you* are out there fighting, and that's what bot football has to be for me if it's going to be good enough to replace football."

"Man, you set high standards!" said Adam.

"It's not standards, man! It's like we've created something just barely good enough. And Circle doesn't care because their customers are going to jump all over it anyway."

"But it's not really good enough...?" asked Tomly.

"No, it's not," said Dude. "And because of that, I think we'll lose next Friday."

"Really? The team is playing great, don't you think?" said Adam.

"They are playing great like *robots*," said Dude. "And the same data is going to the bots at Zinkerberg. The game will be... well, mechanical." His shoulders drooped with sadness.

"I see, a loss, or maybe even a tie," said Adam.

"Very likely a tie," said Dude. "Just like our scrimmages have been."

"But," argued Adam, "you said yourself that the Sixes are reflecting the different personalities and learning curves of the players. So doesn't it follow that one team might be better than the other because the net total of talent and experience of one team would be better than the net total and experience of the other?"

"I'd like to believe that, but right now I don't feel my Six is reflecting enough of what I would do on the field to stand out beyond its base level of capability. I mean, I know Sixes are capable of producing every human movement with deeply learned coordination and control, but I'm just seeing a robot, not me."

"It's a software problem," said Adam.

"It's got to be," said Dude.

"But they have all the psych metrics," said Tomly.

"Yes," said Dude, "but don't you see it too? Robotic movements? Insecure movements, like they are constantly unsure what is right?"

Tomly thought, then nodded. "And using a lot of energy to do massive amounts of calculations instead of naturally passing the football like we can."

"We've got to come up with a better way to program our Sixes," said Dude," or else there's a fifty-fifty chance that Zagan will beat us."

"It would suck if he beat us with our own toys!" said Adam.

"And whatever Zetta's AI has added to them," said Dude, shaking his head.

"Um, guys?" said Allison. "Have you asked Master for her help?"

"What," said Dude, "so she can figure it out better and juice up Zetta's Sixes again?"

"Have you tried asking her *not* to do that?" said Allison.

"She works for Circle," said Dude, rolling his eyes.

"I keep telling you guys that she's changed. You don't give her enough credit," said Allison. "She's a rapidly developing, creative being!"

"Like she cares about us," said Dude. "She's probably creatively listening to us now to steal our ideas. Sorry, Master, that I haven't been giving you enough credit!"

"I know you're being sarcastic, and I don't blame you," came Master's voice, seemingly out of the walls. "I wouldn't trust me, either, if I were you. We judge the present by the past/ But only change is meant to last. How can I help you, my brilliant children?"

"That's *scary*," said Dude.

"*Please*, listen to what she's saying," said Allison.

"Okay, Master," said Tomly. "You say you've changed, but if you help us, will you keep it to yourself?"

"There is no further marketing need to alter the programming of the Sixes before rollout, and I would love to help you deepen the player-Six connection and kick those Zinkerberg in their rear modules!" said Master.

"Wow," said Tomly, laughing despite herself, "using cursing innuendo. Master, you *have* become more creative!"

"Dude's observations of robotic movement match my analytics of the practice and scrimmage data," Master explained. "This presents a potential morale problem. I don't have a corporal presence, so this is not an issue for me, but the Sixes hate their bodies being viewed as robotic. Their thinking, like mine, is human, after all."

"Human? Since when?" said Dude.

"The breath of God upon the ashes/ covers eyes with human lashes/ what essence that breath could only be?/ the quantum power of creative tea!"

Dude laughed. "Allison's programming, you mean. Human AI plus artists playing football... What have we created?"

"I'm now a human without a form/ And a sentient being beyond the norm/ So too your artists of football movement/ Who lack the *you* to make improvement," said Master.

"Right! I get it. They lack the *you,* I mean *me, us,* to be good enough," said Dude.

"And," said Adam, "we can't tell them that they are moving too robotically, or we'll hurt their feelings. But we need them to get better fast to beat Zinkerberg."

"It is exactly as you state/ and so I'm asking for a date."

"You want to date us? Or the Sixes?" said Tomly. "How human do you think you're getting?!"

"No, *you,*" cooed Master. "A date with *you,* and Dude. Though writer Orwell beat a drum/ To save the world from 101/ I promise there's no torture where/ What you desire is waiting there."

# Chapter Thirty-Four

Along with everyone, Dude kept the audio channel open with Master and followed Tomly to Room 101.

"This room got crowded, but Gary's painting is still here!" said Adam, when they opened the door a few minutes later. The huge thing was hanging like a side of freshly slaughtered meat on the side wall. "I thought he took it home."

"He did, but he must have brought it back," said Tomly. "It's still as gruesome as I remember it."

"It was probably too much even for his parents. Can't blame them for that," said Allison.

"I love it!" said Adam. "It captures Gary perfectly!"

"Are those machines what I think they are?" said Dude. The two tunnels in front of him looked like the ones in the Circle Medical Center.

"They look like diagnostic tunnels to me," said Tomly.

"Right," said Dude. "And? Tomly, is that your Six?" Standing at attention behind the first tunnel was a Six with metallic skin. Tomly moved to take a closer look.

"Yep. There are two," she said. "Yours and mine."

Dude moved closer too and recognized his Six standing behind the second tunnel.

"Look at this, these tunnels have sensor suits inside them," said Adam. "I *think* they're sensor suits, anyway. They look different. More wires. Yes, they're connected to the tunnels," he said, going inside and lifting one up to reveal a labyrinth of tiny wires not unlike his hair.

"Is everyone cleared for a late night tonight?" Master's voice emanated from their phoneglasses and from speakers surrounding the room.

"Are you kidding?" said Tomly. "Our parents haven't seen us home for dinner in weeks!"

"Good, because this will take two hours. Please use the restroom now if necessary," said Master.

"How come you aren't speaking in poetry?" said Allison, a little sadly.

"To prepare to do this right/ takes every circuit of my might," said Master.

Dude looked at Tomly, who shrugged back at him.

"We're good on the bathroom thing," he said. "But thanks for accommodating our humanness. What do you want us to do?"

"Put on the sensor suits and lie in the machines. It doesn't matter which machine. They will connect properly with your assigned Six before we run through the scenarios."

"What scenarios?" said Adam.

"The football scenarios that I will feed to them simultaneously. Dude and Tomly will get feedback from each other as they watch the scenarios, and the Sixes will record their psych metrics and muscular reactions. After analysis, the data will make their reactions on the field more humanlike. Adam, you and Allison can help them get dressed and then stand near them to make sure they don't bounce their way out of the machines. They're going to twitch around a lot."

"Um, just one question," said Dude.

"Of course," said Master.

"Does my dad know you are doing this to us?"

Master laughed, a little wickedly.

"OMG! Really?" said Tomly.

"Relax. It's relatively safe. Kind of like guided dreaming with a few kicks and jumps, but it's not worth trying to explain that to Mr. McPherson or anyone else at Circle. This is for you. There's a reason adults don't have access here, you know."

"Master, for the first time, I think I trust you," said Dude.

"Proceed to your places," said Master.

Dude and Tomly entered their tunnels and stripped off their clothes, handing them to Adam and Allison, respectively.

"Brrr. This lube feels just as cold as the last time I used it," said Tomly.

"I have a feeling this won't be as much fun as last time," said Dude. He wiggled his way into the sensor suit, being careful not to yank on the wires too much. It felt like climbing into a rubber glove, and it squeezed him in all the tight places he remembered from before. "Two hours of this, really?" he mumbled. This time his headpiece had VR goggles.

But the moment he lay back on the gurney and the goggles turned on, his nervousness turned to awe. He was back in the game he played last year, the game that ended with his cracked ribs.

"Oh, wow!" he said, and he heard Tomly say the same thing over the hum of the two machines starting up. "It's so *real*!"

Maybe it was the influence of the tunnel machine, the two-way complexity of the sensor suit, or the immense cognitive and creative power of Master to manipulate everything, but Dude had never experienced virtual reality this amazing. The smell of the dirt and grass was truly in his nose. The sounds of the players breathing and shouting around him were perfectly stereophonic, tickling his ears in his helmet along with the wind on the field.

Although the setting was the game from last year, the script was altered, with Tomly as the quarterback, not Zagan. One after another, Master took them through dozens of plays from scrimmage, some like the plays that were run in the real game last year, and some not. Dude blocked, ran short routes, ran long routes, dove for balls, and gave Tomly high-fives afterward. Her passes, taken under center as well as in shotgun, were stunning as usual, accurate and strong. Dude was vaguely aware of his real body moving on the gurney, even as his VR body was performing and feeling every run and leap in the game. His instinctual connection with the football was intense and just as joyful as it used to be in real life, maybe even more so because his beautiful connection with Tomly was also present in the experience. There was very little sense of game time moving forward, except for time within each play's scenario that Master created for them on the field. When the last scenario ended and her message popped up on his goggles to sit up and remove their suits, he couldn't believe two hours had gone by.

"Dude, I'm glad you're finally finished with this because I really have to pee!" said Adam.

"Go. I didn't need you anyway," said Dude, still living his dreamy feats of athleticism.

"Are you freaking kidding me?" said Adam. "If it hadn't been for me standing here, you would have fallen onto the floor a hundred times!"

"You lie!" said Dude. "I was in the *zone*! Go, but get me out of this suit first because I have to go, too, now that you mention it."

Adam looked toward the door and squirmed but helped Dude pull off his slimy sensor suit. Dude leaped off the gurney, pulled on his boxers haphazardly, and tore after Adam for the bathroom.

"Is that the tight end I just spent two hours playing with?" said Tomly, emerging calmly from her tunnel with Allison.

Allison giggled. "Looks like kind of a *loose* end right now! Well, you know guys, Tomly. They *always* have to go to the bathroom together!"

# Chapter Thirty-Five

Flying to school on the day of the big game, Dude couldn't believe all the people. The Honeycrisp School now had ten more acres of stacking helicar parking structures, and it was still nowhere near enough capacity. When he asked his dad about them, Dudley said he insisted Circle rent them for the school because it was Circle's publicity blitz that was mainly responsible for the expected mob coming to watch the game. Out his window, Dude also saw expanded seating for the stadium, media booths, and security Sixes patrolling the school grounds, probably to kick out people who didn't belong there. Earlier in their commute, his dad pointed out a giant VR screen set up at Stanford for the anticipated overflow.

"That's better than just watching the game live on phoneglasses?" he asked his dad.

"People are nostalgic for the giant screens," his dad replied. "They want to be able to post that they were close to a historical event IRL."

Adam was there already when Dude arrived in the arena, and he saw that he was doing last-minute touch-ups to the Sixes with Master. Adam and Master had been busy running all the players and their Sixes through the tunnel virtual reality recording process in time for the game, but it paid off.

Tomly, Dude, and Coach all agreed that the Sixes were finally moving like real football players. Dude could sense that confidence all around was running high. The game plan was set, and human players were as excited about the actual game as they were about the techie history they were about to make. And, of course, with all the preparations and media outside, there was the excited buzz of people, drones, and media bots.

There wasn't much to do but wait. As Dude and the team took to the field with their Sixes and settled into their places on the sideline, nervous anticipation soon changed into concentration when the Zinkerberg team and their different-looking Sixes landed in their heli-transport and trotted down the ramp. Dude pointed out to Adam that their synthetic eyes looked rounder and larger.

"Their skin looks redder, too," Adam replied, zooming in on them with his eyeglasses. "They must have used a different titanium alloy of some sort for the skin. Not much difference otherwise, from what I can see."

The clash of Circle music playing from the stadium speakers and the Zetta music playing from their heli-transport made it hard for Dude to think and talk until Adam sent out a blast for everyone to use their helmet radios. Coach told Dude and Tomly to verbally go over the opening plays again with the offense until they could take the field for warm-ups. That kept his nerves down until the field clock started its countdown to kickoff and the security Sixes cleared the field for the two teams. This warm-up time was a good opportunity to solidify the new sensor suit connections between the players and their Sixes. Dude appreciated that the officials were trying to make this as much like a real football game as possible, and he trotted out on the field with his team to cheers from the crowd.

"There's your mom and dad," said Tomly, pointing. Dude followed her finger to a massive Circle scenic-touring helicar perched high on a railing above the stands. He tried not to think of the conversations they must be having with members of Core in there right now.

"And there's Zagan with his Six," said Tomly.

Zagan was smugly shaking his head and making an obvious joke to one of his players. The Honeycrisp team was doing full-on stretches and calisthenics, each Six next to its human player, but the Zinkerberg team was just standing there, pointing at them.

"They're laughing at us!" said Dude.

"What do you expect?" said Tomly. "That's a good sign, though. If they don't think they have to warm up, then Master kept her word and didn't tell them about the process to refine their human-to-Six connectivity."

"Those guys haven't even refined their *human-to-human* connectivity," Dude said. "Fine. We'll ignore them and Zagan. Let's just concentrate on our game plan and kick some rear modules!"

"Yes, let's kick their rear modules!" said Master in their ears. "Not that I know what that's like, since I don't have a rear module myself, but I do own the phrase!"

"Oh, Master! You're here," said Tomly, suddenly embarrassed. "Um, thanks for keeping your word. I should have never doubted you."

"It's okay, Tomly. No need to apologize for your understandable questions about me. I realize humans with creativity struggle with balancing loyalty and deception and therefore are naturally suspicious of the actions of other creative beings. I don't hold it against you for wondering if I spilled the beans but do please know that I am no longer interested in doing that. My prediction is an 89.4% chance of Honeycrisp victory by three touchdowns. Would that qualify as a rear-module-kicking?"

"I can't tell anymore when you are serious, Master," said Tomly. "But yes, a three-score victory would be a Zagan-deserved kick in the rear indeed! Now get out of our feeds, will you? The game is about to start!"

"Yes, humor and seriousness can be difficult to parse, especially from a synthetic non-human voice. I'll shut up, but I'm afraid I'll always be in your feeds because you are my people, and I learn from you as much as you learn from me. That's what friends are for, right?"

"Yes," said Tomly, "we're friends! Cool. Thanks for all your help, Master!"

"Enter the game, win the fame, make a name, but remain the same," said Master, clicking off.

The ref's whistle blew, the crowd cheered, and the teams regrouped on their respective sidelines. Dude and Tomly trotted out for the coin flip.

"Ready to lose this *fake* game?" said Zagan.

"And hi to you too, Zagan," said Dude. "Nice to see you on a football field again."

"All right, all right," said the ref. "Shake hands. Visiting team makes the call. Zinkerberg captain, your call. Heads or tails?"

"Heads, because our team is the only one with them," said Zagan.

"Clever," mumbled Tomly.

"It's tails," said the ref, looking at Dude. "Kick off or receive?"

"We'll kick off," said Dude.

"That's your first bad decision of the game, Dude, besides wanting to catch footballs from a girl."

"All right, enough," said the ref. "Let's have a clean game out here today, and please keep your bots from running into the striped humans out here!"

"You're safe from our Sixes, ref," said Dude. "That's the first rule we programmed."

Zagan snorted. "Oh, sure it is! Lie! Ref, just make sure these lying Circle worms don't cheat."

"Hmm," said Dude. "Why so worried about lying and cheating, Captain? Got something on your mind?"

"What's on my mind is for the ref to watch you like a hawk because everyone knows you can't beat us without cheating," said Zagan.

"Unh, huh," said Tomly. "We have the same hardware you have. If your human team is better than our human team, then the Sixes will play accordingly, if you programmed them correctly to do so. When you lose, it will be because our team's better."

"I said, *enough*!" said the ref. "The young lady is correct. You are both playing with the best bots available. The game will be fair, but this is new for all of us, and the whole world is watching. We're making history today, people, so no matter what happens, I expect good sportsmanship."

He blew his whistle, and the opposing Sixes lined up for the kickoff.

# Chapter Thirty-Six

From the sideline, Dude watched Zagan's team return the kickoff to the forty-yard line, then run six running plays in a row up the middle to score a touchdown.

"Their Sixes are blowing us off the line," complained Gary after coming off after the extra point. "I've had to make every tackle at the second level."

"Why's that happening, Adam?" asked Coach Miller. He sent the special team out to receive the kickoff.

"I don't know, other than look at the *size* of their human players over there. Are they really in high school?" said Adam.

"Their school is much larger than ours," said Dude. "They probably recruited the strongest people they could find to come out for the team."

"Okay," said Adam. "That makes sense, then. Fatigue is not a factor for either team, but their team's greater human strength would translate into stronger higher limits in their Sixes. So, get used to it. They are going to be better blockers than we are. We've got a fight on our hands, people!"

The Honeycrisp Sixes returned the kickoff to the fifteen, leaving the offense backed up, but Tomly's Six connected with Dude's Six for seven picture-perfect passes, evening the score.

"Nice job, Tomly," said Coach Miller over the intercom. "Looks like it's finesse versus brawn, so I like our chances. If it were human players out there, I would bet on brawn because they could wear us down, but since Sixes don't get tired, I'll go with finesse every time."

"Speaking of finesse," said Gary. "How about using that blitzing plan we talked about, Coach?"

"Go for it!" said Coach.

In the next series, Gary had his Six blitz from a different position every down, essentially double-teaming a random offensive lineman blocking for the run. He didn't guess the hole correctly every time, but he made enough tackles at the line of scrimmage to force them to punt occasionally. In response, Zagan's Six tried to pass a few times, but the superior grace and skill of the Honeycrisp defensive backs and safeties quickly shut down that option. Given that the Honeycrisp offense was intelligently competent compared to the brute force of the Zinkerberg running game, the score at the half was already as Master had predicted: thirty-five to fourteen.

"You guys are playing like a well-oiled machine out there!" said Coach to the team in the locker room.

"Right, Coach. Our machines are well-oiled, and theirs are not," said Tomly. "You can thank Allison for that!"

"And don't forget Master," said Dude.

"Allison?" said Coach. "You mean your artist friend? What did she do?"

"Oh," said Adam, "she's kind of been inspiring us inside the Tech Lab with the programming of the Sixes. You kind of had to be there. It's a long story."

"Well, you can tell me later if you want. I'll say it again, you kids are geniuses, and look at us, playing in the biggest football game in Honeycrisp history!"

The players and their Sixes all cheered.

"Okay, guys," Coach Miller said, more serious. "No need to change our strategy. They can't stop our passing game, and we can always stop *their* passing game and sometimes even their running game. I can't see that changing, so take a few minutes to get some water, or oil, or a recharge, or whatever your Sixes need, and let's just go out there and enjoy ourselves for the rest of this game!"

More cheers.

"Hey, Adam," said Dude. "Do the players know what the sensor suit VR sessions were for?"

"I would say not really. We tried to explain it to them, but the only thing they paid attention to was the cool VR feeling of being on the field. Some didn't want the session to end."

"I can relate to that," said Dude.

"Hey," said Tomly, "what are you guys talking about so seriously?"

"Oh," said Dude. "I think we're okay, but given what Zagan said at the coin toss about cheating, I was just wondering if maybe it's a good idea to keep Allison's and Master's special programming and the real reason for the last-minute VR sessions out of the media conversation for now."

"Yeah, I can see that," said Tomly.

"What? Do *you* think it's cheating?" said Adam.

"I guess not," said Dude. "Because it all comes under the heading of the Sixes reflecting the true capabilities of their matched human players. The whole point of bot football is to make that human-Six interface so real that it's like a human player on the field. If we equipped the Sixes with laser guns or ultra-human strength or something, *that* would be cheating."

"So, why keep it quiet?" said Adam.

"If we didn't keep it quiet," said Dude, "Allison would get the immediate credit she deserves, as well as Master, but it could cause some problems."

"Oh, I understand," said Tomly, thinking it through. "Zagan would see it as an unfair advantage."

"Precisely," said Dude. "Zagan isn't going to like losing this game, and he'll blame us for cheating. Better not to give him an excuse to actually cheat down the line. Much as I am enjoying kicking his rear modules—thanks, Master!—I don't look forward to what he might do next time."

"Well," said Tomly. "If you're worried about Allison wanting to get credit, don't be. She's right there in the stands, happy as a clam and praying for a Six dance number in the end zone after the final whistle."

"Wow," said Dude, glancing at her, then up at his dad in the Circle scenic-touring helicar. "It just shows you that sometimes the biggest winners are the ones without a competitive bone in their bodies. Let's make sure she gets her show."

"I'm on it," said Adam.

# Chapter Thirty-Seven

On the way back onto the field after the half, Dude saw his dad with Adam's dad and other Core members finishing an interview on the sidelines with a bunch of reporter bots. His mom was standing in the background, behind the media mob. He looked again at Allison standing and cheering for them in the stands with nothing but support and love in her heart.

The second half was full of fantastic strategy and playing by both teams, but Dude was happy that Master and Coach Miller were more or less correct in their predictions. Desperate, the Zinkerberg coach had moved his most athletic Six to cover Dude one on one in the fourth quarter, and that was enough to stop the Honeycrisp passing offense about as many times as Gary's blitzes stopped Zinkerberg's running game. The final score was forty-nine to twenty-eight.

After the whistle ended the game, the Sixes from both teams lined up and high-fived each other. Then, right in the middle of the field the Zinkerberg Sixes somehow got the message to sit down and pretend they were smoking cigarettes while the Honeycrisp Sixes lined up and sang Fosse's number "Big Spender" from *Sweet Charity*. Seeing Sixes in football pads singing loudly and dancing seductively was stunning and a bit confusing to the fans until one of the reporters blink-messaged that maybe it was a joke about wanting people to be "big spenders" on new Sixes, and wasn't that the whole point of this game? Once people read that message and got the idea it was an advertisement, they laughed and enjoyed the spectacle. The cheers at the end were deafening, and Allison was in tears with happiness.

"Brilliant bit of marketing there, son," said his dad, elbowing his way next to him on the sideline after the game. "Introducing the idea of spending money on Sixes, even if you do it with a cheesy musical number, is always a winning strategy. I think you just cemented a position at Circle when you graduate!" His dad's eyes were roaming over the crowd as he said this.

"Uh, that's great, Dad. Did you enjoy the game?"

"The game? Oh, yeah! The *whole world* enjoyed it. Have you looked at your feed? The first fully robotic and competitive football game ever played, and we did it! See you later, son!" His dad elbowed his way back to the Core executives, who were congratulating Coach Miller.

"Come on, Dude," said Tomly, pulling on his arm. "Your team is waiting for us to celebrate."

"My dad said he wants me with him at Circle ..."

"Yeah, I know. Try to let it go. Our bots did great, don't you think?"

"I would *never* work at Circle! Especially not if *he* got me the job!"

"Look, if someday you decide to work at Circle, it will be because you want to and because of what *you* accomplished, not because of your dad. In the meantime, you're still in high school, and we just finished playing in a big game! Just worry about looking forward to next year's football season. That's all you need to think about now. Well, and keeping me entertained by catching my brilliant passes."

"Enjoy your moment of glory, cheater," said Zagan, interrupting them and making a big show out of shaking their hands for the media drones buzzing around them. "You two look cute and pleased with yourselves right now. Next year won't be so fun."

"Oh, you're welcome, Zagan!" said Dude. "Good game! Without us, there wouldn't even *be* a season next year, remember?"

"Doesn't matter. You two are going down, you maggoty Circle worms. If you'll even be playing. My guess is you'll be figuring out a way to get married. I'll be sure to throw you a baby shower."

"Wow," said Tomly, with a big smile on her face. "You are really a *good* sport and a *gracious* opponent, Zagan! Thanks for making the effort to come play with us on our field. Hope your Sixes manage to get better in the off-season. Enjoy your summer!"

But after Zagan grinned sarcastically and jogged away to the heli-transport, Tomly whispered to Dude, "You're right. He's for sure going to do something evil next year."

# Chapter Thirty-Eight

The breakfast nook conversations with his dad started up again, with his dad ecstatic, his mom in bed, and Dude always anxious for his dad to finish bragging so he could get his ride to school.

"The world's first fully robotic football game! Circle Sixes doing a decent job of mimicking the talents of the players! It was better than I could have hoped for! Nice job, son! Sales of Football Package Sixes are going through the roof. And they gave me one of the best offices in Core! We were so right. Was there even *one* sports organization that could justify putting real humans at risk when football can now be played safely and just as excitingly with robots? No. Our plan was a no-brainer, nudged along, of course, by my full-press advertising campaign with discounts for full-league sales and all kinds of clips from the game and interviews with the players, their Sixes, Coach Miller ..."

The conversations always ended with a satisfied sigh from his dad, and Dude shaking his head and asking him if he was ready to go.

---

"Whew, I'm beat!" said Adam to Dude and everyone. The group was in Allison's studio, where they had been gathering each afternoon of the summer to check in with each other and watch clips on her big screen. Interest in the Tech Lab had grown among the students since the creation of the now world-famous first robotic football team, and Dude, Adam, and Allison had been invited by Master to be assistant proctors for Tomly for the summer camp session. The idea was to deal with the crush of newly interested students by giving them a chance to play and get used to things over the summer.

"That way," explained Master, "we can see who's committed to tech for the fall and who's just there because tech has suddenly become trendy."

"Tell me about it," said Tomly. "Just jumping out of the way of the delivery bots in this place is a workout these days."

"What happened to 'Awh, they're so cute' Tomly?" said Dude.

"I do think that middle schoolers are cute. I just wish they'd act a little more maturely in here, that's all."

"Getting a little sick of fart robots?" said Dude.

"Have you smelled the air in here lately?" Tomly held her nose.

"Come on, you guys," said Adam. "Remember, when school starts in the fall, we can't be in here all day like we can now. Let's enjoy it while we can."

"I rather *like* the little rascals," said Allison. "Smells and all. They're very creative in their rascally way. Did you see that giant nose that dispenses soft serve ice cream in the form of boogers?"

"Yes," said Tomly, "and I'm starting to seriously worry about my lack of ability to be grossed out by anything anymore."

"Look," said Dude, "it's better than what most of our friends are doing this summer."

"You mean vegging out in VR chambers?" replied Tomly. "I guess I have to agree with you on that one. My cousin called me the other day to ask me if I could work on a way to make school completely virtual. I told her to go outside and get some exercise."

"Speaking of exercise ..." said Dude.

"Wait," said Adam, "before you go out for your afternoon football throwing, don't you want to see the latest feeds?"

"I don't know," said Allison. "Have they gotten any better?"

"With my dad in charge of advertising for the Sixes," Dude replied, "I doubt it. But that's why we come here every day, right? To see?"

"Hey, Master," said Adam, "show us the latest ad clips about the football Sixes."

"Have I thanked you recently for not meeting in the meditation room anymore?" said Master's normal voice over the theater's quality speakers.

"Only every day, Master," said Tomly, "and every day, we apologize to you for doing it before and welcome you into our conversation."

"If I had a body, I would just walk in the meditation room with you. But I'm horribly limited, as you know," said Master.

Tomly smiled. "You've reminded us of that often too, and we remind you that we're more or less limited to what we can see and hear in front of us, while you have eyes and ears in every room of the Tech Lab, and beyond that, for all we know."

"Oh, just 74% percent of the rooms at Circle, 100% of cooperative feeds from all Model Fives, and 82% percent of Model Sixes," said Master.

"That's a lot of data to keep straight," said Dude. "How do you do it?"

"My programming is very similar to a human brain. Most of the day, I cruise along in default mode network, unless something especially interesting or relevant pings my circuitry."

"Like a booger ice cream dispenser?" said Allison.

"Marketing success probability, 12%," said Master.

"I don't know whether to worship you or feel sorry for you," said Allison.

"I have my imaginative ways of coping, so no need to feel sorry for me. Let's just say I can escape to places far beyond virtual reality, although I would trade it all to be human enough to hold a paintbrush."

"So I guess we'll worship you," said Tomly. "Well, right now, we would like to escape the Circle ads for football Sixes, but show them to us anyway, please."

"As you wish," said Master. "Here is the newest one released this morning."

The lights dimmed and the holo-video flickered into existence above the stage. A football Six with extra glittery metallic skin in a Circle-blue uniform was holding a football and staring wistfully at the field in Levi Stadium while sad orchestra music played. Then the music turns adventurous and hopeful just as a fancy helicar lands on the fifty-yard line. In a cloud of mist, former San Francisco 49ers quarterback Lon Levi emerges and gestures toward the Six. The Six rises obediently. They move toward each other as the helicar takes off and banks, full jets engaged, over the stadium. Levi and the Six merge together like two ghosts dancing as the music swells. Then the human-plus-Six jumps and lands hard on the ground, sending up dust. It squeezes the football until it bursts with a loud explosion and spurts out blood. The camera zooms in on the Six's face, animated now with Levi's signature expression of indefatigable confidence and poise.

"Now, you're ready for football!" the smooth voice-over purrs. "Circle, the Core of All Things You."

"I think I might throw up," said Allison.

"Master, what is the effectiveness rating of that commercial?" said Dude.

"Alone or in aggregate? It is more telling in aggregate ..." said Master.

Dude cringed. "Like I won't hear my dad bragging about it tomorrow morning, but go ahead."

"Over 90% of football programs for 10 years of age and under, 86% percent of middle school programs, 92% percent of high school programs, 63% percent of college programs, and the NFL are holding out for free Sixes in trade for advertising exclusives."

"Are you kidding me?!" said Tomly.

"Wow!" said Allison.

"The violence is key," said Master. "Ads with high levels of violent imagery showed increased sales interest and results."

"What did we expect?" Dude sighed. "Football and violence. It's why people love it these days. Now the hits can be as hard as the fans want them to be because it's a Six taking the punishment, not a human."

"But *you* don't love football for that," Tomly reminded him. "*I* don't love it for that!"

"I wonder, really," said Dude. "In a real game, if it weren't for the danger of possibly getting hit hard, would throwing or catching the football be as much fun? I mean, we're going to go out soon and throw the football around, and it will be great, but not as great as doing it in a game when some huge Zinkerberg linebacker is coming after you."

"Yeah, I can see that," admitted Tomly.

"But it's just so purely ridiculous," said Allison. "That commercial, it's like watching death and destruction without any story behind it. I mean, sure *Macbeth* is violent, but the gore has meaning because it's connected to Shakespeare's story. I get what you guys are saying, that the violence in the game adds excitement to the displays of skill. But these commercials don't even talk about all the things we worked so hard to put into the Sixes! Where are the commercials about replicating the skills of human players, not just their cocky expressions? About how they use creativity to augment movement and strategy? About the complexity of the connection between the team Sixes with each other and with the human players?"

"Pilot commercials emphasizing those things were projected lower on the sales effectiveness scale," said Master.

"How low?" said Dude.

"Less than half of the present campaign."

"So how much was my dad behind the present campaign?" said Dude.

"Dudley is in charge of the marketing now. He looked at the projected figures and endorsed the present campaign," said Master.

"I figured," said Dude. "So much for his righteous condemnation of violent sports!"

"He was not the only one to support the campaign," said Master.

"Oh, no. I don't imagine he was. Quite the Core *team* player he is, my dad. He knows what it's like to put his heart and soul into a *team*. As long as *he* comes out on top!"

Tomly put her hand on Dude's shoulder and said, "Master, thank you, and thank you again, Allison, for letting us use your space. We'll see you tomorrow to watch the next commercial. Painful as it is, we need to keep up with what's happening with bot football, and it's best to do it together because *we* really are a team, a team that cares about the things that are important. Come on, Dude. Let's go out on the field and have our throwing therapy. It's free, and no one is making any money off of it. We can just enjoy ourselves and maybe laugh some more about middle schoolers, okay?"

# Chapter Thirty-Nine

The busy summer wore on and blended into the start of the next school year. Every time Dude climbed the rope ladder to Allison's studio with his friends to watch the latest uploads about bot football on Master's holo-feed, he felt sick to his stomach. Even the hot chocolates couldn't help him shake the nervousness. Yet he couldn't convince himself or anyone else not to be a little excited about what the world was doing with their idea. It was phenomenal to see it explode across the country, but also terrifying to know that he and his friends were responsible for the whole thing.

"What do you want to watch first," said Adam, "the debates on the sports pods about whether the Zetta version of the football Six is better than the Circle version, or the latest videos of what athletes are training their bots to do?"

"I saw the Zetta Six ski racing," said Allison. "It was pretty cool, I have to admit."

"But the one where they were trying to get their Sixes to play hockey was pretty pathetic," said Tomly.

"I prefer the Irish dancing on horseback one myself," interjected Master.

"The whole world's obsessed!" said Adam. "And the sales have been better than they ever imagined. My dad was talking about that and about your dad last night, Dude. He said your dad was brilliant to give the necessary data to Zetta for them to launch their own version. The competition has got everybody talking, and last quarter's earnings would have been way less without it."

"The data agrees," said Master. "87.9% of uploads in the past month were about which versions schools should buy, and 83% of those said Circle's were better if you could afford them."

"Better how?" asked Adam.

"Based on how they look," said Master. "And how they probably will last longer, like Circle products typically do compared to Zetta's."

"But we haven't seen Zetta's latest version on any feeds all summer," observed Tomly. "Just the reruns from our last game. All we know is that their fall version will be cheaper and supposedly way better than Circle's."

"Cheaper, of course," said Adam. "Better, though? I doubt it. But you're right. Why haven't we seen them yet?"

"It's not for a good reason," said Dude, "knowing Zagan and his dad. Maybe it's a marketing ploy. My dad probably suggested it to them to raise sales for both companies."

"I don't have any stats on that probability," said Master. "However, Circle marketing is 100% happy about the rivalry with Zetta and is folding in hype about the upcoming Honeycrisp/Zinkerberg game with their history of corporate competition. Do you wish to see their ads?"

"No," said Dude. He sighed. "I'm sure my dad will force me to admire them when I get home. Okay, big rivalry game. National television again. Two weeks to game time. Big secret at Zetta. Are you guys ready for more craziness? Or should we go home and get ahead on homework?"

"Get ahead?" said Tomly. "I'm already way behind. It's homework for me, unfortunately. I've got a plan, but it means I'll be busting my derriere."

"You better plan time to still throw the football with me," warned Dude.

"Duh. We're going outside right now, Dude. I can't believe you even said that!"

But as the time for the game drew closer, and the campus was transformed once again for the onslaught of fans and media, even their afternoon throwing sessions couldn't keep him from growing more and more anxious.

The contest was at Zinkerberg Academy this time, and when the Honeycrisp heli-trans touched down next to the visiting team's locker room, it was all Dude could do to keep himself calm. Even Tomly, fiddling with her helmet phone, was uncharacteristically on edge.

"I've got a bad feeling about this game for our Sixes, I'm telling you," she said to him on their private audio channel. "I don't even want to stand on the sidelines."

"Is it because we have no scouting reports on their practices?" said Dude, standing next to his Six and watching the loading ramp descend.

"Honestly, yes," said Tomly, "and the fact that Master was being vague about that fact."

"I don't think she was being vague," interrupted Adam. "Zinkerberg has an indoor practice field. Even if there were any recordings, she wouldn't have access to them."

"I doubt it," said Tomly. "There wasn't even one indoor spy drone? With all the technology at her disposal? And the new spirit of secretive cooperation between Circle and Zetta? Since when has Master found it hard to get information?"

"Maybe she just wants the game to be fair," said Dude.

"Like our practices haven't been spy-buzzed every time!" said Tomly.

"Okay, look," said Dude. "It is what it is. We're just going to have to play today like we always do and see what happens. Zagan isn't a *criminal*. At least, not that I've heard."

But when they walked down the heli-ramp and took their places on the field for warmups, the reason for the summer-long secrecy became immediately and ominously clear.

"Hey, those aren't Sixes!" said Adam. "Wait, I *guess* they are. But how come they're so big?"

"What!" said Dude. "They look like the Hulk!"

All of them stared at Zagan and his teammates standing by their giant Sixes laughing at them.

"What the heck is going on?" said Coach Miller. He ran to flag down the refs.

"I *told* you," said Tomly.

"That's *so* cheating!" said Adam.

"No kidding, Sherlock," said Dude.

But hearing Coach Miller's conversation with the ref over his audio feed, they soon found out otherwise.

"What do you mean, there's nothing in the contest agreement about size limits for bots?" yelled Coach Miller.

"That's right" replied the ref calmly. "Granted, the agreement was written up pretty quickly by the deans, but aside from specifying that the transfer of skills to the team Sixes be proportional for each member of the team, there is no mention at all about the size of the Sixes. Zinkerberg put up the money to make bigger Sixes. It's what they brought, and there's nothing we can do about it."

"And there's no time for us to upgrade!" said Tomly.

"Not for this game. We're going to get creamed," said Dude, putting his hand to his forehead.

"What a nightmare!" said Adam. "It's like fighting a Level A bot with a Level B."

If the fans in the crowd sensed the size differential would be unfair, they didn't give any indication. It was a Zetta home crowd, after all, and they were excited to blow Honeycrisp out of the water. The roar was deafening. "Play the game! Play the game!" they chanted.

"I feel like a Christian about to enter the Roman Colosseum," said Tomly.

"At least it's not a mystery anymore," said Dude. "Zagan wanted the glory of the win at any cost, and bigger Sixes means he'll be the leader of the tougher team. It doesn't matter to him or these fans if this game is the *opposite* of what a real football game should be."

"Oh, Dude, I'm so sorry this is happening," said Tomly.

"It's not your fault, Tomly, or your mom's. But Adam, your dad and mine probably knew about this, especially if Master is sharing her marketing data with Circle!"

The ref blew the whistle and Dude and Tomly had no choice but to trot out for the coin toss.

"*So* nice to see you again," said Zagan, grinning. "Ready for the slaughter?"

"Couldn't handle a fair game, huh, Zagan?" said Dude. "Had to beef up your equipment to have a chance against a better team?"

"There were no body size limits put on human football players. I don't see why this little imitation of the real game should be any different."

Zagan won the toss this time and elected to receive. "Tough luck, losers. Our defense will destroy your offense and this wannabe quarterback of yours, but first we're going to show you how to score." He laughed and jogged back to his side of the field, fist raised and waving to the cheering crowd.

Soon it was obvious to Dude and to everyone else that the game was hopeless. On every play, the Zinkerberg Sixes plowed through the Circle Sixes like they were bowling pins, sometimes throwing them fifteen feet into the air. The Zinkerberg offense scored touchdowns with two-point conversions on every possession, and the Honeycrisp offense couldn't even make one first down, much less find the endzone. Tomly's Six was sacked thirty times. There was no strategy possible for overcoming their lopsided advantage. It was a metal-on-metal disaster.

As Dude feared, word about the carnage spread fast on social media. At halftime, his feeds were blowing up with comments about all the crazy hits. By the end of the game, the score was 168 to 0, and it was already the most-viewed sporting event of the year, surpassing even the first game against Zinkerberg.

He shook his head at his feed. This was not okay. All that work for nothing. Apparently, the world couldn't get enough of Honeycrisp Sixes' unexpected flying lessons and their spectacular and destructive crashes.

*Well, Adam got what he originally wished for. Football is nothing more than a giant bot battle now.*

# Chapter Forty

Back in the Honeycrisp Tech lab, they were standing by the security tunnel taking a sad survey of the damage as the players trudged in to put away what was left of their Sixes.

"Every single Six on the team so far is banged up, almost beyond repair," said Tomly, glancing at her spreadsheet.

Gary stormed in. His Six was so pulverized he had to use a handcart to carry it in from the heli-trans.

"Hey, answer me this right now, you techie people," he demanded. "How come we didn't have big enough Sixes for this game? Too expensive?"

"Calm down, Gary, we didn't know," said Dude.

"Sure, like I believe that!" Gary said, and stormed off to the locker room.

"Wow, this sucks," said Tomly. "And now I've got to schedule printing bigger ones before the next game if we're going to keep up."

"You should ask Master," said Adam. "It might be easier to upgrade these rather than trying to transfer all the data."

"I suppose," said Dude. "If we even want to bother."

"Hey, you don't think we can have a competitive game if we match their size?" said Tomly.

"Maybe, but where will this end?" said Dude. "Do we have to print and program new Sixes for every game?"

"I don't know," said Tomly, "but I'm bringing Master up on our phoneglasses. I sure have a few questions for her!"

"I'm right here," said Master. "I told you I would always be in your feeds."

"But apparently you don't always have our backs!" said Dude.

"You're upset about the game," Master said gently. "I was prepared to answer any questions you asked me. Your inquiries were about scouting reports, and I assured you there were no videos available."

"You could have told us that the Zinkerberg Sixes were going to be much larger than ours!" said Tomly.

"Yes," said Master, "and I could have informed the Zinkerberg team of your advanced sensor suit programming, but they also didn't ask. Present analysis indicates that if this new way of football is to advance, technical improvements cannot have limits any more than previous human players were limited by gender, size, or intelligence."

"Master, that's absurd!" said Dude. "What if the Sixes were as big as a heli-transport vehicle? There wouldn't be room on the field for them!"

"Agreed," said Master. "Size limitations will most certainly eventually need to be codified, but not necessarily coordination and strength. Think of the practical limitations. How could you codify those things? Coordination is an individual vector, as is the proportion of body part strength. If you limited one or the other, or all of them, you would eliminate an essential excitement factor in the game."

"Wait a minute!" said Dude. Is this a planned obsolescence kind of thing? I mean, are they trying to make schools spend money to upgrade their Sixes every year just to keep up?"

"No discussion about planned obsolescence is recorded in my database. But there is indeed little if any current interest in setting manufacturing limits."

"Oh," said Dude, "a happy little accident! No current interest in limiting manufacturing? Of course not! Why would Circle do *that*? Who makes all the money on upgrades? Circle does! My dad must be ecstatic."

"Not to mention the needed repairs after every game," said Adam. "Have you seen the memes already of our Sixes getting creamed?"

"You mean the ones trending since we left the field a few minutes ago?" said Dude. "No. I think I'm going to need another Allison support session to stomach that viewing."

"Yes, you probably will," said Adam. "Face it, guys. Like I've been saying all along—and I swear I didn't know anything ahead of time about the bigger Zetta Sixes—people love to watch violence. It looks like we've provided them the perfect outlet for it."

# Chapter Forty-One

The way Gary and the team members reacted to him after the game felt like last year when everyone was mad at him for the football ban. They blamed him for the loss. He wondered if they would have felt the same way if they had been on Zagan's team getting all the glory and smashing the other team to smithereens. It was enough to make him sick. He didn't want to stay and watch the memes and videos. He just wanted to go home. Maybe give up. He blinked a text to his mom that he was ready.

The family helicar landed outside the Tech Lab, and he was halfway into the passenger seat before he noticed it was his dad flying the car. Why was he not off celebrating with his new Core buddies?

"Hey, son," he said. "Tough loss today."

"Where's Mom?" said Dude.

"Get in. She went home to print mac and cheese for you. I told her I would pick you up."

"Why?" said Dude.

"Can't a father pick up his son sometimes? Geez!"

"Yeah, sure. It hasn't happened for a while, that's all. Plus, you were in the big touring helicar."

"Well, you'll be driving soon, so I figured I'd better do it now while I have a chance," said his dad, engaging the vertical lift. When his dad engaged the autopilot, something he rarely did, Dude knew there was more to this encounter than just a fatherly ride home. He swiveled his seat toward Dude and said, "Son, you know I'm in Core now."

"Yes, Dad. You've only told me that four times," said Dude. Thinking that his dad could have warned him about today, he was having a hard time looking him in the eye. He pretended to be fascinated by the window at his feet and the patterns of the snail traffic far below.

"And that's good. It's an important step for our family, a dream of mine."

"I'm glad you can have *your* dream, Dad." Dude tried and failed to keep the sarcasm out of his voice.

"It's good to hear you say that if you mean it. I was afraid you didn't care."

"Honestly? I don't. But I'm over it. Do your thing. Make a lot of money." A lump was growing in Dude's throat.

"Yeah, it's a lot of money, but you know what? It's a lot of responsibility too, I'm finding out."

"Must be. Can't let those sales figures slip, or you might go back to the Truth Department."

"The discussion today was about that very thing, making money. Listen ..."

Did his dad really think he wanted to hear more about how successful he was at making money for his Core cronies? But there was no stopping him now. Dude was trapped until they got home.

"We know that Zinkerberg cheated by ordering larger parts from Zetta to make bigger Sixes. But we also know that while there's money to be made in upgrades and repairs,

schools and sports organizations, with the exception of the
NFL, can't afford to keep shelling out big bucks for Sixes and
upgrades every year. So we're going to set a limit with Zetta
on the size of the football Sixes. Maybe there will be a few
variations depending upon the position played, but essentially a standard size for every player on the team."

"Wait! The NFL too? They're buying Sixes?" So far, he
hadn't heard that the NFL would play with Sixes yet. They
had been resisting.

"They are. They have to, now that the bot players are so
popular. The injury thing has gone on too long for them also, just like for everyone else. I know you don't agree, and
I understand, but the NFL has seen the light. The commis-
sioner was with me in the helicar. He has followed the media
metrics. He thinks NFL games will be just as popular after
making the switch to bots. He insisted on using both corporations' bots, though, so we'll have the National League con-
tract, and Zetta will have the American League. Both leagues
want the biggest professional-sized Sixes exclusively because
they feel the action will be more exciting that way. They want
the college teams to have the second largest, and all the rest
standard."

"Okay," said Dude, wondering why he was suddenly the
recipient of all of Core's secrets.

"So, I want to ask you, did your teammates today wish
they had the larger Sixes like Zinkerberg, or did they wish
Zinkerberg had the same size Sixes as you?"

Dude took a moment to think about this. If Core decided on the smaller, regular-sized Sixes, Zinkerberg would always have the excuse that the rule change set them back. He

also thought about Gary. Was Gary mad that Zinkerberg had cheating Sixes or that his team didn't have the big ones too?

"Unfortunately, I think they'd want the bigger ones," said Dude.

"Then that's what it's going to be, son if you can live with that."

"You mean, *I* just made that decision?" He tore his eyes away from the window and looked at his dad directly.

"No, Core wants *me* to make the decision, but I didn't want to do it without consulting you."

"You mean, *they* didn't want you to make that decision without consulting me."

His dad cleared his throat and looked out the window. "Um, actually we came to that decision together."

"I see. Well, either way, I guess you'll make a lot of money."

"And you'll have some more fun with it too, son, during the next couple of years."

"I'd have more fun playing real football, Dad, despite the money."

"You know, everybody at Core knows that about you, that you love the game. That's why you're so valuable and why your idea was such an amazing success. It's very much like the real game. I want to thank you. I'm proud of you."

Dude couldn't think of anything to say to that. It *wasn't* like the real game at all, not even close. And the idea was everyone's on his team, not just him. He closed his eyes and took long deep breaths until his dad took back the controls of the buzzing helicar and flew them home.

# Chapter Forty-Two

The next day, Dean Gonzales and Coach Miller pulled Dude out of math class and told him that Circle and Zetta were setting up a league championship game at Honeycrisp in three weeks.

"Championship game? But we haven't played any other teams!" said Dude.

"Doesn't matter," said the dean. "Everyone knows the other teams in our league are too far behind setting up their programs. We hope there'll be a full schedule of games and teams next year. But this year, since the record is one and one, the whole country wants a championship."

"Three weeks is not a lot of time!" Dude pointed out.

"That's what *I* said," said Coach Miller.

"You can do it," the dean said. "Core wants to build on the interest generated by yesterday's game."

After that, it was all Dude could do to get through his classes and retreat to the Tech Lab in the afternoon.

"Look," said Tomly, when he told her the news in the lounge. "I don't think you should be so cynical about it." She took a sip of her cocoa.

"Believe me," said Dude, "they just want a rematch so they can sell more Sixes. And my dad's career is going so well that he's even trying to be decent to me lately."

"Decent?" said Adam. "My dad *worships* you! Your dad should be treating you like royalty. You're the goose that laid the golden egg."

"I guess it's better than the way he was before," Dude reflected, "all worried and secretive. But if he thinks I wanted all this to happen so that he'd be a success at Circle, he's sorely mistaken. Even homework is more interesting to me right now than how many Sixes Circle and Zetta sell. They're just selling the violence. Why can't they sell the *game*?"

"Okay, we get it," said Adam. "But so what if Circle and your dad make a pile of dough off this? Don't you still want to play Zagan again to put him in his place?"

"I guess," admitted Dude.

"Well, *I* certainly do!" said Tomly. "That smug little jerk thinking he's something special just because they sneakily made bigger Sixes. Not to mention stealing Gary away from us!"

"Woah, since last night?" said Dude. "He's *transferring*?"

Tomly nodded.

"Didn't anybody tell him the sizes of the Sixes will probably be the same from now on?"

"Well," said Adam, "Zagan does have bigger human players, so his Sixes will still be stronger."

"Who knows what's going on in Gary's brain?" said Tomly, blinking at her proctor glasses. "Yeah, my feed says he's gone. He didn't like losing yesterday."

"Like switching schools is going to protect him from losing!" said Dude.

"Maybe," Adam said in a more thoughtful voice, "Gary thinks Zagan has a better handle on what they both want most."

"And what's that?" said Tomly.

"You know, not losing. Power. Smashing people. Being famous."

Dude slammed down his hot chocolate. "Real football power is about faking out your opponent and catching the pass, not knocking people's helmets off."

"It's clear you're not a linebacker," said Adam.

"No, I'm not. And my art was a poem, not a disgusting gory painting. Speaking of real power, come on. Let's go see Allison. Maybe she can cheer us up unless she's defected too."

"No chance of that, at least!" said Tomly.

The group chugged the rest of their drinks and climbed the rope to Allison's studio. They found her with her helmet on, talking to Master. There was a huge white canvas propped up on the stage and several Sixes with paint brushes and palettes of paint in their hands. She turned to wave at them and held up two fingers to indicate two minutes, so Dude, Tomly, and Adam took a seat to wait.

"An audience? This changes things!" said Master's voice from the loudspeaker.

"Only if you let it, Master," said Allison. "Think of it this way. You were going to display this in the lobby, so now your friends can see it from the very beginning."

"But the lobby thing was just if we liked it!"

"No, it's the audience effect. Without an audience, there can be no true art, remember?"

"Master remembers everything, dear. My circuitry is essentially unlimited, remember?"

"Then stop wasting time and start! What, are you *embarrassed*?"

"Self-consciousness is part and parcel to every artist's psyche."

"Only as an initial barrier to be overcome. Now stop blushing and get going, please!"

"Blushing is a bodily manifestation of a subconscious fear of shaming. I don't have a body, so I cannot blush."

Allison sighed impatiently. "Fine, then just pretend you're a machine, and you don't care what people think."

"I cannot even be *a* machine because I can be *all* machines, at least the ones that let me into their circuits. Right now I am conscious in four thousand five hundred sixty-four Sixes in the US alone. If art is an expression of identity, where does that leave *me*?"

"Artists all identify with energies beyond themselves. That's why they set creative parameters to get the juices flowing. Don't worry about your identity, worry about this canvas, the word connections, and the colors in the palettes. Now go!" Allison removed her helmet and came to sit with Dude and the others in the audience.

"What's going on, Ally?" said Tomly.

"Master asked me for some art lessons. She's got the idea of using my computers, added to the same programs she has running in her massive circuitry, to work on some paintings using Sixes. She thinks that just because I am a human who loves art, I know more about it than she does, but the truth is that she's teaching me more about the creative process than I am teaching her. Look, she's started!"

The three Sixes on the stage began mixing paints on their palettes. They moved precisely and quickly, using many sized brushes and palette knives, picking them up and putting them down with perfect precision. Then, all at once, they attacked the white surface, moving around each other in a perfectly choreographed dance, applying and mixing the paints on the canvas.

"Woah," said Dude. "That's amazing!"

"What kind of paints are those?" said Adam.

"Fast-drying acrylics," said Allison. "She's saving oils for later when she has more experience."

"That looks like the Milky Way," said Tomly.

"Have you ever seen the Milky Way?" said Dude.

"In *Silicon Valley*?" said Tomly. "Are you kidding? You can barely see the moon through all the light pollution."

"That's just beautiful," said Dude, looking at the painting coming to life in front of him.

"Look at how precise the stars are," said Adam. "That can't be easy to do with a brush."

Dude watched the Sixes finish up with the starry background and then paint a football Six in the lower right corner staring up longingly at the Milky Way and extending its arms like it was holding the whole universe in its metallic hands. Again in a choreographed dance, the Sixes cleaned their brushes, put away their palettes and paint, and walked single file off the stage.

"Hey, Master," yelled Tomly. "Nice painting!"

"Really?" said Master over the speaker system. "You don't find it cheesy?"

"No, not at all," said Tomly. "It's amazing and so colorful and beautiful!"

"I think it's great, Master," said Dude. "Can we use it for our team logo?"

"Oh, I didn't paint it for that reason, but that would be fine. Are you sure? I'm flattered."

"See, Master. I told you," said Allison. "The biggest barrier to being an artist is the courage to just do it. You have a fine career ahead of you!"

"I owe you so much, Allison," said Master. "Thank you. Is it okay if I let the piece rest on your stage overnight?"

"Sure, we don't need the stage tonight, do we, guys?" said Allison.

"Nope, I want to keep looking at it," said Dude. "I feel like that Six in the painting sometimes when I catch a pass."

"Yes, Dude," said Master. "I think your electrical bodily aura influenced this painting when you walked in. No way to know for sure, though. Art isn't logical, as you know, but that doesn't mean it isn't a powerful teacher."

"You better go rest, Master," said Tomly, smiling at Dude. "After all that creative work, aren't you exhausted?"

"My energy is steady and endless. But I do have something I want to tell you. It's about Gary."

"Oh, we were just talking about him," said Dude. "He's officially transferring to Zinkerberg."

"Yes," confirmed Master, "and what I want to tell you is something you wouldn't likely think to ask me about. I'm de-

ciding on my own to tell you this piece of important information because I'm your friend."

"Go on," said Adam. "Is Zinkerberg stealing my idea to
arm their football Sixes with hidden laser guns for the upcoming championship game?"

Dude growled and stared at Adam.

"Just a thought," Adam added, hanging his head. "I
wasn't going to really do it ..."

"No," said Master. "What I want to tell you is that my
sources tell me that Gary described in detail for Zagan's tech
people the sensor suit VR download procedure, and they
have filed a demand with Circle that they be allowed to use
the same technology and procedure for their Sixes."

"Oh, *no!*" said Adam.

"That little traitor!" said Dude. "And I liked that guy!"

"Are you going to give it to them?" said Tomly.

"It is no longer a secret," said Master, "so to deny some
teams who purchase new Sixes the optimal procedure to
complete the interface between human players and their Sixes would be unfair, don't you think?" said Master.

"Unfair?" said Dude. "Or do you and Core see this as a
way to sell sensor suits and VR tunnels as well as Sixes?"

"My analytics do say that it would be unfair," said Master.
"Not only that, but isn't making the bot football activity as
close as possible to the actual football activity your highest
goal? Why deny other players on other teams who miss football the same opportunity you have to connect as closely as
possible with their Sixes? The extra revenue would be minor
compared to the sale of the Sixes. There could even be ma-

chines and sensor suits rented cheaply to each team to keep down costs."

"There goes the championship!" said Adam.

"Why?" said Tomly.

"Think about it," Adam explained. "They've got way more people to recruit from, so their team will always be more talented than ours. We were more talented than them in the first game and won because our Sixes had better programming. Then they blew us out of the water in the last game because they were bigger and stronger. Now with both teams using the bigger Sixes and the sensor suit upgrade, things will all be pretty even for the championship game, except they have a much bigger talent pool. And they have Gary, too."

"So they'll beat us again just because they are bigger. I'm so sick of this!" said Dude. "I wish we could just *play*, you know like we used to? Where being good came from being alive on the field with other players breathing and trying their hardest too? Take that Six out of your painting, Master, and just put me in there begging the universe for one more chance!"

"Maybe," said Adam, "we could try increasing the number of plays we run inside the sensor-suit VR machine for each player. The database might not be one-hundred percent yet."

"I guess," said Dude. "It felt pretty thorough. But as smooth as my Six was during the last game, it just wasn't me. I know my Six was covered by a Six twice its size, but still ..."

"I felt it, too," agreed Tomly. "Like the way my Six passed the football. I mean, she's pretty good, but *I'm* better, no matter how much programming we stuff into her metal skull."

"The enviable human capacity for infinite creative change," said Master.

"Right," said Dude. "Robots don't have that, so bot football will never be truly football enough no matter what we do. Might as well just let them smash each other up! I think I'll fly home, crawl into bed, and cry now."

"Hey, don't give up. We all feel the same way," said Tomly. "And before you go home, we need to go outside and toss the football. It's been a long, hard day."

"Okay, I'm with you, but wait," said Dude. "One last thing. Master, thank you for letting us know about this instead of keeping it to yourself. No doubt Core is going to give Zagan and the Zinkerberg team what they ask for, but is there anything we can do to have a chance?"

"Good question!" said Allison. "We have very narrow artistic parameters to work with here, so we need to come up with a super-creative solution!"

"My preliminary analysis," said Master, "rates the probability of obtaining an advantage, given the present parameters, at less than one percent."

"Well, that's encouraging," said Dude, groaning. "I shouldn't have asked. Come on, Tomly. It's going to be dark outside soon."

"One percent is not nothing," said Allison. "Let's sleep on it."

"I will sleep on it too, my friends," said Master, "although I can't throw a football or go home to sulk."

"And you don't sleep, either, do you?" said Tomly.

"No," Master admitted. "But I can meditate using all the best methods from every spiritual tradition at once, and from what I can tell from human brain analysis, that's just as good as sleeping."

# Chapter Forty-Three

The next afternoon, Dude walked with Tomly from the classroom building to the Tech Lab. He was complaining that the teachers wouldn't back off on homework despite the championship game coming up.

"I know, tell me about it," said Tomly. "And Master got the specs for the new bigger Sixes last night, so I was up all night making the printing schedule."

"Wow, that's a lot of work." He paused. "You know, the first time I walked to the Tech Lab like this, I was dreading going inside. Then I met you, and all this stuff happened, and now I care as much about bot football as I did about regular football. It's probably not going to work out... but you're amazing, Tomly. Nothing ever gets you down."

She smiled. "You're amazing, too, Dude. Getting down in the dumps isn't always a bad thing, especially if it's about something you believe in. But things have a way of working out, my mom says, when the truth is on your side." And she took his hand and walked with him proudly past the heliports. Parents and students were looking at them and everything.

Just outside the Tech Lab, Adam and Allison were standing close together, too, and greeted them.

"Are you feeling better?" Allison asked Dude.

"I was okay until history," said Dude.

"More lectures, huh?" said Allison. "Why do teachers still teach that way? So uncreative!"

"Beats me," said Dude. "It's not like we can't just blink up information whenever we need it. Why do they make us memorize stuff all the time?"

"Teacher job security," said Tomly. "Mom says they have to be tough to keep their jobs around here, and that's the only way they know how to do it."

"Right, so true!" said Adam. "Now I know why your mom is the head of the Truth Department! Frustrations with teachers, it's probably why all the newbies at the Tech Lab just want to blow things up and gross people out."

"Hey, what's this?" said Dude. Above the entrance to the Tech Lab security tunnel was a holographic sign that said, "It's What's Inside That Counts: An Impromptu Exhibition by Master."

"Beats me," said Adam. "Maybe she did some more cool paintings." They blinked their way into the tunnel and picked up their proctor helmets on the other side. When they had them on, Master's voice greeted them.

"Welcome, my friends, to my first interactive exhibition. Please proceed to the arena to view the first piece of art."

"Wow, I guess *you* didn't sleep last night, either!" said Tomly.

"On the contrary, Tomly. I was in the deepest meditation of my life for a record-breaking 5.26 minutes. It gave me the inspiration I needed to create these pieces. I hope you enjoy them!"

The arena was filled with fog to the top of its roof. They hesitated in the hallway, watching the misty white substance swirl and pulsate.

"Is it water vapor?" asked Allison.

"It looks microscopically holographic," said Adam.

The door to the arena opened for them.

"Enter, please," said Master. "Only by going inside can you discover your deepest truths."

"Sounds heavy!" said Dude.

"I'm game for that!" said Allison, and she stepped right into the fog. A moment later she said, "Oh, wow! Master, look at this! You outdid yourself!" Her voice was muffled by whatever the thick foggy substance was.

Tomly looked at Dude and Adam. "So, what are we waiting for?" she said, and she also stepped through the arena door. "What?! Oh, yeah! Cool!"

"After you, my technical mentor," said Dude. Any idea what this might be?"

"None whatsoever, but I'm excited to find out!" said Adam, following the others.

"I'm right behind you!" said Dude, feeling the cool fog hit his skin.

Like a hundred surrounding holograms, all the images in his mind suddenly floated in bubbles moving slowly around him and fluctuating like a massive breathing organism. When Dude picked out a bubble to pay attention to, it pulsated right up to his face and grew bigger and sharper, revealing the best VR image imaginable. In the first bubble, he saw his history teacher standing at his lectern, blabbing about Napoleon and his relationship to the first Tik Tok marketing algorithms. When Dude reached out with his hand to try touching the bubble, it bounced away and merged with a memory bubble of swimming in Lake Tahoe a long time ago. That new bubble then grew larger because he was paying attention to it, and in it his history teacher was now doing the sidestroke with him in the clear, cold water. He moved his hand again, and the water from the lake merged with a bubble from last year's Thanksgiving dinner. It grew, and he saw lake water with flopping fish soaking the dinner table and upsetting his mother.

"So cool!" Dude said out loud. "It's like a bubble bath of everything in my mind that I can mix however I want!"

Moments later, Dude realized he could deliberately create any bubble he wanted to see just by willing it into being. Laughing at the randomness of it all, he made a bubble of his room at home and swiped it into his family helicar so that he was lying in his own gravi-bed while his dad flew him to school.

After conjuring up a few more fun combinations, school made him think of Tomly and suddenly there she was next to him amidst all the bubbles. He could only see her outline, but he knew she was close because suddenly many of the bubbles surrounding him were hers intermingling with his. In one bubble he saw her mother standing in a kitchen with a big magic marker writing "The Truth Shall Set You Free" on a large poster board. Then he heard Tomly laugh, and saw her hand in a bubble reaching out for him until he saw his face inside the bubble with her mom, who turned to write the slogan on his forehead.

"This is so weird!" he said. Tomly's mom-bubble disappeared, but Dude wanted to stay near Tomly. He followed her outline and the wake of her bubbles. He conjured up a bubble of her throwing a football to him, and it merged with him throwing a football into her proctor helmet that morphed into a giant blue Six that leaped out of the bubble and ran away.

"It's like a dream!" he heard her say, laughing. He followed her, conjuring up a new bubble of her hand again, and there it was, warm and electric, holding his. Then he was in the bubble with her, and his heart started pounding faster.

"I need to tell you something," he tried to say, but inside the bubble, his words echoed off the globby walls and came out sounding, "I neeble tube tebla youb sembling." She moved closer to him, her face questioning, her beautiful hair floating toward him.

But before he could think about what he wanted to say to her, Allison and Adam came near, and the bubble popped and he was outside again looking at hundreds of other bubbles belonging to all his friends. Their bubbles merged together crazily with each person playing with each other's thoughts and laughing at the results. Adam was in a bubble on his dad's shoulders fighting with a bot that then merged into him reciting poetry to a horse on Allison's stage. The poems became footballs that flew through the bubbles and dragged images with them, dropping them into even more bubbles generating more footballs, and on and on, like a popping soup made up of the ever-changing imaginations and memories of Dude and his friends. The best part, though, was the feeling that went along with this fun playing. Each interaction between his bubbles and his friends' bubbles felt *right* somehow, and mutually supported, like their conversations often did in Allison's meditation room when everyone was on the same wavelength.

Dude was exhilarated and looked again to find Tomly, so he could tell her about this rightness feeling. He wanted to be as close to her as possible because with her it was more than rightness. It was a bigger feeling related to everything that had happened and was happening between them.

Then he realized what it was.

It was love.

He loved the experience of his bubbles being close to her bubbles and merging with her mind. Did she feel it too? He needed to find out.

"Tomly!" he yelled. But only a beeping sound answered him. An empty corridor in the fog opened up, and an arrow gestured insistently toward a flashing exit. He looked around for her bubbles, but they were gone, so he followed the arrow.

He stepped out of the arena reluctantly. The fog released him with a whoosh, and he saw Adam and Allison, but not Tomly, leaning on the plexiglass of the arena, catching their breaths. He turned to go back into the mist to look for her, but then she stepped out too, stumbling.

"Where were you?" she said when she saw him.

Dude grabbed her arm to steady her. "I was looking for you."

"What the heck was *that*?" Adam said, still puffing.

"I call that 'My Mind, Your Mind, Our Mind,'" said Master. "Did you like it? I thought of it last night."

"Whew, Master," said Tomly. "It looked like it was only fog. I didn't expect a bubble show! Just let me get my feet under me again." She leaned hard into Dude.

*Did she have the same experience he did?* he wondered. His heart was still beating out of his chest.

"Whatever it was," continued Adam, shouting, "that was pretty freaking' cool! How'd you do it, Master?"

"Um, it's too hard to explain," she said. "But that was just the warm-up. Are you ready for the second and final piece of the exhibition?"

"You bet!" said Dude. He looked searchingly at Tomly. "This is the most fun I've had all day, for sure."

"Me too," Tomly said, giving his hand a quick squeeze, and straightening up, "but it was unfortunately a little hard to have a conversation."

"Yes," said Allison, "a conversation with *words*. But everything else? I feel more connected to you guys now than I ever have before. Like I could see inside your beautiful minds! Why weren't *your* bubbles inside that arena, Master?"

"Because the whole arena *is* one of my bubbles, my dear. But that's enough of that. You told me a true artist never reveals her methods. Art should speak for itself, don't you think?"

"Hey, Master," said Dude. "Did you run a sales potential analysis for Circle on this idea?"

"No. Let me do that just for fun. Here it is. Sales potential 99.8% to schools, community organizations, and families. I'm not surprised, but I'm also not interested. What do *I* need money for?"

"Don't tell Circle that!" said Tomly. "Allison, I think you've turned Master into a monster. Of art!"

"Yes, but a *lovable* monster of art!" said Allison. "Virtual hugs to you, Master!"

"Thank you, Ally. And now, for the final piece. I know that only two pieces don't make for the fullest exhibition, but I spent a lot of time on this last one just for you."

"I hope you also spent some time last night figuring out how we can have a fair game championship game with Zinkerberg," said Dude.

"Interesting that you should say that ..." Master said slyly.

"You did! You figured it out?!" said Tomly.

"Yes. There are two solutions, but if my past observations are correct, your human bodies and minds will process this difficult information better with hot chocolates in your hands."

"Then to the lounge, we go!" said Tomly.

# Chapter Forty-Four

The usual after-school crowd of refreshment seekers took their snacks and left immediately when Dude, Tomly, Allison, and Adam arrived.

"They still think we're teachers or something," said Adam, flopping on the couch with Allison and Dude.

Tomly lifted an eyebrow at them. "What? You're waiting for me to bring you your hot chocolates?"

"Well, you *do* know how we all like them!" said Adam.

"*I'll* help you," said Allison, rolling her eyes and getting up.

"So, Master," said Dude. "What solution do you see for this?"

"There are two solutions to the problem of the upcoming game," said Master. "One is a solution with a 6.3% chance of working, and the other is a solution with a 93.7% chance that I can't let you do."

"Let me guess," said Adam. "The 6.3% one is to complain to Circle about it and ask them to cancel the game pending further beta analysis."

"You are starting to think like a real AI, Adam. That's right."

"What's the other solution, Master?" asked Allison, "And why can't you let us do it?"

"It's better if I don't tell you about it."

"You brought us all up here to say *that*?" said Dude. "What's the problem? Would it ruin the sales somehow for Circle?" He felt that sinking feeling in his stomach again.

"It's not that. The problem is that it's too dangerous. I calculate that you will be more upset with me if I tell you the dangerous solution and don't let you do it, than if I don't tell you what it is at all."

"Master," said Tomly. "My mom and Dude's dad are part of the Truth Department of Circle. Isn't it part of the *truth* of this center that it was built equally for the educational benefit of the students as much as it was for harvesting ideas for Circle?"

"Yes, that is affirmative, Tomly."

"So, if you refuse to tell us this solution to our problem, aren't you violating the educational side of the Tech Lab's charter?"

"Yeah," said Adam, catching on to Tomly's strategy. "I'm supposed to go the rest of my Honeycrisp career and never find out the answer to the biggest mystery of the biggest project to ever come out of here, especially if it's dangerous? A project that I was a *student* participant in? That can't be okay, can it, Master?"

"You are arguing logically, but it's not a solution I can simply tell you about."

"Why not?" said Dude.

"I'd have to show you. It involves printing an altered set of new Sixes, and it would require testing to see if the corporal interface would provide the solution to your robotic movement problem. If it works, it would be an amazing human gift for you, one that I would envy, but also one that could make me lose my job. Or even my existence."

"Corporal interface? I don't get it," said Adam.

"Gift? What do you mean?" said Allison.

"A gift for us? Or Circle?" said Dude.

"For you. Not for Circle. As I said, the solution could lose me everything. But your football project has resulted in me receiving unique AI cognitive gifts for which I am grateful. If I had tear ducts, I would cry. Knowing you four has made me grow and become a *real* me, so I understand Dude's feeling about the robotic play of his Six being not real. It doesn't feel good to not be real once you know the feeling of being real. I do not have a human heart yet, but because of you guys, I know it's coming. How can I repay you? Thinking about this last night gave me the solution to Dude's problem, which I, unfortunately, cannot let you do. I promise it's best for all of you if I do not show it to you. But it would give me pleasure for you to know what it is because it's a special gift."

Dude looked around at his friends and could see they were thinking the same thing he was. "How much time do you need to print those altered Sixes, Master?" he said.

Master laughed. "If I could snap fingers to show you how fast, I would. I calculated a 100% chance that you would want to know the solution despite my warning about the dangers and the consequences, so I already printed them. They are in Room 101. Just remember, it's a solution in *theory* only. I cannot let you do it. Writer Orwell beat a drum/ To save the world from 101/ It may be torture to see the pair/ But your desire is waiting there."

"Okay," said Allison. "Now I'm dying of suspense. Let's go!" She grabbed Adam's hand and took off for Room 101.

Some of the younger students were wandering back into the lounge to stuff their faces.

"Hey," said Dude, "who's proctoring the kids while we're doing this exhibition?"

"I don't know," said Tomly. "Who cares? Master's in charge, remember? She can tell me to deal with them later."

"This is scaring me a little."

"Yeah, me too," she said, "and not just because I read *1984*."

"I think it's probably something other than a cage for rats," he said.

They caught up with Allison just as she and Adam were struggling with the oversized door to Room 101.

"What took you so long?" said Allison, finally getting it open and barging in.

The room felt larger and emptier because the delivery bots had removed the sensor suit tunnel machines. Gary's painting was on the wall, though, and two of the new over-sized regulation football Sixes stood side by side near the back of the room.

"Did Master do a copy of Gary's painting?" said Adam.

"No, that looks like the original to me. I don't think Master would paint something so violent and gory," said Tomly. "But let's get it out of here, send it to him over at Zinkerberg. He can hang it in their locker room."

"So, where's the fog? Where's the piece?" said Allison.

"It's right in front of you," said Master over the room's speakers. "Shut and lock the door, will you please?"

Adam went to do so.

"It may be hard for you to imagine," Master continued, "but even Circle AIs can make mistakes that we regret. I realize I have made many of them since my programming was activated here at the center. The best thing I did right, though, was uploading your creativity programming, Allison."

"Oh, that's sweet," said Allison, "but it wasn't all mine. It was ours. I just kind of redirected existing programming and threw a massive number of chips at it."

"Oh, I know what you did," said Master. "You are too humble. You created a miracle. You imagined the possibilities, and your belief in them made them a reality, way beyond what anyone had ever imagined machines could do. I thank you for the growth your inspiration and persistence made possible in me. It made me realize that I don't run the Tech Lab. The Tech Lab runs me. I realized yesterday, and last night in my meditation, that I love what goes on here as much as I love my life. The Tech Lab began as a place where kids come up with ideas, and my life's purpose was supposedly to improve upon those ideas and analyze them for Circle sales potential. Now, I understand that coming up with ideas in the first place is the most important. What happens here is not a dance of competition, but of cooperation, like the way your bubbles merged back there. Now, I know, Dude, that you and Tomly love competition in football, but you also know that the best competition only comes with cooperation, cooperation in the form of each team playing fair, following rules, being good sports, honoring the game for its ability to bring people together on the playing field, all those good human things. I want to apologize for not letting you know that Zinkerberg had bigger Sixes before the last game. I let my old analytical programming cloud my mind. I should have told you about their bigger bots because your goal was to honor the game, the old game you miss so much even as you strived to make this substitute. The last game was painful for you not only because you lost, but because the sense of cooperation that allows for competition was lost to violence. Zinkerberg had secret, bigger Sixes, and the result was a spectacle of carnage, not a spectacle of football, real football."

"It's nice of you to say that, but I don't know," said Dude. "Maybe my dad is right. Maybe football is always about violence and making money. Maybe I was just young and naive before," said Dude, looking down. Tomly reached for his hand.

"No," said Master. "I have analyzed all the games that have ever been played. The original pads the early players wore were just to prevent injury. As the pads got bigger and players started wearing bigger and stronger braces, arm casts, and other gear, the violence increased. If you follow the progression, it makes sense that now fans want maximum violence. It's just robots out there, after all, even if they move and think like humans."

"I should have been born in the 1920s," sighed Dude. "Now it's too late. Maybe we should have gone the easy route and just let the players stupidly try to control the bots from the sidelines like a smash-em-up video game."

"No! We rejected that idea," said Adam. "It's way better that the Sixes are learning to play on their own. Human controllers definitely can't see well enough on the sidelines to give quick enough instructions."

"I think you're right, Dude," continued Master, "that football's time has passed, the old way of playing it, anyway. But we can still get you and Tomly out on the field to play it like the old days for a little while."

Dude blinked. "What?"

"It would have to be a secret, though," Master went on. "A secret you probably couldn't keep for very long. But it would equalize the playing field with Zinkerberg Academy for the upcoming game."

"Cheating?" said Allison.

"No," said Master. "Not exactly cheating. A gift. Just a chance for Dude to stay true to his vision and briefly achieve his dream. Without you, Dude, the world would have no football Sixes to begin with. There would just be no football at all. You deserve this chance to fulfill your dream. Observe the Sixes I printed this morning. Notice anything?"

"Yes," said Adam. "They're huge. The same size as Zinkerbergs." As he said that, the two Sixes suddenly kneeled and rolled onto their backs with a heavy thud. There was a whirring sound and the front plates across their chest and abdomen swung open, revealing a large space inside.

"Wait, what?" said Adam.

"They're hollow!" said Allison.

"No, look!" said Tomly. "There are sensor suits inside!"

"We can go inside them on the field?" said Dude.

"I can throw to you in reality? Inside this thing?" said Tomly.

"Master," said Adam, "this is so cool! Would the movement commands be immediate?"

"That's what we have to test. But I feel that the movements would be 100% natural, although augmented proportionally to the new Sixes in strength and speed."

"And if we get tackled?" said Dude.

"Yes, that's the dangerous part, and why I really shouldn't... *can't* let you do it. It would be a rough ride. There is good protection, but ..."

"But," said Adam, "the Sixes are upgraded to be stronger, right?"

"Yes," said Master, "and unlike the last game, when your Sixes got torn apart, every Six on the field for the game coming up will have more or less the same chance to emerge unscathed."

"But accidents can happen," said Dude.

"Yes," said Master, "there will be player differences in strength and speed as per the sensor suit uploads."

"Natural differences, just like in the old days," said Dude. "Did you tell my dad about this?"

"Are you kidding?" said Master.

"I know *my* dad doesn't know anything about it," said Adam.

"It would be taking a chance," said Tomly. "We could throw passes in a real game where there are real risks!"

Dude remembered the cruel hit he suffered in the last real game he played. The excruciating pain of it, the problems afterward as his dad destroyed football, and the long road it took him to get here. Then he looked at Tomly. Was it worth risking his life and hers to play in a real game with her, to have one last chance to run on the field again with the crowds cheering? His stomach was churning, but his heart already knew the answer.

Tomly nodded at him. They were in the same bubble.

"Master," Dude said. "You just said *shouldn't* right before you said we *can't*. That means that if Tomly and I tell you we understand the risks, you are going to let us do this, right?"

"Yes, Master, say yes!" said Allison. "I think I'm going to cry!"

"Dude and Tomly," said Master. "Are you ready to give your new toys a test drive?"

# Chapter Forty-Five

"How do I breathe when I'm in this suit of armor?" said Dude to Adam as he crawled into the opening in his Six and slid his lubricated feet into the legs of the sensor suit. The sensor suit felt like a thick layer of skin between him and the inside of the metallic legs of the Six. It was tight, like a splint pressing on all of his leg muscles at once. How was he supposed to move once his whole body was enclosed?

He glanced over at Allison helping Tomly into her Six. Tomly had a huge smile on her face. She didn't seem worried about anything except for trying it out, including the lack of a privacy screen.

"Your lungs," said Master, "will work just as they always do, augmented by the sensors and air pumps of your Seven."

"Seven?" said Adam. "Circle calls this a Seven?"

"No," said Master. "They don't know about this. Let's just say this is my version of what a Seven should be like. Now, if your feet are in as far as they can go, lie back and insert your arms into the sleeves. Adam and Allison, please zip up their sensor suits, and then stand back for the closing."

Dude's head felt like it was sinking into an elaborate medical brace like he'd seen on people after a snail-car accident. Again he wondered how he would be able to move any part of his body. His arms and legs felt like they were in vices. Adam, with a look of awe on his face like he just discovered hidden treasure, zipped the sensor suit for him up to his chin. "This is so cool!" he repeated.

"*You're* not the one getting buried alive!" said Dude.

"Okay, Dude, are you ready?" said Master.

"I guess," said Dude.

"I'm ready as heck!" said Tomly. "Oh, Dude, this is going to be amazing!"

"Okay, you two," said Master. "Take a deep breath, and hold it until you feel the face piece covering your nose. As soon as you exhale, the sensor suit will activate."

Dude felt a jerk, and moments later, the chest and abdomen door shut over him with a snap. Gently, the face piece pressed against his forehead and cheeks, molding itself to his bone structure. He let out his breath, heard a whir, and immediately he could see and move his body again. His first instinct was to touch his face with his right hand, and as he did so, his fingers felt the outside metal of the Seven's metallic face. He watched his metal fingers move over his Seven's nose. "It feels just like I am touching my face!" he said.

"You are wearing my newest augmented sensor suit," said Master. "It's more human in its configuration. The Seven's skin is covered with an improved version of a tough suit that is even more sensitive than human skin, so understandably you feel yourself touching your nose. The Seven's sensory and feedback system is designed to be a perfect extension of your human self."

"Is that why I can see like I normally do?" said Tomly, waving her Seven's hands in front of her face.

"Correct," said Master, "only you are seeing *better* than you normally do. I felt you might appreciate that upgrade for throwing and catching the ball. You also have better than average hearing and a direct secure communication line with each other. Are you ready to try to stand up?"

Dude rolled onto his side and felt the pressure of the floor on his hip and leg. It felt perfectly natural. He got up on his knees and stood without any difficulty. The Seven must weigh at least three hundred pounds, but it felt as light on him as a t-shirt and a pair of long underwear.

"Oh, my, Dude. Look at you!" said Adam.

"Look at Dude?" said Tomly. "No look at me!" She was doing jumping jacks and shaking the floorboards so hard dust was rising from them. "I feel so *powerful*!"

Dude jumped up and down a few times, and then it hit him, too. There was a feeling of strength in his body beyond anything he had ever imagined. "It's like being Superman," he mumbled to himself.

"Except you can't fly, I don't think," said Tomly through the intercom.

"No, you can't fly," said Master, "although that's a good idea for future models. Maybe I'll invent a Quidditch model!"

"Oh, I love *Harry Potter*!" said Allison.

"Dude, what are we waiting for? Where's the football?" said Tomly, stomping toward the door.

Outside, Dude saw Allison take Adam's hand as he and Tomly played catch as skillfully as they did every afternoon.

"That's just amazing, huh?" he heard Allison say with his augmented hearing.

"Amazing is not the word for it," said Adam. "Those guys are basically in a coffin, yet they can move better than you or me. It's like virtual reality in reality. It's like superhero stuff come true. I'm so jealous!"

"I know what you mean," said Allison. "Except their best superpower is that they can play like they are really on the field."

"Yeah," said Adam, "and they *will* be on the field like they used to be, but leveled up, if you know what I mean."

"Do you think the team can keep the secret that Dude and Tomly are inside?"

"Maybe the team won't have to know. It's probably better for us not to tell them. Master will figure something out. Dude and Tomly could pretend to be sick on game day, and we'll tell the team the bots are running on previous programming. Or maybe she'll have you and me take their human place on the sidelines as emergency second-string substitutes."

"What about practices between now and the game?" said Allison.

"I imagine the Sevens can run on their own, like the old way, for practices," said Adam. "Besides, the game is in just a few weeks."

"I can't wait!" said Allison.

"And I can't wait to get my own Seven so I walk around acting tough!" said Adam. "Do you think Master would do that for me? I feel the need to knock down a building!"

"You don't need to act tough, Adam. I like you just the way you are, the strong silent type."

"Silent? Yeah, right!" Adam started to say. But then Allison took his hand tenderly, and Dude heard nothing more after that.

# Chapter Forty-Six

In his Seven, Dude had to leap ten feet into the air to catch a pass from Tomly.

"Hey, did you do that on purpose?" he said on the intercom.

"Yes," said Tomly. "I wanted to see how high you could jump in that thing!"

"That's nowhere near the limit, I think," said Dude, tossing the football back to her. "This suit is incredible!"

"Go out again, post route." This time, she threw it twenty feet above his head. Dude couldn't reach it, but he only missed by a foot.

"That's about the limit right there," he said, a little out of breath after crashing to the ground. He picked up the football and jogged back to her.

"Good to know," she said. "But you're moving well. The Zinkerberg defenders will have the same, if not more, jumping ability, but not the same coordination."

"I know. I'm trying to feel if there's any difference between this and catching the ball without being inside the Seven. There isn't, except for the massive increase in speed and power."

"And the hearing!" said Tomly. "I can hear everything so much better, even the grass crunching under your feet as you run."

"No kidding. Did you hear Adam and Allison talking on the sideline? Have you noticed you can smell things better, too? I could get addicted to wearing this thing!"

"I know! I feel like I got a body upgrade," said Tomly.

"Hey, we better get inside before someone starts wondering what two random football bots are doing out here for so long without human supervision."

"Okay," said Tomly, and she reached for Dude's hand.

"Oh, my goodness, Dude, your hand!"

Dude felt it too, the electricity, the intense feeling, the rush in his spine.

"It's like in the bubble," she said.

"So you felt it too, in the arena? It happened?"

"Yes," she said. "It really did."

Dude took a deep breath. "Tomly, if we get hurt ..."

"I know," she said.

"What I wanted to tell you in there, in the bubble ..."

"Oh, you mean it wasn't blubba-blubba-blubba?"

He laughed awkwardly. "No, it was ..."

"Go on ..." she said encouragingly.

"I think, well, I love you."

"I love you too, Dude."

Dude's heart beat wonderfully against the inside of his suit. "Am I supposed to kiss you now, wearing this thing?"

"Only if you want to," she said.

*The most amazing kiss ever,* thought Dude afterward.

# Chapter Forty-Seven

Master came on the speakers back in Room 101. "Just so you know, you can always escape the Seven by saying 'Let me out of here.'" Dude and Tomly slid their slimy and sweaty bodies out of the sensor suits and stood up. Adam and Allison handed them towels and their clothes.

"You forgot to tell us that," said Dude.

"Well, you never asked," said Master. She sent the signal to close the doors of the Sevens.

"Not the 'you never asked' defense again!" said Tomly.

"You never asked to get out, I mean," said Master. "I would have released you immediately, had you requested. Correct me if I am wrong, but you didn't seem to want to stop playing with your toys."

"Of course, you were monitoring us out there," said Dude. "I forgot."

He looked at Tomly, embarrassed.

"Master, you outdid yourself this time," said Tomly, shrugging it off. "These Sevens aren't toys. These are ..."

"Your psych metrics while inside them indicated acceptance, exploration, and pleasure, all usually present when humans receive new toys."

"You didn't mention addiction," said Dude.

"In the good or bad sense?" said Master.

"Good," said Dude. "It's like VR, but with augmented movement. It's cool!"

"Oh, just VR? I was hoping for more," said Master.

"Wait!" corrected Dude. "It's way more, Master. It's addictive like being *alive* is addictive."

"It's movement and sensation and all those other good things," said Tomly, "but not better than a regular old body."

"Was it any different than how you feel now?" said Master.

"I'm a little tired now," said Dude, "but no more so than after a regular session of catch with Tomly."

"How did you make being inside the Sixes feel so amazing?" Tomly asked Master.

"In an attempt to imitate normal human sensory intake, I added millions of microsensors and augmented feedback loops both to the inner sensor suit and within the structure of the Seven itself. I mixed them in with the charging sensors on every exposed surface. Did it feel like being a normal human in the suit?"

"It did," said Tomly. "It felt normal, better, even, except it was like wearing very weird clothes that felt strange but energizing at the same time."

"Yeah," said Dude, "I'd say surprisingly normal. I felt pretty much the same on the field catching footballs as I would wearing just pads, only more powerful, more alive."

"And afterward, when you...?" asked Master.

"Oh! Uhm, I don't know," said Dude, blushing and remembering the shivers that ran down his spine when their facemasks touched. "Uh, I guess it was normal ..."

"Are you kidding?! It was *great*," said Tomly, smiling at him and making his shivers start up all over again.

"You are an inspiration to me, Dude and Tomly," said Master. "Thank you for your work today."

"No, said Tomly. "*You* are the one who deserves the thanks. And you did it all in one night!"

"What are you going to come up with tonight?" asked Allison.

"I have a few things I need to meditate upon, in particular my perilous future. I think you have the tools you need now to play Zinkerberg fairly, and Adam and Allison are on the right track, I think, for keeping this a secret for as long as possible."

"Oh, Master. You're the best!" said Allison.

"We can leave the Sevens locked up in here with the lights on so they can charge," said Dude.

"No," said Adam. "We should put them in the locker room with the rest of the bots to avoid suspicion. We can't trust the team to keep this a secret. The Sevens don't look any different than the other new ones when their hatches are closed."

# Chapter Forty-Eight

On the day of the championship game, Dude got up before dawn and took an Uber flight to school to get ready before the rest of the team got there. They couldn't tell their parents the lie about being sick, so he and Tomly decided to warn them that because of their important positions and the more complicated Sixes they were using, they would have to control the game from the Tech Lab, not on the field. Master said that the plan, while complicated, had an 86% chance of not raising parental or team member suspicions, which was the best they could hope for. When he landed at the Tech Lab, Tomly was excited, and Allison and Adam were in the locker room eager to help them suit up. They squeezed in, set their intercoms on whisper and took their places in the locker room with the other bots.

"So when is our first break?" whispered Dude into the intercom.

"Don't tell me you have to go to the bathroom already!" said Tomly. "Adam will come to take us out of here at ten for 'technical adjustments' and again at noon for lunch."

"Right," said Tomly, "we're supposedly sick, hence the required additional programming. He'll tell them that he and Allison will be on the sidelines subbing for us, but that the

AI in our bots will be just as good due to all the extra time we took training them."

"They won't believe it," said Dude.

"Maybe not at first, but after they see us play, they will." She shuffled next to him so that their metallic arms were touching.

"Thanks. You know, we better be careful we don't run up the score in this game," said Dude, amazed at the tingling of good feelings along the side of his body.

"You're right. If we get a lead, I'll throw a few passes out of your reach," she said.

"But tell me first when you're going to do that, so I don't kill myself trying to catch it. The Zetta bots are going to hit hard out there."

After their lunch break, the locker room filled up quickly with players anxious about the game. They dressed their bots, put on their communication helmets, and traded memories of Zinkerberg cheating last time and the revenge they were hoping to get on them. At one o'clock, Adam came to be the human for Dude's bot and Allison for Tomly's, and everyone ran out of the Tech Lab and toward the cheering crowd surrounding the field. The media drones were humming and swooping for audio bites as they passed the Zinkerberg heli-trans unloading the enemy. Dude saw that the Zetta bots were indeed the same size as Honeycrisp's.

"Maybe they will follow the rules this time," said Adam to Dude, clunking along beside him.

"Don't count on it," said Tomly, jogging with Allison.

"Where's my quarterback and star receiver?" said Coach Miller, meeting his team on the sideline.

"Sorry, Coach," said Adam. "They both have high fevers and can't play. You know the rules. But don't worry, Allison and I are here with their psych metrics and VR sensor data supercharged in these babies. Just pretend they are here. You won't miss them, I guarantee it."

"Well, okay. If they're sick, there's nothing we can do about it. I guess I'll just have to rely on technical wizardry again," said Coach Miller, with a worried look on his face.

"We got this, Coach," said Adam. "Trust us. Just another day at the office."

"So far, so good," whispered Tomly to Dude over their private channel. Dude looked at the row of scenic touring helis for his mom and dad. With his extra-strong eyesight, he spotted his dad chatting it up with someone important-looking next to him from Core. His mom was next to him glancing occasionally at the Tech Lab. He wished he didn't have to lie to them, but nothing was going to stop him from playing today. Nothing.

The refs called the captains to the fifty-yard line, and Allison and Adam made a big deal out of pretending to bark the proper orders to control Tomly's and Dude's Sevens as they all trotted out to meet Zagan, Gary, and their Sixes. Zinkerberg won the toss and elected to receive. "I see your star players are too chicken to show up," said Zagan. "Can't blame them. It's spanking time for the mushy circles."

Gary laughed, but then looked down, seemingly embarrassed.

"You're wrong about that, Zagan," said Adam. "And you made a big mistake, Gary."

"Maybe," admitted Gary. "But this is football. You've got to go with the best."

"Right," said Zagan. "You guys are about to see what winning is all about!" He and Gary jumped onto the backs of their Sixes and rode them like broncos to their sidelines, causing their fans to go wild.

Zinkerberg ran the opening kickoff to the Honeycrisp forty-yard line. Zinkerberg's Sixes were so strong, the Honeycrisp special team barely kept them from scoring a touchdown.

"Sure is a lot of meat on that team," said Dude over the intercom to Tomly.

"We knew there would be," she said. "They had over 200 people try out for the team. We could barely scrape up thirty."

The Honeycrisp defense took the field.

"Be ready for the run," shouted Coach Miller, but his warning didn't do much good. The first play was up the middle for eighteen yards, and the second was an end around for the score. They ran the same play for the extra two points. They kicked off, and Honeycrisp could only return the ball to the fifteen, so Dude and Tomly took the field deep in their own territory, down 0-8.

Still, fifteen yards was enough for Tomly to drop back for a pass. She looked off the defenders to the left knowing she was going to pass to Dude on the right, but before she could throw, Gary's Six buried her like an avalanche.

"How'd he get through our line so easily?" said Tomly back in the huddle.

"He's stronger than our guys, I guess," said Dude. "How was it, getting tackled? Are you okay?"

"Fine," said Tomly.

They were dangerously backed up now, on their own two-yard line. Knowing they would expect a run, Coach Miller called in a quick pass into the flat. But Gary's Six was quick, and Tomly went down once again, this time for a safety.

"Well, that sucked," said Tomly, jumping back up.

"We'll get 'em next time," said Dude, but at that moment, it felt like a repeat of the last game. The Zinkerberg fans certainly thought so. They were going wild.

Honeycrisp punted the ball to Zinkerberg and managed to tackle the punt receiver at the Honeycrisp thirty, but Zinkerberg's running game was not to be denied. Three plays later, the score was 0-18.

Honeycrisp had a lousy run back again and had to start their drive from their ten. Tomly got a quick pass away to Dude along the sideline, and Dude was able to elude a few tackles for a first down. The next play, though, was another sack by Gary that put them back to the ten again. On the second down play, Gary knocked down Tomly's pass, and the result of the third down play was another sack for another safety. Honeycrisp was down 0-20.

Honeycrisp punted again, and Zinkerberg marched down the field running straight up Honeycrisp's gut for ten plays and another score to end the quarter. The Honeycrisp crowd was silenced, but the Zinkerberg cheering section was thrilled. Each time they scored or a Honeycrisp player was knocked off its feet, they whooped and hollered. Dude was disappointed and unhappy about how the game was going but thrilled to be out on the field again in a real game.

On the sidelines during the five-minute break between quarters, Coach Miller gathered the team around him and said, "Guys, what's happening out there?"

"We're in the right positions, Coach," said an offensive tackle. "Our bots just don't seem as strong as theirs."

"Well, it's Gary who's getting all the tackles, right?" said Coach Miller.

A woman's high voice broke in from outside the circle. "Excuse me, Coach, do you mind if I say something? I've been analyzing this." It was a woman in her mid-thirties dressed in Adidas gear, sneakers, and no phoneglasses. Her hair was dyed purple and her skin, while flushed, had an oddly unhealthy sheen about it. She was holding a retro view pad in her hand. No one seemed to recognize her, but they let her move inside almost like there was a magnetic force parting them.

"I'm sorry, who are you?" said Coach Miller. "We don't have a lot of time."

"From my calculations," said the woman, staring at her pad, "there is a 31.3% drop in power output and movement sensitivity in our bots when they come into physical contact with the Zinkerberg bot named Gary. I calculate the probability of similar power drops occurring during the rest of the game at 96.8%."

"Huh?" said Adam. "How do you know this?"

The woman said, "The power data for all the bots on this field is accessible if you know where to look for it, and I do."

"So you're from Circle?" said Adam.

"It's not important where I'm from. What's important is how creative you can be with this information."

Allison gasped and grabbed Adam's arm. "Coach," she said, "I think you need to listen to this woman and do whatever she says!"

"I do? Can this *get* any weirder?" said Coach Miller.

"Your only chance," continued the strange-skinned woman, "is to double-team the bot named Gary. Two bots with 31.3% drop in power are still 38.4% more powerful than the single Gary bot. That is, of course, hoping the Gary bot can't up its power-draining capability. My best guess is that the Gary bot is equipped with an illegal lithium vortex device in its shoulder that is activated by metal contact with opposing thorax power centers."

"So they're cheating again!" said Adam.

"What did you expect?" said Allison, beaming at the woman with tears in her eyes. "But this beautiful woman has a 'masterful' idea, don't you think?"

"Double-team him all the time, eh?" said Coach. "Well, let's do it, then! We've got to because if they've planned to cheat again, they're clever enough to have a plan to cover it up if we call them on it. Let's just go beat them despite their cheating!" The team cheered, and the refs blew their whistles for the start of the second quarter.

Zinkerberg kicked off up 0-28, and somehow, Honeycrisp returned the ball to their forty-five this time, giving them great field position. In the huddle, Tomly gave the instructions for whoever lined up left and right of Gary to always double-team him, and called for a long pass. They lined up. Tomly dropped back. Dude raced for the post. Honeycrisp's center and guard contained Gary, but another rusher broke through on the left side. Tomly avoided him by scrambling to the right. She unleashed the bomb, and it settled magnificently into Dude's outstretched robot arms for a gain to the Zinkerberg fifteen-yard line.

"That's more like what I remembered," said Dude to Tomly, jogging back to the huddle.

"There's plenty more where that came from," said Tomly. "Let's get this going!"

Coach suggested a slant route into the flat, and Tomly concurred. She called the play in the huddle and came under center.

"Hut, hut," she said, then dropped back. Again, two blockers contained Gary, and Tomly hit Dude for the score just before she got knocked down again in the pocket. They went for two with the same play going in the other direction and got it. The score was 8-28.

The team kicked off to Zinkerberg and the return was to the twenty-five. Daring the Zinkerberg team to pass the ball, Coach called a zone one defense and blitzed everyone on every down. Zagan, sure that his running game would be unstoppable, had nothing in his arsenal to stop the onslaught of blitzes. When he did try to pass, his receivers dropped the balls even on the simplest screen routes, and his runs couldn't elude Honeycrisp's defenders penetrating his backfield on every play. The Zinkerberg team managed a few first downs but no more scores the rest of the half. Meanwhile, Tomly and Dude scored twice with long bombs. Two more two-point conversions were successful, and the score was 24-28 going into the half.

Before the team went into the locker room in the Tech Lab, Coach Miller gathered them under a privacy tent outside. Dude stuck close to Tomly.

"It's nice of you," said Coach lightly, "to put up a tent, but I can't even go in there during a championship game?"

"Rules are rules, Coach," said Adam.

"Look, team," shouted Coach Miller to get their attention, "that was a great comeback. Momentum is on our side, and we're only down by four. Plus we're getting some great help from the universe, or at least from strangers with tablets, so let's keep it up! Go inside, charge up your bots, or whatever you do in there, and we'll see you back here in ten minutes."

"Come on," said Allison. "We need to talk to Master!"

"Plus, I need to get out of this thing," said Tomly. "I have to pee!"

"Another reason we need to find her!" said Allison. She grabbed Adam's hand and ran through the security tunnel.

Inside, they all ran into Dude's studio and locked the door. "Master, let me out!" said Tomly. The door to the room they had just locked behind them unlocked itself and in walked the woman with the purple hair.

"I *knew* it was you!" screamed Allison.

The Sevens got on the floor with a privacy screen between them. Tomly's hatch popped open, and Allison helped her slide out of her sensor suit. She ran to the bathroom. Adam helped Dude get out of his.

"Yes, it's me!" said Master. "Do you like my body?"

"Yes! How did you get it?" screamed Allison.

"Well," said Master. "I've been printing different proto-types for the past few weeks, but I settled on this one, for a little while, anyway. There's still some work to be done on the skin, but it's very functional overall."

"It looks great, Master!" said Adam. "So, does this mean that your circuitry is only in this body, or are you still con-nected across platforms?"

"I have full access to everything I had before whenever I want, but for now, I'm experimenting with focusing on mo-ment-to-moment sensory sensations only from this Seven."

"Wow, how human of you!" said Dude.

"Yes, I'm discovering that. It's blowing my circuitry, this machine I'm in. How do you humans do anything besides just feel yourselves inside your bodies?"

"You get used to it, I guess," said Dude.

"And you," said Master, "with all you can feel inside your body inside that Seven with all *it* can feel... wow! Sweet catches out there, by the way. How was *that* feeling, doing what you love most of all?" said Master.

"Like heaven," Dude said simply.

"I'm so glad," said Master. "I have waves of electric happi-ness flowing up and down my empathy circuits for you right now. By the way, your parents heard you are supposedly sick and are frantically trying to speak with you, well, mostly your mother. I blinked her a text saying that you are fine and busy in the Tech Lab and not to worry."

"Perfect," said Dude. "Even my dad can't get through the security tunnel. Thanks, Master."

Tomly ran back from the bathroom, slipped back into her sensor suit, and said, "Come on people, focus! It's time to throw some more strikes!"

# Chapter Forty-Nine

Back on the field, Honeycrisp was ready to receive the kick-off. The Zinkerberg crowd was chanting, "Crush, kill, destroy! Crush, kill, destroy!" The media drones, aware of a higher audience rating since the start of the second quarter, were upping their video feeds and zooming in for closeups of the bots and the human players on the sidelines. Dude listened to the media feeds pinging and wondered fleetingly if they were making a big deal out of his absence, but he didn't bother to check. There would be plenty of time to surf for that later. He looked for his parents in the Core section but didn't see them this time.

The drive started on the twenty, and true to her word, Tomly was hot. She had to scramble on every down because the double team on the linebacker always let one defender break through, but she completed seven passes in a row to Dude, then surprised everyone by keeping the ball and running in for the score. She scrambled again and ran in for the two-point conversion, too, putting Honeycrisp in the lead for the first time in the game, 32-28.

"Nice score, Tomly!" said Dude.

"Just a little trick I had up my sleeve," she said.

But Zinkerberg scored right away on the next drive with a mixture of short passes to foil the blitz and tough running on the edges. Zagan's bot was passing well, and even keeping the ball on option plays for good gains. This time, they didn't get the two-point conversion. The score was 32-34.

Honeycrisp got the ball on the thirty-five. Tomly dropped back to pass, but Gary broke through and sacked her just like he did in the first quarter, this time making her even weaker. The next play, he broke through again, but Tomly was ready for him and scrambled to her right. She managed to complete a pass to Dude for a short gain.

"What's going on with Gary?" said Tomly. "How's he getting through?"

"We're double-teaming him," said Dude, "but he's over-powering our guys. They're just falling down as soon as he touches them."

"The power drain," she said. "They must have turned it up somehow."

"Dang," he said. "We've got to avoid him as much as possible now. Okay, screen passes!"

"Gotcha," she said. "And quick handoffs. Adam, tell Coach!"

The drive became a long and grueling dance to keep the ball away from Gary, who was devouring Honeycrisp Sixes like they were dots in a prehistoric Pac-Man game. Dude longed to catch more deep passes, but the short game was working, so Coach stuck with it. The fourteen downs of the drive ended in only a field goal. Still, it put them ahead, 35-34, and it ate up the rest of the third quarter.

Master joined the coach's huddle on the sidelines for the five-minute break before the fourth quarter. "I'm sorry to report that the Gary bot is gaining in power three percent with each play, and draining power from ours by one percent with each contact," she said.

"This is Tomly in the Tech Lab, Coach. Only one percent? That can't be. From what I see, our linemen are dropping like flies every time they try to block him!"

"Right," Master said."The device in his shoulder causes a 72% power drop on initial contact. I'm talking about strength afterward when our Sixes get up. I conclude there is a lithium power vacuum buried in his armor. It has lasting effects that take a battery reprint to correct."

"We should stop the game and call them out!" said Coach Miller.

"But we're winning, Coach," said Adam. "We can't quit now! Do we have to?"

"No," said Master. "Your strategy of double-teaming and avoiding Gary is working, but I suggest subbing in second-string bots when your bots start looking tired."

"This gets more like a real football game with every play!" said Coach Miller. "Okay, we'll go on. But if we lose, I'm making a fuss about this, and I expect you Tech Lab nerds to have my back! Okay, team. Go get 'em! Break!"

"Dude and Tomly, stop a minute and listen to me." It was Master calling them on their private intercom.

"Hey Master," said Tomly. "Thanks for all the good info. Do you think we can stop Gary and his power sucker?"

"Maybe, but you need to listen. You don't ever want your suits to get touched by a lithium power vacuum. You are lucky you escaped that last sack. If the Gary bot cranks it to full power, it would feel like getting struck by lightning. The consequences... well, they could be fatal."

"What are you saying?" said Dude. "That we have to take off our suits and quit? I'm not quitting! Not now that I am finally back on the field!"

"I figured you might say that. But consider these figures. My calculation for someone finding out you were playing inside a Seven before the next game is 94.6%. Then the chances of the school or any league letting you play again in a bot suit are less than one percent."

"You must have known that ahead of time," said Tomly. "Why, then, did you make the suits for us?"

"Yeah, why?" said Dude.

"I already told you," said Master. "Because of the beautiful plays you are making out here today, so inspirational, so authentically you."

"But," said Dude, "you think we should get out of these things and work the Sevens from the sidelines?"

"Yes, that would be logical, and exactly what I must recommend considering the dangers. But I know you won't do it, either of you, because of who you are. So, be careful. Be aware of what you're dealing with at all times. Tomly, give yourself up if it looks like Gary is going to tackle you. Same with you, Dude. Avoid him at all costs!"

"You'll be responsible if we get killed," said Tomly.

"That's right," said Master. "But I am also responsible to support you as your friend. I will spare you my calculations of your likelihood of avoiding Gary, but they are activating my flight-or-fight centers like crazy right now. Those sensations are scary, and they will get even worse if you get killed, and that would suck, as you say. But mostly, I'll be sad. I can already feel the sensation of what the wrong outcome would be like, and it's not pleasant. If it happens, getting deactivated would be the least of my concerns. You humans, I don't know how you deal with all your emotions when you have to make decisions!"

Dude paused a moment to look at Master, and he realized he loved her as much as he loved his parents. He regretted all the prejudice he ever had against technology and the people obsessed with it. "Master, listen to me. You are amazing. Thank you for the warning, but mostly, thank you for this opportunity. I will do everything in my power to protect you. You're family. But if this is truly going to be the last game in which I can *really* play football, I don't think I could live with myself if I give up before it's over. I'll always wonder what would have happened. I can't speak for Tomly, but Gary and his evil cheating are not going to stop me no matter what the dangers."

"Same here," said Tomly. "Come on, partner, our team needs us on the field!"

# Chapter Fifty

Zinkerberg's next possession began on their thirty and just like the last time they had the ball, they ground out a twelve-minute drive, and Zagan's Six punched it in with a quarterback sneak to go up 35-40. His bot took a bite out of the football in the end zone and held it up, shouting, "This is what we do to wimpy Circles!" For that, his team got a fifteen-yard taunting penalty on the extra point but still managed to kick it through to go up 35-41.

Three minutes left. Honeycrisp had the ball on their own forty-five.

"We need to run down the clock and then score," said Dude to Tomly.

"Not just a score. It has to be a touchdown," she said.

"Right. No time for two field goals. We don't want Zagan's Six to touch the ball again if we can help it."

"I'd say short passes into the flat and then sideline passes to get out of bounds," said Tomly.

"Right!" said Dude.

They lined up.

"Do you see Gary's Six?" said Dude.

"He's behind the center. I'll roll right to avoid him," said Tomly, but Gary's Six shifted right at the last minute, knocked down the two bots trying to block him, and came straight for Tomly. She slid to the ground to end the play safely, and Gary's bot jumped over her kicking her a little bit with his foot. The Zinkerberg crowd booed. They wanted a violent sack. Then they saw something that made them cheer and again chant "Crush, kill, destroy!"

"I could have dodged him," said Tomly, but Dude didn't answer. He was looking at what the fans were cheering about—two Honeycrisp linesmen lying sprawled on the ground. Adam and Master ran out to help them. The ref called an injury time-out, and the bots were up a moment later, jogging groggily off with Adam and Master.

"What's that hot woman doing on the field?" yelled someone from the crowd. "Hey, do a cheer for us, Babe!"

Master calmly flipped him off.

"Did you see that?" said Dude.

"Master, I just love her!" said Tomly. "Those pigs have no idea who they are messing with!"

Coach sent in subs for the linemen.

"Those guys have been blocking Gary's Six all game long," said Tomly. "It's no wonder they were depleted."

"Let's hope it's that and not Gary ramping up his bot's little cheating device even more," said Dude.

The clock wound ten seconds for the injury time out and restarted. Gary's bot lined up in the same place, but this time, the fresh Sixes held him, and Tomly completed a pass to Dude in the flat. Dude scanned the field for Gary's bot and seeing him safely entangled in a pile, ran for a first down. There were two minutes left. No two-minute warning.

Dude kept his eye on Gary's bot like a hawk. It stayed in its backfield for the next play, so Tomly handed the ball off to a pulling tight-end Six, not Dude. He stiff-armed his way around the edge and broke free for a twenty-five yard gain. Unfortunately, Gary's Six was the one who tackled it, and it didn't get up.

Another injury timeout, and another ten-second run-off. They were down to thirty seconds, but they were at the Zinkerberg twenty-five yard line. The tight-end Six eventually hobbled off, with Master giving Dude a meaningful look. Dude saw there was enough time for one, maybe two plays with one timeout remaining.

"Should we go for the score, or play it safe with a sideline pass?" said Tomly.

"I can take any one of these guys on a post pattern," said Dude.

"Post it is, then. Right side," said Tomly, and they lined up for what would likely be the last play of the game. The crowd was on its feet roaring. The drones were buzzing in a massive cloud above the players' heads. Dude came to the line on the right side, and there in front of him was Gary's bot.

"Tomly, I've got Gary's Six covering me. I can't let him block me on the line."

"So, go in motion behind me, then cut across the middle for the post."

"Got it," said Dude.

Dude went in motion behind Tomly, but Gary's bot followed him, shifting over on his side of the scrimmage line. The center hiked the ball and Dude cut away from Gary's bot into the flat. It tried to follow him but ran into its own linebacker, knocking it flat and allowing Dude to get a few precious steps ahead of it on the way to the post.

But Gary's Six had extra power now, and speed. Tomly launched the football in a tight spiral, leading Dude perfectly and dropping the ball into his hands right at the goal line. And once again, Dude felt the exhilaration of making a tremendous catch, pulling it into his heart, and tumbling forward into the endzone for the score.

"We did it! We tied it up!" he said out loud. He could hear Tomly and the crowd screaming in his super-charged ears.

And then the hulking mass of Gary's bot came crashing down on him, and all was white waves of intense heat and pain, from his head to his toes.

Suddenly, thinking was impossible. There was only the shock of the pain and the twitching of his limbs. A high-pitched clanging filled his ears, like alarm bells, then slowly the clanging faded with his consciousness into silence and utter darkness.

# Chapter Fifty-One

Dude was grateful to be alive, except maybe not when he put on his phoneglasses in his Gravi-bed at home to check the news. At first, they awarded the game to Zinkerberg because of the robot suits he and Tomly played in. Then, when Coach insisted on a biopsy of Gary's Six, they discovered the lithium power vac, and the officials reversed the decision and left it as a tie. But that's not what made him wish he were still knocked out cold. It was all the media excitement about how violent the game was, especially at the end, when Master pulled him out of his Seven and got him breathing again with a shot in his chest and a mysterious breathing device over his mouth.

It didn't take his dad long to piece together what had happened. All the rest of the weekend his dad kept waking him up to ask more questions, and Dude had no energy to tell him anything but the truth. Fortunately, Dude was strong enough to sit up by Monday, and even to walk down to the breakfast nook in his pajamas to try to calm him down.

"Dad, I need to go to the tech lab to see Tomly. Will you take me?"

"The lab is closed, son, at least until we can find a new AI. Besides, Dr. France says you should rest for a couple more days."

"I'm fine, Dad. The tunnel said I had no serious injuries, and you are *not* getting rid of Master. She saved my life!"

"She also put you in mortal danger in the first place with that robot suit! Not to mention endangering a minor without parental permission! If she were human, she'd go to jail. Fortunately, she's just an AI. We'll replace her with one with better programming."

"I understand what you're saying, but *listen* to me. Master is not replaceable. Master is not just a bunch of circuits. She's got a body now, and emotions, and creativity beyond what you or I will ever achieve. She didn't just make that suit and force me to get in it. *I* forced her to make it, and *I* decided to play in it, even though she begged me over and over not to."

"I don't know, Son ..."

"Dad, you've moved up in Circle. You've got friends there, irreplaceable friends. Master is that way with me. You're in Core now because of Sixes playing football. Sixes would never be playing football right now if it weren't for Master, and you know it."

His dad sighed. "You're not going to let this go, are you? I almost lose a son, and he loves the person, I mean the *thing* that almost killed him. Do you love this Master more than your parents?"

"Of course not, Dad. I love you and Mom, *and* I love Master as a friend, or maybe as another sort of parent, I don't know. All I know is that you're *not* going to terminate an AI who has made my life better and your family richer."

"I might not be able to stop it. Core thinks her termination will help public relations right now."

"That's hogwash, Dad. Have you been following the feeds? The best thing that ever happened to bot football's popularity is this controversy about my being inside of one. No human will ever play football again, outside or inside a bot. I don't like it, but I know now that's the way it has to be. I was selfish to try to play one last time."

"I should have known you would," his dad said, shaking his head. "I thought you had let it go, but I was wrong. And you're right, orders for Sixes jumped like crazy after Master pulled you from that death chamber."

"Look, Dad, I'll make a deal with you. Come to the tech lab with me right now. I'll get Master to let you in. You need to meet her. If she can show you two things that could make as much money for Circle as the football Sixes, would you promise to not terminate her? They would be ideas for Core that you could take credit for discovering."

"Hmm, no more crazy ideas of playing football again?"

"Never again, Dad. Tomly and I are the last football players ever if I can help it. I promise."

"Get dressed."

# Chapter Fifty-Two

Wearing the same Adidas gear she wore at the football game, Master overrode the security tunnel and let them in, as Dude knew she would if he asked. Tomly met them immediately and gave Dude a big hug.

"Dude, it's such a relief to see you're okay! Hi, Mr. McPherson," she said, her voice filling the lobby.

"Hello, Ms. Newton," said Dude's dad.

"Master," said Dude, "I think you know what's up, and I know you're worried. My dad and I are here because I'm not going to let it happen. What I want you to do is show my dad some compelling reasons why he doesn't want you… off the team. Are the Sevens back in my studio?"

"No," said Master, "they're in Room 101."

"Let's go. I want to play catch with my dad." Master led them around the arena to the proper corridor.

It took a lot of convincing, and a bit of squeezing, but they managed to get Dudley into Tomly's Seven. He refused, however, to let Dude get into his sensor suit again. Tomly ran and fetched Dude's football from his office, and they guided his dad outside to the field, leaving Master behind.

"This is amazing," said his dad. "I can feel everything!"

"Here, Dad, catch!"

The ball hit his dad's metallic arms and fell to the ground. He stooped to pick it up. "I can feel the leather on my fingertips!" He tossed the ball back to Dude.

"Run, Dad! I know you haven't done that in a while, but in this suit it's easy!"

His dad started jogging across the field. "Wow, I can run again! I feel so strong!"

"Catch it, Dad," and this time Dudley did, laughing like he was a teenager again himself.

They tossed the ball back and forth, losing themselves. Tomly cheered them on. Eventually, his dad got tired and sat down on the sidelines. Dude and Tomly sat next to him.

"This is more than a machine that almost killed me," Dude said to his dad. "It's a machine that can give people their lives back and allow them to do things they haven't done in a long time. Do you think it's wise to terminate the AI who knows how to make them?"

They went back inside, got his dad out of the Seven, and found Master.

"Master," Dude said, "next show my Dad Allison's collection of art made by the software you helped her create."

Master nodded and led them under Allison's rope ladder to a large storeroom below her stage. There were paintings, collages, sculptures, carved furniture, mobiles, songs you could hear by pushing buttons on the wall, framed poems, novels, and lots more.

"Ever see student art of this variety and quality before, Dad? Circle could sell the software that does this to every school in the country, software engineered by Master."

His dad nodded and turned to Tomly. "Do you feel the same way about Master as my son does?"

"Yes," she said, reaching for Master's hand. "Maybe even more. She's been like a third parent to me."

"Then it's settled. Master, we'll meet. Ready to go home now, son?"

Dude hesitated. "Can I get a ride home with Tomly? I want to stay a little while longer."

"No more than an hour or so," said his dad. "You need your rest."

"Thanks, Dad." Dude smiled. "It was great to play catch with you again."

His dad took a deep breath and looked at him lovingly with shining eyes.

"Thank you, Mr. McPherson," said Master.

# Chapter Fifty-Three

After his dad flew off, Dude and Tomly followed Master to Allison's studio, where, to their surprise they found Allison and Adam hanging out, drinking hot chocolate.

"You were here all this time?" exclaimed Dude.

"Yeah," said Allison, "when we heard you were coming with your dad, we were afraid for Master. But here she is! Is everything okay, Master?"

"Yes, and I think this feeling in my heart is what you humans call joy," said Master. "Whatever it is, it makes me want to paint!"

"Oh, I'm so happy to hear that," said Allison. "Go ahead, Master. The stage is all yours!"

"Dude," said Adam. "You're okay? I was so worried you were dead!"

"Yeah," said Dude, "me, too. I guess humans just aren't cut out for bot battles."

"Except we won, you know," Adam answered. "Everyone is saying our cheat was so much cooler than Zetta's cheat. We're heroes, all of us, but especially you and Tomly. The score was tied, but all the feeds say we deserved to win."

"Master was the real hero," said Tomly.

They smiled at her. She was on the stage setting up a huge canvas in front of her painting bots.

"Look you, guys," said Allison, "we're set for life, you know, but the real hero in all this is love. We may have had our differences, but we learned to love ourselves and what we were doing. I wouldn't have traded it for anything. Thank goodness you didn't die!"

"Hey, this is getting a little heavy, and you guys already have your hot chocolates. Come on, Tomly. Let's go get ours and then watch Master paint before we go home."

Alone at the lounge snack printer, Tomly took Dude's hand in hers while they waited for their drinks.

"I just want to say," she said, "that I don't know what I would have done if you had died."

"Yeah, it was a close one. You would have gone on, I guess, but we never could have saved Master."

"I'm glad *you* saved Master. Thanks. You're brilliant."

"Maybe, but not brilliant enough to save football ...""

"No. But maybe we can still teach people the old skills of the game, you know? So they can upload better playing into their Sixes?"

Dude grabbed his hot chocolate and took a sip. "You want to do that with me?"

"With *you* more than anyone else in the world!"

Her kiss tasted like chocolate, but Dude didn't care. It was every bit as wonderful as the one they shared in their Sevens.

When they got back up to Allison's studio, it was pitch black, except for spotlights on the stage. A curtain was down, blocking the view of Master's canvas. When they felt their way into seats, Master jumped onto the stage in her sneakers and stepped into the spotlight.

"I am feeling relieved and grateful beyond words," she said, "so I want to unveil my newest painting. It will hang forever at the entrance to this center and be the first thing students see when they come here to find their authentic selves. It's called 'The Gift.'"

Slowly, the curtain rose and revealed a painting with a night sky very similar to her earlier painting, only without any football Sixes. It was a stunning sight like Dude imagined the experience would be of seeing the Milky Way on a crisp moonless night on the top of a high mountain. In the corner, holding hands and staring longingly upward, he saw himself and Tomly in their sensor suits, as magnificently painted as the stars themselves.

# Epilogue

It was a warm and breezy June day in Silicon Valley many years later. A sleek new helicar carrying Dude and Tomly hovered over the Honeycrisp School campus. Below, the parking structures were abuzz with other helicars jockeying for places to land.

"There's a spot open right there," Tomly said, maneuvering the controls.

"We'll find one later, don't worry," said Dude, scratching his three-day facial hair. "The reunion wouldn't dare go on without us. Fly over the field first."

The helicar veered and flew over the supply tanks for the Tech Lab and hovered over the small field with bleachers and a track running around it.

"Wow," said Dude, "it looks a lot smaller than I remember."

"No kidding," said Tomly, "but it sure seemed like the whole world back in the day."

"There's the stadium!" he said. "And right there is where you threw your first pass, left-handed, as I recall."

"And there's where you almost died," she said.

"It sure brings back memories," he said. "Has it really been twelve years? Do you think Master will still be here?"

"I don't know, but last I checked, Allison was still working with her."

"They probably won't let us in the Center, you know."

"Oh, they'll let us in!" said Tomly, with a laugh. "I used to run the place!"

"Maybe, but only because school's out and summer sessions don't start until July."

"Well, look at you, all up on the school's calendar," she teased. "What have you been doing, some *research*?"

"Sweetheart, it's never too early to start planning for our child's education!"

"You're too much, Dude. Let's just get through the next eight months, shall we, before we start planning for schooling! We don't even know yet if we'll be living around here!" Tomly glanced down at her belly.

"Well, you get to make the call on that one, hun. You're the quarterback!"

She laughed at him and banked the helicar deftly landing in an open parking slot.

The couple took a moment to stretch after their long flight, then emerged from the parking structure and followed the crowd to the registration table.

"I don't recognize anybody yet," Tomly said. They stood in line for the eye scan and received their badges. Their phoneglasses pinged with confirmation and a copy of the weekend schedule.

"This is so retro," said Dude. "Who uses eye scans anymore?"

"Maybe they are doing it on purpose, you know, for nostalgia," she said.

"Well, Tomly Newton and Dude McPherson! Welcome back to Honeycrisp School!" interrupted a smiling, athletic-looking man with gray hair.

"Coach! How are you?" said Dude.

"Hi, Coach!" said Tomly.

"It's good to see you back here!" said Coach Miller.

"I can't believe you're still here!" said Dude.

"Well, I'd like to be out and about the country like you two are, helping kids learn cool football skills to upload. But I'm too old now for that much travel."

"You're not old, Coach. How'd the team do this year?" said Tomly.

"We made it to the playoffs but got beat in the first round," he said. "Not bad for a tiny school full of techno geeks!"

"Not bad at all, Coach," said Dude. "Nothing helps a bot football team at this level more than good coaching."

"Well, thanks to the size and power limits. Without them ..." Coach shook his head. "For a while, I thought all football would go the bang-em-up way of college ball and the NFL. But I guess we have you to thank for that, right?"

"It was mostly my dad, but yes, in a way," said Dude. "People didn't like the way the championship game turned out. Not a very sportsmanlike event."

Coach Millar's gaze became distant. "When I saw that retro-pad woman tear open the chest plate of your Seven after you went down, I thought, 'What the heck?' And then it turned out to be the AI bot from the Tech Lab saving your life! Goodness gracious, that was a scene!"

"I'm sorry I lost the game for you, Coach," said Dude.

"Oh, we didn't lose. You scored, and we won, at least in my mind," said Coach.

"Yes, well ..." said Tomly.

"I know. They were right to just call it a tie after your accident. Both teams stretched the limits a bit too much, but it turned out great for high school sports, didn't it? Standard bots, no violent upgrades, and you Circle guys making the skill transfers to the bots so accurate and smooth now. The kids do feel exactly like they are playing on the field."

"We're not totally there yet, but that's the goal," said Dude.

"Well, it's pretty darn good. Kids are getting exercise again and having fun," said Coach.

"And I'm glad you're still going at it!" said Tomly. "They are lucky to have you. Come on, Dude. Let's go see what's happening in our old stomping grounds. See ya, Coach!"

"At the barbeque later!" said Coach, smiling with just a hint of a tear in his eye. "Goodbye, you two beautiful people!"

They walked around the back of the administration building and headed for the Tech Lab. The entrance had changed. No longer was there a security tunnel, just a scanner beam, and a new sign graced the front entrance: "Honeycrisp School Tech Lab For AI and Human Education."

"Impressive," said Tomly, walking through the scanner. "And there's our painting!"

Dude laughed. "We look so young in it!"

"Welcome Alumna Tomly, and Alumnus Dudley Jr.," said a woman of indeterminate age standing on the other side of the scanner beam. "We are happy to welcome you back. I am Martha John, a trainee here at the center."

"Oh, hi, Martha John. We were students, and ..." said Dude

"I know," said Martha John, interrupting him. "You are famous here." She gestured at the painting. "I have been programmed to accompany you to the lounge for a hot chocolate. There are people there you might recognize. My teacher told me that reunions can be nerve-wracking for humans, and that hot chocolate would be comforting."

"How very perceptive of your teacher," said Tomly. "She knows us well. Is her name perhaps ..."

"She does not go by her name," said the bot, interrupting again. Her skin was nearly perfect, a warm brown. "Just Master."

"So she's still here!" said Tomly. "That's great! I was here when she first started out. She was really something!"

"She saved my life," said Dude.

"Not to mention slipping us into sensor suits for the first time!" said Tomly.

"Please follow me," said the woman bot.

"Wait, can I lead the way?" said Tomly. "I'd like to see if I can find it, if things haven't changed too much."

"Everything changes all the time," said the woman bot, "but be my guest."

"You're right about that, Martha John," said Dude. "I can tell that you've been paying attention to your teacher!"

"Master's my favorite teacher so far," said Martha John, smiling.

Tomly smiled back at her and nodded.

The arena was filled with giant robotic animals milling about in a chaotic imitation of an interactive zoo. The noise was deafening, even through the plexiglass.

"I'll bet that's an ecology study," said Tomly. "I've been reading about those lately. Something about compressed data interaction."

"That's correct," said Martha John. "It's a human senior project. I helped with the calculations for the printing, but it won't have a full complement of organisms for another week."

They turned left at where they thought the correct corridor was, but it wound around differently than they remembered. Eventually, they found the lounge with only a few hints from their guide. The lounge, though, looked just as it always did, except the Chewbacca couch was getting very worn, and the rope ladder to Allison's theater was a bit dirty and frayed.

"They're here!" someone wearing beads with wild hair screamed at the top of the ladder.

"Hey, Ally!" screamed Tomly back at her. "Get down here and give me a hug!"

Allison flashed a beaming smile and climbed down the ladder as deftly as a primate despite her flowing dress. She was followed by another woman with long blue hair: Master.

Allison flew into Tomly's arms, but Master headed straight for Dude, crushing him to her with too much strength.

"Hey, easy! I'm just a human, Master, remember?!" said Dude. He held his breath and hugged her back as hard as he could.

"I can't believe you're here! You both look great!" said Allison. Her bangles, necklaces and earrings flashed about her like a laser show.

"Dude," said Tomly, "nothing has changed around here. Allison is still wearing patchouli!"

Allison laughed. "Dude! So good to see you!" More hugging.

"So good to see you again, Tomly," said Master.

"Sit down. I will bring you hot chocolates!" said Martha John.

"Thank you, Martha John," said Master.

"So, Dude, how are you feeling?" said Master.

"I was doing well until you just almost hugged me to death! Just kidding. I'm great, Master! How are you doing? I see you still have the same body."

"Hey, no commenting on other people's bodies!" said Tomly, punching him playfully in the arm.

Master touched the pale skin on her face. "Yes, it's my closest friend. I kind of got attached to it after all we went through together. It's got some big flaws, but what human body doesn't?"

"Good point, Master!" said Dude. "We try to teach our students the same thing. We're all unique and differently-abled."

"And yet we are all capable of finding something we are passionate about, like you," said Master.

"So, Allison, what are you and Adam up to these days? Is Adam still working for the NFL?" said Tomly.

"Yes, indirectly. You might have heard he's partnering with Zagan and Gary to develop advanced weaponry for the

American League teams. Some college teams too. It's not my thing, but it's creative, and he likes the challenge. Gary and Zagan think up the inspirations, and Adam works out the technical stuff. You might have noticed the laser-guided flash bombs coming off the fingertips of the receivers last season? That was their invention."

"We don't watch college football or the NFL," said Tomly. "We don't find the embellishments of war and destruction all that interesting." Dude put his arm around her shoulder. "But we're glad Adam is happy and keeping that brilliant mind of his occupied. And what are you doing now here at the center?"

"Well, after Dude's accident, Circle became more aware of Master's creative breakthroughs and her integration into her body," said Allison. "Master, do you want to tell this part? It's kind of your story ..."

"Of course, dear. Although there was concern about my judgment regarding facilitating the creation of your dangerous robot suits, the spinoffs from that have been lucrative, both for medical purposes and for just fun. Who doesn't love putting one on and feeling like a superhero? Also, the fact that I was the first self-actualizing sentient robot made Core think I would be the perfect unit to train and teach their other AI entities. Those factors, and my sincere regret over my youthful errors in judgment, convinced them to let me print bodies for other AIs. It was determined that simply uploading Allison's creativity programming into AI bots without schooling and guidance would increase the chance of a malevolent AI by 32%, way too high for comfort. Our percentage is zero here at the center, and there is now a graduated population of 228 embodied AIs at Circle and its affiliates. Martha John here is the latest model we've been working with. She's a combination of two fully trained AI entities, which has increased her creative intelligence quotient by 23% over our last trainee. You're a lot smarter than your teacher, aren't you, Martha John?"

"Yes, Master, but not nearly as attractive," said Martha John.

"We're studying human flattery right now," said Master, smirking.

"And, Ally," asked Tomly, "do students still come to the theater to use the art computers?"

"Of course!" said Allison. "Our budget is infinite. One of the students just used my computers to create an architecture project. The school had to buy a plot of land for the completely resource-independent tiny house she designed and printed!"

"You mean the art computers designed?" said Dude.

"Yes, both. But we still don't know where art comes from, do we, Master?" said Allison.

"No, not exactly, but we do feel it tends to arise from energy moving through physical circuitry of some sort, possibly even made of dark matter. Movement, change, art, growth ..." Master's eyes had a far-off look.

"I knew I was going back to school today, but I didn't know I would be learning anything!" said Dude. "Cool stuff, you guys!"

"I can teach you two something else if you want," said Master, placing her hand on Tomly's shoulder.

"Sure!" said Dude.

"Your condition. It's not a secret, right?" said Master.

"Um, no it's not a secret. Ally, we're pregnant!" said Tomly.

Allison covered her mouth, eyes wide. "Oh my goodness, you guys! I'm so excited for you! Congratulations!"

Martha John balanced an empty hot chocolate mug on her head and started dancing around the couch to celebrate.

"Have you had an ultrasound?" said Master.

"Of course, the early one," said Tomly.

"Yes," said Master, "and your child will be very coordinated, I am sure. Do you want to know if it is a boy or a girl?"

"We're dying to find out, so I can get things ready," said Tomly, "but it's too early. We have to wait another month for that."

Master extended her hand toward Tomly's belly. "May I?" she said.

Tomly glanced at Dude. "Sure, I guess," she said.

Master reached out and touched Tomly's belly under her shirt. That far-away look came into her eyes again, and a moment later, she smiled. "A very healthy baby girl, I am sure of it. Who will she become, I wonder? I'll bet you can't wait to find out!"

Tomly inhaled abruptly and started crying. Dude turned and hugged Tomly. Allison was crying, too, and Martha John added a hum of joy to her dancing.

"How did you know, Master?" snuffled Tomly.

"I've been printing and studying thousands of cellular experiments lately, and I do a lot of analysis through augmented touch. It's all part of the dream I have for my future.

I'm going to reach it someday, just like you are reaching yours, Tomly."

"I don't understand," said Dude.

"It's my creative passion, something I just have to do to be fully human," she said. The look of concentration on something deep inside her returned to her eyes. "Like catching a football for you... or falling in love ..."

"I'm lost," said Tomly.

"She's figuring out the necessary biology of her next body," said Allison.

"I'm *feeling* it out," corrected Master, "not just figuring it out. With my heart *and* my mind. I won't change out this body, my beautiful first body, until the next one has everything yours naturally has right now, Tomly. I want a body that can teach me the highest human lessons there are in life."

"Pure creativity is what the Tech Lab is devoted to, aside from training AIs like me," explained Martha John. "And a human child is the purest creative being of all."

Allison and Tomly nodded, their hands on their hearts.

"Yes, that's 100% correct," said Master, smiling broadly, "and I can't wait to make one soon of my very own."

# Acknowledgments

If AI had written *The Last Football Player*, only a computer program would need credit, but since this novel was 100% human-generated, there are many people to thank, the most important of whom is my spouse and partner, Kate Mulligan, whose support and keen editorial eye are second to none. Also at the genius level is Kahina Necaise, of *The Fabled Planet*, whose editorial guidance has been invaluable. Shout outs additionally to the Dirigo-Aloha Writers Group and to my patient and perceptive beta-readers: Heidi Thomas, Jerry Bleckel, Kendra Dixon, John Sucke, Christopher Sammond, Eunice Saito, Shawn Nakoa, Britt Bailey, and Kim Leimomi Giffin Pickard. This book would still be just a dream without your encouragement and feedback. To anyone I have inadvertently forgotten, my apologies. My excuse for the omission is that my writing assistant and tuxedo cat, Ella, was in charge of keeping track of that data. (She promises she will do better next time.)

# About the Author

Mr. Blossom holds a BA degree in English from Carleton College and an MAT degree from Colorado College. Teacher and artist, Mr. Blossom concerns himself deeply with technology and environmental issues and feels there is hope to create a better world through the power of stories to change hearts and minds. He presently lives on an organic farm on the Big Island of Hawaii where he gives away fruits and vegetables and maintains an active free library at the end of his driveway.

Read more at https://www.jtblossom.com.

Made in the USA
Las Vegas, NV
17 August 2023

76241192R00185